Dear Diary,

Sometimes it seems that crisis follows crisis for this family. I shouldn't complain. I'm so proud of my children, and I'm delighted that at least some of them seem to be finding love. But the Maitland troubles don't seem to be over yet. . . .

I still can't believe it. My little Beth is being accused of murder. How could anyone think that bright, carefree, loving Beth would commit such an act? My maternal instincts tell me to exert every ounce of Maitland influence to protect her, but Beth feels that this would make her look more guilty than the circumstances already do. She believes her innocence is the only protection she needs. And she seems to think that the two detectives assigned to her case are fair, competent and open-minded.

What a night it's been. I'm sure the police will soon see they have the wrong suspect. Nobody can truly believe our Beth guilty of such a crime.

This, too, will pass. It must.

Dear Reader,

There's never a dull moment at Maitland Maternity! This unique and now world-renowned clinic was founded twenty-five years ago by Megan Maitland, widow of William Maitland, of the prominent Austin, Texas, Maitlands. Megan is also matriarch of an impressive family of seven children, many of whom are active participants in the everyday miracles that bring children into the world.

When our series began, the family was stunned by the unexpected arrival of an unidentified baby at the clinic—unidentified, except for the claim that the child is a Maitland. Who are the parents of this child? Is the claim legitimate? Will the media's tenacious grip on this news damage the clinic's reputation? Suddenly rumors and counterclaims abound. Women claiming to be the child's mother materialize out of the woodwork! How will Megan get at the truth? And how will the media circus affect the lives and loves of the Maitland children—Abby, the head of gynecology, Ellie, the hospital administrator, her twin sister, Beth, who runs the day-care center, Mitchell, the fertility specialist, R.J., the vice president of operations, even Anna, who has nothing to do with the clinic, and Jake, the black sheep of the family?

Please join us each month over the next year as the mystery of the Maitland baby unravels, bit by enticing bit, and book by captivating book!

Marsha Zinberg,
Senior Editor and Editorial Coordinator, Special Projects

ARLENE
JAMES

The
Detective's
Dilemma

Silhouette Books

Published by Silhouette Books

America's Publisher of Contemporary Romance

SILHOUETTE BOOKS
300 East 42nd St.,
New York, N. Y. 10017

ISBN 0-373-65067-1

THE DETECTIVE'S DILEMMA

Arlene James has been writing for twenty-one years and considers herself truly blessed. Not only has she been able to pursue a career she loves, but she was also able to enjoy the luxury of being home with her children as they grew. Now that her kids are happily married, she's approaching her writing with new ardor.

Arlene's marriage, always a source of inspiration, also seems to be getting better as time goes by. She and her husband grew up, met and married in Oklahoma—years after attending the same school unaware of each other's existence. She was a young widow, and he was smooth enough to convince her to marry him after their first date! Is it any wonder she writes romance?

I'm a most fortunate mother.
I have two truly wonderful sons, and now I have two truly
wonderful daughters-in-law. Both are bright and beautiful
(inside and out), women who actually deserve such fine
men. I thank God and my husband for such dear sons. I
thank my sons and their in-laws for such dear daughters.

So this is for Ross and Monica, and Joseph and Heather.
You have made me very proud. Again.
I love you all. Mom.

CHAPTER ONE

BETH'S HANDS curled into fists. Immediately she relaxed them and tamped down her impatience. She looked at the serious mien of the tall, dark detective lounging on the corner of the table at which she sat and felt the sudden urge to laugh. It was all so utterly preposterous. Murder. How could anyone suspect her, Beth Maitland, of murder—even if the unfortunate victim was her ex-fiancé's wife? She'd much rather have flirted outrageously with the handsome detective than committed murder to assuage a broken heart, had she ever had one. What she would do, however, was answer these silly, repetitive questions.

"I went to the children's garden in the courtyard of the day-care center to be certain that the bulbs planted that day were properly covered. No, we weren't expecting a freeze," she said flippantly, "but it *is* February, and as you well know, in Texas the weather is never certain. I didn't go back to my office. I never saw Brianne. I certainly didn't kill her."

"Yet we know she was going to see you," the detective persisted, looming close enough for Beth to catch a whiff of the sandalwood in his cologne.

Despite his stern, almost menacing demeanor, he was a devastatingly attractive man. Standing at least a couple inches over six feet and whipcord lean beneath a well-tailored suit of black sharkskin, Ty Redstone was definitely of Native American descent. Ink black hair, swept straight back and chopped bluntly at the nape, had been tucked behind his perfectly formed ears, calling attention to his squarely sculpted jaws and chin. His cheekbones were high and prominent, with slight hollows beneath, his lips wide and mobile. A long, thin nose and straight, slightly jutting brows lent a hawkish appearance to his almond-shaped brown-black eyes. A high, wide forehead bespoke intelligence, and his coppery skin was as smooth as a child's, with the exception of a pair of tiny crow's feet, one at the outer corner of each eye. Had he not been convinced that she had murdered Brianne Dumont by strangling the night before, Beth could have formed quite an amazing crush on the man. As it was, she could merely sigh and repeat what she'd been saying for the past two hours.

"I didn't see her. I had no idea she was even in the building."

"But her husband says—"

"I don't care what Brandon says," Beth snapped, momentarily losing her composure, "I didn't see her!" She constantly wavered between humor at the ridiculousness of being accused of murder and anger at the seriousness of it.

Her attorney, a handsome, middle-aged man named Hugh Blake, intervened. "My client has answered this question repeatedly. Either move on, Detective, or we will."

"It's all right," Beth answered him, drawing another deep breath. "I've said it before. I'll say it again. I did not ask Brianne to meet me at the Maitland Maternity day-care center or anywhere else. If Brandon says I did, then he's lying or mistaken."

"You weren't jealous of her for breaking up your romance with Brandon Dumont?"

"No."

"And there was no feud between the two of you?"

"Not as far as I was concerned," Beth insisted. Leaning forward, she placed a hand flat on the ugly gray table near the corner where Detective Redstone sat. "I know I told my friend Katie Carrington that it was Brandon who ended our engagement and I pretended to be upset,'' she said, ''but that was a lie. Brandon asked me to say that he was the one who wanted out, and I didn't see then what harm it could do.'' She sat back, waving a hand dismissively. ''I just wanted it over with. Even before I found out Brandon was fooling around with Brianne, I knew the engagement was a mistake. Brianne was just the excuse I needed to end it. I didn't kill her. I had no reason to. Heck, I was *glad* she wound up with Brandon. Better her than me.''

''Your story just doesn't check out, Miss Maitland,'' Redstone's partner, Paul Jester, said bluntly. Sprawled casually in a stiff chair at the end of the rectangular table, he seemed the more easygoing of the two, with his pale blond flattop, pink apple cheeks, blunt nose and plump lips. He looked comfortably rumpled in khakis, sport shirt with open collar and tweed jacket with baggy elbows, a true contrast to Redstone's dark good looks and tailored clothing.

Jester shifted forward, both elbows propped on the tabletop, and went on, repeating facts already established. ''Mrs. Dumont checked into the Maitland Maternity Clinic at five forty-five, noting in the guard's reception book that she had an appointment with you. At precisely six-fifteen, you check out, just at the moment the security guard on the desk is changing, so no notice is taken of the fact that Mrs. Dumont is still inside. At six-twenty the cleaning lady finds the body in your office and sounds the alarm.'' He sat back, spreading his hands. ''Now what are we supposed to believe?''

Beth shook her head. ''Make what you must of it, Detective. I'm telling you that I had nothing to do with the murder. I always check out precisely at six-fifteen. The registry will verify that.''

Redstone leaned down, getting right in her face. She noticed that one of his small white teeth was chipped, the one left of center on the bottom, and shivered with sensual awareness—of a man who suspected her of murder, yet!

"Mr. Dumont swears that you set up the appointment with his wife via the telephone that very afternoon," he said.

She shook her head. "I didn't."

"He says, in fact, that you've been harassing his wife since the day of their marriage."

She looked Redstone straight in the eye. "I don't know why he's saying these things, but they *aren't* true."

"And," the detective went on relentlessly, "you yourself told Ms. Carrington that he, not you, ended the relationship."

"My client has explained that repeatedly," Blake said. "This protracted interview is beginning to border on harassment, gentlemen."

"Look, Ms. Maitland," Paul Jester said soothingly, ignoring the attorney. "It happens. We know how it is. Your fiancé dumped you for another woman. You called her into your office after hours to tell her exactly what you thought of her. She got smart, hit a nerve. Before you realized what you were doing, you picked up something and wrapped it around her throat...."

Beth was shaking her head, her eyes blazing angrily. "No, no, no. It wasn't like that. I never touched her. I never even laid eyes on her. I certainly didn't kill her."

"That's enough," the attorney asserted. "You have my client's statement. Nothing has changed in the last two hours or more."

Jester sighed and shot a look at his partner, who got up off the corner of the desk and paced toward the door. Halting, his back to Beth, Redstone brought his hands to his waist and bowed his head. After a moment, he looked over his shoulder, studying her unapologetically, one hand covering the lower part of his face.

"I didn't kill her," Beth said to him, sensing that he was

the one she had to convince. "As God is my witness, I never even saw her. I wasn't jealous. I don't know why Brandon is lying. All I know is, I didn't kill her."

The door opened, and Megan Maitland, Beth's mother, stuck her head inside the room. "How long is this going on?" she demanded. Her white hair had been swept into a neat French twist high on the back of her head, adding to the air of authority that always surrounded her. "Haven't you badgered my daughter enough?"

Attorney Blake, a good friend of her mother's, stood. "I think we're finished here," he announced firmly.

"I should hope so," Megan said. "We have a press conference scheduled in less than an hour, and I want my daughter there with me."

Beth frowned at the notion of the press conference awaiting them at Maitland Maternity. The press had been rabid wherever the Maitlands were concerned. First, a baby had been abandoned on the clinic's doorstep with a note that claimed he was a Maitland. Then Connor O'Hara, a Maitland cousin no one had ever seen before, showed up, followed by his girlfriend, Janelle, who claimed to be the baby's mother. And all while Maitland Maternity Clinic was planning its twenty-fifth-anniversary gala. Now a murder had been committed in Beth's office at the clinic day care—and Beth was the prime suspect. She'd rather thumb her nose at the press pack than give them anything, but even a press conference was preferable to being booked for murder. She stared at Ty Redstone, trying to decide if he was going to arrest her. Finally, he nodded.

"You can go for now, Ms. Maitland, but don't leave town, and be prepared to make yourself available to us on short notice."

Blake clamped a hand around Beth's upper arm, helping her to her feet. He held out her jacket for her. "Good day, gentlemen," she said, looking at Ty Redstone. "Wish I could say it had been a pleasure." With that she walked out the interrogation room door and straight into her mother's waiting arms. The appalling events of the past several hours had drained her, so she allowed her mother to rock her gently from side to side while Hugh Blake quietly praised her for her aplomb and assured Megan that he would pressure the police to find the murderer quickly. Megan thanked him for his help. Beth lifted her head, and together the three of them walked out of the downtown Austin police station.

Ty CLOSED THE DOOR on the sight of Beth Maitland standing huddled within her mother's embrace. After years of this work, he was relatively unaffected by such displays, but something about these Maitland women got to a man. Every one he'd met so far was a real beauty, including the mother, who had to be sixty if she was a day. But then these rich types could afford whatever mysterious beauty treatments kept them looking so young and lovely. Not, he had to admit to himself, that beauty treatments of any sort could make a woman's legs as long and slender as Beth Maitland's, or nip her waist in so narrowly that he could span it with his two hands. He dismissed such thoughts, turning to his partner and the matter at hand.

"So what do you think?"

Paul leaned back, balancing his chair on two legs, locking his hands together behind his head and propping his crossed ankles on the table. "I don't know. Seems like a pretty airtight case on the surface."

"No kidding." Ty ticked off the incriminating evidence. "She has the motive and the means. The timing is perfect. The body was found in her office. And the dead woman just happens to be the new wife of her recent and former fiancé. Add to that the statement of said former fiancé—now the widower—that she set up the appointment via telephone, and what you have—"

Ty looked at Paul, and Paul looked at Ty. Together they said, "Too easy."

Bowing his head, Ty clapped a hand to the back of his neck. "I'm always spooked when they're too easy."

"The old hound is smelling a fix," Paul said blithely. It was a break-room joke that Ty Redstone could smell a frame a mile away despite a steady wind—and for good reason.

"Suppose you break it down for me," he said, ignoring Paul's attempt at humor.

Paul rocked forward and pulled his legs down from the table. He extracted a small notebook from his coat pocket, unclipped a pen from it and flipped it open, preparing to demolish their airtight case. "Okay. First of all, strangling is a man's MO. Even with a garrote, it takes strength over time to get the job done, and an unbound victim of the same approximate size can put up a pretty fierce struggle."

Ty nodded. "Women usually conk their victims over the head, shoot 'em full of holes or slowly poison them to death. They don't strangle them with a thin, flexible weapon. What do you think it was, by the way?"

Paul shrugged. "Some sort of cord would be my guess. Too thin for a belt or rope."

"Right," Ty said, "so a woman doesn't usually strangle her victims." He lifted a cautioning finger. "But we both know that means nothing. Under the right circumstances, anything goes."

"Granted," Paul said, "but if she really does check out at six-fifteen every night and we can prove it, then it's an established pattern that anyone who knows her could use to frame her."

"We need the logbooks for at least a year," Ty said, beginning to pace the room as Paul took notes. "We'd better pull the phone records for Maitland Maternity Clinic and the residence." He snapped his fingers. "Check to see if Beth Maitland has a cell phone, too. If she's been harassing the happy couple, we'll find some sign of it.''

Paul scribbled it all down. "Got it."

Ty paced the narrow confines of the interrogation room. "What do you think happened to the murder weapon?"

Paul shrugged. "Nearest trash bin, probably."

"We searched with a fine-tooth comb," Ty reminded him.

"She must have taken it with her. I kept expecting you to ask about it."

Ty shook his head. "If she hasn't gotten rid of it, I don't want her to rethink and do it now."

"You figure she still has it?"

"Maybe. Anyway, we won't have a decent idea what Brianne Dumont was strangled with until forensics has done their bit. No sense trying to look for it until we do. Make a note to ask forensics for an early determination," Ty instructed. Paul dutifully made the note. "Okay, back to the breakdown."

"One big consideration," Paul said, "is that we only have Dumont's word for it that the Maitland dame set up the appointment with the victim."

"Or that she harassed her," Ty said, picking up the thread of the argument. "And since Dumont was seeing Ms. Maitland until fairly recently, we can assume that he's spent a good deal of time around the maternity clinic and the day-care center."

"Which means he could probably get himself in and out without being seen," Paul concluded. "There's a working theory. He baits the trap by telling his wife that Beth's asked to see her."

Ty stopped pacing and brought both hands to his hips. "I have to wonder why she would go for that, meeting the other woman on her own turf, especially if the other woman was displaying threatening behavior."

Paul shrugged. "Maybe she wanted to apologize—Maitland, I mean."

"Or maybe there was no harassment," Ty said, theorizing, "so the Dumont woman had no reason not to make the meeting."

"Makes sense," Paul concluded before returning to his theory. "On the other hand, he could've killed her, dumped the body in the office and fabricated the meeting to allay suspicion."

Ty shook his head. "Too tricky, even without a blood trail." He came to a halt and brought his hands to his waist. "We have to do some reconnoitering."

"Until we discover a hole in the dike," Paul agreed. "Then we pull the plug and let the truth flood away the lies."

"You sound as if you're convinced we'll find that hole," Ty said.

"Yeah, maybe. There's something that's been bothering me from the get go on this one."

"Oh?"

Paul nodded. "It's like this. The woman is rich and beautiful."

And she has a freewheeling sexuality that fairly sings to a man, Ty thought but didn't say. He knew that Paul, being happily married, wouldn't say it, either, which was not to infer that he hadn't noticed. Ty showed his agreement with Paul's assessment by nodding.

"A woman like that's got to be beating 'em off with a stick," Paul went on prosaically. "What's she want with a cold fish like Dumont? Any guy who would break up with Beth Maitland and marry another woman within forty-eight hours, well, he's not the love of anybody's life, if you ask me."

"Definitely not the sort you'd kill over," Ty agreed. "Now, all we've got to do is prove it." *And hope we don't make the case against Beth Maitland in the process,* he told himself, surprised at the sentiment.

Paul nodded thoughtfully and scratched his ear with the tip of his pen, leaving a bright blue mark. Ty smiled. Paul Jester was a good detective, a fine father and husband, an excellent friend, but he was always doing goofy stuff like marking himself up with those damned ballpoint pens he carried. Ty cleared his throat against a chuckle and added a query to the list.

"We'd better do some digging into Dumont's background as well as Beth Maitland's, just to cover our butts."

"And don't forget our victim," Paul said, writing.

"Good point. Now I'll tell you something about this case."

"What's that?" Paul asked, looking up. Ty knew that, given his ancestry, the guys around the office fancied him something of a shaman with his predictions and hunches, but he knew himself to be a purely logical man who made good deductions—not that he was averse to cloaking his expertise in a thin veneer of Crow mysticism. In this business, a man needed every edge he could get, and Ty was rightfully proud of his rich Native American heritage.

"I'll tell you right now," he pronounced sagely, "that this thing is going to come down to a face-off between Brandon Dumont and Beth Maitland. I, for one, think we'll only hear the truth when we get the two of them in the same room together at the right time. Meanwhile..." He let the statement hang there, but Jester was quick to finish it.

"Meanwhile," he said resignedly, getting to his feet, "we've got a lot of work to do."

Ty waited as his partner shoved his chair under the table and walked around it. Then he turned to the door.

"You've got ink on your ear," he said as they went out together, just loud enough for the other guys in the wardroom to hear. Paul was still scrubbing at the offending mark long after the laughter had died down.

"YOU DID WELL, BETH," Hugh Blake told her. "I don't want you to be discouraged. The police are a long way from concluding their investigation, so there's a chance the real murderer will come to light. If they do charge you, I promise you we'll fight them on every front. Just stick to the truth and try to relax. All right?"

She nodded and thanked him for his help, then allowed her mother to usher her into the limo. Beth sighed, letting her head fall back on the warm leather upholstery. It wasn't particularly cold, but Beth pulled her fitted brown corduroy jacket closed.

"My poor darling," Megan said, sliding onto the seat next to her and laying a comforting hand on her knee. "How could anyone suspect one of my children of something so heinous? Especially you! Everyone knows you wouldn't hurt a flea. You're much too fun-loving and playful."

"I don't think fun-loving and playful preclude murder in the eyes of the law, Mother," Beth suggested with a wan smile.

Megan shuddered. "I still can't believe they suspect you. It's just ludicrous, and they'll see that. They will."

Beth tried for another smile and was saved the effort when the chauffeur slid the divider window open. "Back to the clinic, Mrs. Maitland—Ms. Maitland?"

"Oh…yes, thank you," Beth replied for the two of them. "I'm a little distracted today. Sorry."

"No problem," the driver assured her, sliding the window closed. An instant later, the vehicle shifted into gear and swung easily across the parking lot. Beth lifted her head. Enough self-pity. Time to face this mess head-on.

"I'm worried how this is going to affect the clinic and

day-care center," she said bluntly, and Megan immediately
rushed to defuse her concerns.

"Don't be silly. Everyone knows this is nonsense. As
Hugh says, it'll all blow over soon and—"

"Mom," Beth interrupted firmly, "the press has cruci-
fied us over the paternity of a babe left on our doorstep.
You can't believe they'll ignore an accusation of murder."

"No one has accused you of anything!" Megan cried.
"You've been questioned. We all have. That's all it is or
will be."

"Let's face facts, Mother," Beth said gently. "I'm suspected of murdering my ex-fiancé's new wife in my office.
The press is going to play this only one way."

"Let them," Megan insisted sternly. "Everyone who
knows you will realize how absurd their implications are."

"But those who don't know me will wonder," Beth
pointed out, "and that could hurt the clinic. Just when
we're ready to lay one scandal to rest, another pops up. At
the very least, the twenty-fifth-anniversary celebration will
suffer."

"Not at all," Megan assured her. "Most of the invitations have already been accepted. After today's announcement that the parents of our darling Chase have come forward, the rest will come around. You'll see."

All Beth could see at the moment was that she wasn't
going to be able to shake her mother's staunch belief in the
victory of truth and the ultimate invulnerability of her family. But then, she didn't really want to. Unfortunately, all
she could do was pray that nothing and no one else did it
for her, and that was exactly what she did for the remainder
of the trip to the clinic.

Traffic was worse than usual. The limo crawled or stood
still more often than not, so they were almost late for their
own press conference. They had time to run through the
clinic to the back hall. The other members of the family

were waiting for them, and they gathered around as soon as Beth drew near, offering hugs and asking questions.

"Are you all right?" Ellie, Beth's twin, immediately demanded. Identical to Beth except for the shorter hair and lighter lipstick, Ellie seemed to have found a new confidence since her marriage to Sloan Cassidy. Not wanting to subject the family to any more publicity, the two of them had secretly eloped over the New Year, much to everyone's delight. Beth smiled and nodded to reassure her sister. Ellie's tailored, sleek business attire and short, neat hair contrasted sharply with her own, eclectic ensemble of broomstick skirt, boots, cropped sweater and corduroy jacket. Ellie, to Beth's mind, was the intelligent one, the professional one, not that Beth would have traded places with her. She loved working with children. Ellie's career choice as Maitland Maternity's administrator seemed deadly dull and unnecessarily stressful, but Beth couldn't help feeling that Ellie secretly garnered more respect than she did as the director of the day-care center. That belief, however, did not color her great love for—and pride in—her sister.

"What happened at the police station?" her brother R.J. wanted to know.

Mitchell was right beside him. "Those idiots didn't charge you, did they?" he asked.

Beth shook her head. "No."

"Of course they didn't," her older sister, Abby, insisted. "Who in his right mind would suspect our Beth of murder?"

"You might be surprised," Jake said, holding himself, as usual, at a little distance from his siblings. He had whispered to her as she was leaving for her interview with the police detectives that, if push came to shove, he had a few connections who might help them get at the truth, but Beth knew that she wouldn't ask him to pull any hidden strings for her unless she saw no other hope. Jake was much too protective of his shadowy life, and she didn't want to jeopardize that privacy.

"This will have to wait," Megan instructed calmly. "We have a press conference to conduct. We're going out there and present a united front to that mob of jackals. We have nothing to hide, nothing to be ashamed of or worried about. Remember that, all of you."

Anna, who usually skipped these occasions since she, like their brother Jake, had no professional connection to Maitland Maternity, stepped up to link her arm with Beth's. Ellie took the other arm. Abby stood next to their mother, with R.J. and Mitchell flanking them, and Jake brought up the rear. Megan lifted her chin, as regal as any queen, then she put out her hand, shoving open the door and leading them all onto the railed landing that lent itself so perfectly to this sort of thing.

Flashes went off. Cameras started rolling. There was a general jostling of bodies as reporters surged closer, jockeying for position, microphones swaying over their heads. Megan stepped to the microphone mounted on the railing and lifted both arms in a gesture of welcome.

"Thank you for coming." Immediately she was bombarded with questions.

"Mrs. Maitland, have the baby's parents been identified?"

"Who has been charged with the murder at the clinic?"

Chelsea Markum, cool and professionally commanding with her vibrant auburn hair and beauty-queen looks, elbowed her way to the front and demanded, "Is Jake Maitland involved with some terrorist organization? And who is this mystery woman he's brought into your midst? Does it have anything to do with the murder?"

Jake muttered something best unheard and edged away from the lights. Megan laughed. "My goodness, Chelsea, what an active imagination you have." She ignored Chelsea's pout and waved down the remainder of the questions.

"I'm here to announce that the parents of the infant child left on this very doorstep at our last meeting have, indeed, come forward."

"Who's the father?" someone called.

"The father is a distant relative who desires to remain nameless," Megan went on calmly. "He and the child's mother are working to put their lives back together and provide a loving home for their son. Surely you realize that this was an act of desperation on the mother's part. Now that the father is aware of the child's existence, the couple are working through their differences. Please, I beg you, allow them the privacy necessary to accomplish this."

"Are you saying that none of your sons fathered this mystery child?" someone asked.

Megan seemed to pause, then said in a strong, clear voice, "None of the fine young men you see standing here with me today had anything to do with that child's conception. Now, that's all I'm going to say."

"But what about the murder?" Chelsea Markum demanded, having recovered from her set down. "Can Maitland Maternity survive this new crisis?"

Beth stiffened, but Megan shook her head. "The tragedy that occurred here last night has nothing whatsoever to do with Maitland Maternity."

"Isn't it true that the dead woman caused the breakup of your daughter Beth's engagement?"

Pointing to another reporter instead of acknowledging Chelsea Markum, Megan tried to ignore the question, but Beth knew it was hopeless. She stepped next to her mother and leaned toward the microphone.

"No, that isn't true," she said evenly.

"But the police suspect you, don't they?"

"You'll have to ask them that," Beth said dismissively.

"In fact," Megan said, once more taking control, "these questions really ought to be directed at the police. I believe the detectives working this case are one Ty Redstone and Paul Jester. Why don't you ask them these things?''

Beth chuckled inwardly. Poor Redstone and Jester! Her mother had effectively sicced the press on them. She wondered if Ty Redstone would blame her for it, then purposefully pushed thoughts of the attractive detective from her mind. She had more important matters to address—and the perfect forum in which to do it. Once she'd made a public statement, her mother could not gainsay her, and Beth was utterly convinced that this was for the best.

''I have something else to say,'' she announced over the buzz of questions flying at them. She shot her mother an apologetic glance. She hated to do this, but she knew that she must. The reporters grew surprisingly quiet. She could see pens poised over handheld notebooks, microphones straining forward to catch her every word. She didn't make them wait. ''For the record, I have no idea who killed Brianne Dumont or why. It certainly was not me. However, my family and I are grieved by this tragedy and want to see the person responsible brought to justice. Given the circumstances, I can understand that some might link me with the crime even though I had no part in it, and that being the case, I am taking a leave of absence from my position as head of Maitland Maternity day-care center until this mystery is solved and the guilty party is found.''

The murmurings this time came from behind her, from her family, but she'd made the decision, and she knew it was right. She knew what she had to do. Cooperating with the authorities was fine, as far as it went; trusting them to exonerate her was something else again. She was not going to sit idly by waiting for someone to rescue her. Her chin went up in a gesture so reminiscent of her mother that her siblings smiled.

Megan took firm control of the situation once more and brought the press conference to a swift conclusion. The final questions came, as usual, from Chelsea Markum, who shouted at Beth and Jake as the family returned to the relative privacy of the clinic. It was only as she prepared to break the news of her leave of absence to her staff that Beth realized life as she knew it had drastically changed, perhaps forever.

CHAPTER TWO

BETH QUICKLY DISCOVERED that the intention of proving her innocence and actually doing it were two different things. Where did one begin? After much thought—and she'd had lots of time for that these past two days—she was convinced that she was being framed for Brianne's murder. The question was, why? Try as she might, she couldn't imagine what anyone could have to gain from framing her, and yet she could find no other explanation. One other thing had become clear to her: Brandon Dumont was her strongest suspect.

She was saddened and angered by this. She had once had strong feelings for Brandon. At least, she had tried to make herself believe that she *could* have strong feelings for him. That belief had waned even before she'd discovered that he was sleeping with Brianne, and had been put to death by Brandon's insinuation that his betrayal was somehow her—Beth's—fault.

She had dismissed her anger, telling herself that his response smacked of jealousy and was beneath her, that it was best to put the whole relationship behind her. She had dismissed Brandon's avowal that she would regret breaking their engagement and tried to lessen his anger by agreeing to tell everyone that he had instigated the breakup himself. Given the tales he was telling about her supposed harassment of Brianne, she had to wonder if that was part of the setup. Why else would he lie to the police? Or had Brianne, for some absurd reason, convinced him that the harassment was taking place?

She was brooding about it all in the mansion nursery, watching a sleeping Chase from the comfort of a well-placed rocking chair, when Megan entered and brushed a kiss on the top of her head before tiptoeing to the crib to worship little Chase with her eyes. Knowing her mother would want to talk, Beth got up and moved toward the door. Megan turned on the baby monitor and followed.

"I'm so glad you kept him at home with you today," she said softly when the nursery door was closed behind them. "The press was all over the place."

Beth sighed. "Truthfully, it was selfishness on my part. I needed something to *do,* and he's such a sweet baby."

"Won't you come back to the day-care center?" Megan asked quickly, but Beth shook her head.

"I can't, Mom, not now. It's just not fair to the employees and patients, not to mention the children."

"If this is about the twenty-fifth-anniversary celebration," Megan argued, "we're in good shape there. Most of the invitations were accepted before this happened. Even those who had previously sent regrets have decided they can come, after all, and the acceptances are still trickling in. Honestly, sweetheart, no one suspects you of having anything to do with that poor woman's murder."

"Please, Mother, let's not argue. My mind's made up."

Megan sighed. "You always were strong-willed. But if your mind's made up..."

"It's the best thing. Now, tell me, how was your day?"

Megan looped an arm around Beth's shoulders as they strolled side by side down the hall. "It's better now. I'm looking forward to a long hot bath and a quiet dinner, frankly." She grimaced and came to a halt. "I forgot. I asked you to invite Janelle and Connor to dine with us this evening. Oh, well. They aren't really company. They're family, aren't they."

Beth faced her mother across the hallway. "They may be family, but they aren't coming to dinner because I never got a chance to invite them. Janelle didn't show up for her visitation today."

"That's odd." Megan's brow wrinkled. "There was no one at the guest house when I stopped by after lunch, either." Megan had come home for lunch to see Chase and had visited the guest house on her way to the clinic. Beth couldn't help feeling that something didn't add up properly with Janelle and Connor, and it bothered her that her mother didn't seem to share her concern.

"I thought Janelle was anxious to spend time with the baby," she said pointedly.

Megan bit her lip. "So did I, but perhaps she and Connor just need some time alone together. They haven't been reunited very long, you know."

"Seems to me they'd want their child with them," Beth said.

With a wave of her hand, Megan dismissed the observation. "Soon enough all the formalities will be met and we'll have to give baby Chase up to his parents' care."

"Maybe so, but if he were my child, he'd have been here just long enough for the DNA tests. They're simple procedures, after all."

"It's like I said," Megan insisted, not quite meeting Beth's gaze, "Connor and Janelle need some time to work things out between them." Beth sensed that her mother was more troubled than she wanted to admit, and finally Megan confirmed it. "Maybe I'd better go over there later, be sure everything's all right."

An excellent idea, Beth thought. "You have your bath," she told her mother. "Then we'll have a quiet dinner and walk over to the guest house together."

Megan smiled and laid her forehead against Beth's. "Have I told you lately how much I love you?"

"Uh-huh, but it's always nice to hear."

Suddenly Megan grew serious, cupping Beth's face in both her hands. "I worry about you, darling."

"I'm fine, Mom." It was true. She hadn't murdered Brianne, and she wasn't going to let anyone frame her for a murder she hadn't committed. It helped that she had the Maitland influence and money behind her—and Jake's connections, too—but her real strength was the truth. She kissed her mother's smooth cheek. "You're the one with too much on her plate right now."

Megan sighed, but then her chin went up again. "It'll all work out," she vowed, and Beth, at that moment, did not doubt that her mother was right.

JANELLE ANSWERED the door in her bathrobe. "Megan, Beth, how sweet of you to drop by."

To Beth's ears, her words sounded just the opposite. "We haven't interrupted anything, have we?"

Janelle gave her a brittle smile. "Of course not."

"We just wanted to check on you, dear," Megan said, striding past Janelle into the tiny foyer of the guest house. The sapphire blue wool of her cape swirled and fluttered as Megan removed it. Beth caught the flash of irritation on Janelle's lovely face and smiled. Apparently Janelle was feeling somewhat proprietorial about her lodging, but it would never occur to Megan to wait for an invitation into her own guest house, and Janelle ought to realize that by now. A smile smoothed the flash of irritation as Janelle followed Megan, leaving Beth to close the door.

"Well, I'm glad you did," Janelle was saying. "I was feeling a little lonely, actually."

Megan and Janelle were settling onto the comfy couch in the small living area when Beth wandered into the room. She couldn't say why she disliked Janelle. Oh, she'd tried to like her, for Megan's sake if nothing else, but something about Janelle rubbed Beth the wrong way. The small house felt overheated after the coolness of the clear February night, and Beth pushed her waist-length orange jacket off her shoulders, draping it over the chair that stood to the side of the small entry.

"When you're lonely you can always visit your son," she said, to see Janelle's reaction. "You knew Chase would be at the house with me today. I expected to see you there."

Janelle seemed shocked, but then she blinked her big eyes until they teared. "I know. It's just that it's so hard to see him when I know I can't take him home with me."

"Seems to me you could fix that easily enough," Beth pointed out.

"For your information, I've sent for the necessary paperwork," Janelle informed her coldly. She was all warmth and smiles when she turned to Megan, though. "That's what Child Welfare wants, isn't it? A birth certificate?"

"I think that would work nicely," Megan said. "I'll speak to them to be sure."

Knowing that her mother relished having the baby in the house, Beth refrained from pointing out that the DNA testing would be quicker, and Megan deftly changed the subject.

"I stopped by earlier to check on you, but you were out."

Janelle waved a hand. "Oh, that. Connor took me to lunch, then I had some shopping to do. I brought so few things with me, you know."

"I knew it was something like that," Megan said. "Did you have a good day, get everything you need?"

"Yes, thank you."

"Forgive me for interrupting," Beth said unrepentantly, "but where exactly did you have to send for that birth certificate?"

"What looked like panic flickered across Janelle's face, but then she smiled, one hand fluffing her hair nonchalantly. "Why do you ask?"

"Just wondering."

"New Mexico," Janelle said.

"New Mexico!" Megan exclaimed.

"I wound up in Taos after Connor and I parted," Janelle explained haltingly, "just wandering around, looking for someplace to settle."

Megan made some reply, but Beth wasn't listening, her attention claimed by a noise from the back of the house. She could have sworn that someone was moving around in the bedroom.

"Is someone else here?" she asked sharply, barely aware that she had interrupted Janelle's complaints.

"What?" Janelle asked loudly. Megan lifted a slightly censorial eyebrow at Beth, and she immediately apologized.

"Sorry. I thought I heard something."

"You don't think we have a prowler, do you?" Janelle said loudly, a hand pressed to her chest.

It was all Beth could do not to roll her eyes. What she thought was that Connor was hiding in the bedroom, and she couldn't imagine why he would feel the need. "No, of course not," she said.

Janelle heaved a dramatic sigh. "Oh, thank goodness. It's so quiet here at the back of the property."

"We're very safe," Megan assured her. "The whole compound is walled, and we have an excellent security system. I hired the guards and had everything tested and upgraded after we brought Chase home and the press interest mushroomed."

"How good you are," Janelle said, almost purring. "I sensed that about you, you know, before I brought my little babe here."

She made it sound as if she'd left the baby in Megan's arms instead of dumping him on the clinic doorstep, Beth thought irritably. She couldn't help wondering why her mother was buying this act so completely, and she disliked watching Janelle's patently false gushing.

"Do you mind if I get a drink of water?" she muttered, already moving into the foyer.

"Of course not. You just help yourself," Janelle answered with exaggerated politeness.

Beth strode through the foyer and the dining nook, with its ice cream parlor table and matching pair of blue-striped chairs, past the short counter and into the kitchen with its bright white cabinets and cobalt blue countertops. She opened a cabinet door and took down a drinking glass, then filled it with water from the tap. Leaning a hip against the counter, she sipped the cool, sweet water and tried to figure out why Janelle irritated her so much.

Something occurred to her, and she drained the last of the water in one long gulp, then placed the empty glass in the sink. She strolled back the way she'd come and was about to step into the foyer when the sound of her mother's voice reached her, and she automatically paused. Only belatedly did she realize why. Secrets. The tone of her mother's voice was the one she used when discussing secrets. What secrets could her mother have to discuss with Janelle, of all people?

"No doubts," her mother was saying. "But no one else understands about Connor. How could they?"

What was this about Connor? She cocked her head, ready to catch every word, then it occurred to her that she was eavesdropping. Purposefully, she moved into the room. "I was just thinking," she said to Janelle, "I'm sure Child Welfare would send for the birth certificate for you. They could probably get it electronically."

Janelle stared at her with her mouth open. Megan immediately seized on the notion. "You know, that's right."

"Uh, yes," Janelle said, blinking rapidly. "Yes. Except, um, I—I'm not sure the birth has been recorded yet." She flapped a hand ineffectually. "I didn't have the baby in Taos, actually. It's so expensive there." She glanced uncertainly at Megan. "I moved to a little town north of there.

I—I only saw the doctor a few times, and I never did understand anything he said, his accent was so thick.''

"Was he Mexican, then?" Megan asked.

"I think so."

"Of course. Well, New Mexico isn't the end of the world," Megan said soothingly. "The papers will come, and until they do, Chase will just have to stay where he is."

"But you can always visit," Beth pointed out, "as often as you want." Which so far hadn't been very often, she mused.

Janelle fluttered her eyelashes and smiled gratefully. "You're all just wonderful," she sighed, and Beth wanted to strangle her. She almost laughed, considering that's what the police thought she'd done to Brianne Dumont. But Brianne had never engendered any dislike in her, not the way Janelle did, and even Janelle was as safe with her as Chase in his crib. Now, if she could just convince Ty Redstone and Paul Jester of that...

JANELLE CLOSED THE DOOR behind her unwanted visitors and folded her arms, fuming. That damned Beth. She could handle Megan. The woman was so besotted with her grandson and so anxious to believe that Petey was her long-lost son Connor that she'd do almost anything Janelle wanted. But Beth was a problem—and another problem was not what they needed just now, not after who she'd seen at the Austin Eats Diner that day. All that crap about New Mexico and sending off for the birth papers ought to buy her some time—time to come up with something else. First things first, though.

"You can't keep ignoring the kid," her dolt of a husband pointed out, appearing in the doorway of the bedroom.

"I know that, you idiot! But that's not our biggest problem at the moment."

She began to pace. Damn, she'd thought for sure that

she'd killed that bitch Lacy the day she'd dumped the kid. If the diner hadn't been so crowded at lunchtime and she hadn't been wearing sunglasses and a scarf, her face might have triggered Lacy's memory. With the amnesia gone, Lacy would remember that she was Chase's mother, not to mention the small fact that Janelle had tried to kill her with a blow on the head.

"What did you say they were calling her?"

"Who?"

Rage surged through her. The man looked like a movie star, but he was as dumb as a stump. If not for her, he'd still be working a two-bit construction job in Las Vegas, but what a damned nuisance he'd become! Was it too much to ask that he have enough intelligence to follow a conversation? She picked up a brass bookend and hurled it at him.

"Lacy Clark, you overgrown booby! Who else?"

He dodged the bookend and waited to see if she'd pitch the other even as he muttered, "Oh, her."

"Yeah, *her*," Janelle said, sneering, "the woman who gave birth to our Maitland meal ticket." She drove a hand through her long, dark hair. "Damn! I knew it. I knew she wasn't dead. Blast her! Why couldn't she have just died in that alley?"

"At least she doesn't remember anything," Petey said hopefully. "You heard that woman at the diner say she has amnesia. She can't tell about you trying to take the baby or hitting her if she can't remember."

Janelle turned a hard look on Petey. "And what if she gets her memory back?" she demanded. "We can't trust she won't. We have to shut her up permanently. We don't have any other choice. If that Goody Two-shoes gets her memory back, we're through here. We lose *everything*. We have to make certain that doesn't happen."

Petey studied her warily. "What are you thinking?"

"We're going to finish the job," Janelle said coldly.

"Lacy Clark should have died in that alley. The only way to fix this is to finish what I started that day."

"You're saying we have to kill her."

"It's her own fault," Janelle declared. "If she'd just given me the baby like I'd planned, instead of changing her mind at the last moment, we'd be safe. Now one of us has to make sure she never remembers."

Petey grimaced. "Me, you mean."

"Can you think of another way?" Janelle asked coaxingly. "Darling, I've already tried and failed. I've done all the planning and setting up. God, I invested months in that woman, winning her trust, convincing her the real Connor didn't want her or the brat. I'm just not strong enough to do this one last part. And we're so close to getting our share of the Maitland millions."

With a sigh, Petey lifted a hand to the back of his neck. "I'll take care of it," he said simply, and for the first time since lunch, Janelle relaxed somewhat. This husband of hers did have his uses, and if she managed him right, she could have everything she deserved and wanted. She swayed across the room, pulling loose the sash at her waist.

"When?" she pressed. "How?"

Petey shrugged and eyed the lissome, naked body she displayed for him. "Soon. I'll figure something out."

"No one can ever connect us with her murder," Janelle purred, reaching out to place a hand on his chest.

"They won't," Petey promised, leaning toward her.

"They'd better not," she growled, grabbing him by the hair and pulling his mouth down to hers.

Her husband liked to play it rough once in a while, and she was willing to give him what he wanted often enough to keep him in line, especially since he worked so hard to give her what she wanted—and just now she wanted Lacy Clark dead.

TY PUT HIS HEAD DOWN and determinedly ran the gauntlet, his strides long and sure as he said, "No comment," throwing the words left and right. He shoved through the heavy glass door of the Austin Police Headquarters building, leaving the reporters to the mercy of a windy February afternoon. As he hurried toward the elevator, he nodded to various officers in and out of uniform, clerks, secretaries, attorneys and at least one judge racing for the private entrance with a police escort following in her wake. The elevator opened and Ty stepped aside to allow several others to get out. Finally, he slipped inside and stabbed the correct floor button with an index finger. He held his breath as the doors slid closed, leaving him mercifully alone.

Putting his head back, he sighed in relief. What a day! Press dogging his every step, superiors ringing him up on his private cell phone to demand explanations, interviews that turned into Beth Maitland testimonials. If he hadn't already been inclined to think the woman innocent, he'd have greatly resented all the heavy-handed support that was coming her way. The same, however, could not be said for Brandon Dumont.

The picture coming together of the poor widower was of an image-conscious, somewhat shady, self-important social climber who routinely inflated his background and his income. He had a reputation as something of a ladies' man, and several of the ladies reported being carefully cultivated, only to be thrown over when a more socially prominent candidate appeared. Beth Maitland would have been the social pinnacle of Dumont's romantic pursuits, while the woman he'd married had been utterly devoid of social consequence. As far as Ty could tell, the murdered woman had been nothing more than an attractive accountant in Dumont's office, a step above a bookkeeper, until Dumont had married her. If it had been a love match, it had been a volatile one, since at least two people in a restaurant had heard them arguing recently, though neither could say about what.

The elevator came to a halt and the doors slid open. Ty stepped out at a swift stride that carried him across the hall and into the squad room. It was warm, too warm, and he slung off his lightweight, black leather overcoat as he navigated the corridors between cubicles to his, which he shared with his partner. Paul Jester sat at the desk facing Ty's, talking on the telephone. He glanced up as Ty hung his coat on the hanger he kept there for that very purpose. Paul quickly got off the phone and rocked back in his creaky chair to prop his feet on the corner of his desk, smiling like the proverbial cat that had eaten the canary.

"Our friend Dumont has been indulging in a little high-stakes day trading," Paul revealed gleefully. "That's the next thing to gambling, and he's playing with borrowed money. Looks like he's in over his head and trying desperately to get out. The Feds are asking questions about his business, and three investors in the last six months have filed complaints and disputes with him over his handling of their funds. Plus, the wife had a small life insurance policy, and she changed the beneficiary just two days before her death."

Interesting information. "Dumont is the beneficiary, of course," Ty surmised.

"Yep."

"Who was the original?"

"Her brother."

"He lives in California, right?"

"Right. It's a small policy, thirty thousand, but Dumont's already filed the claim."

Ty rubbed his hands together, pulled out his chair and sat. As motives went, it wasn't much, but instinct was whispering that they were on the right trail. He was determined to be thorough, though. He had recognized in himself a disturbing tendency to *want* to believe Beth Maitland. Something about that woman got to him on a very elemental level. Whipping out his notebook, he prepared to report what he had learned. "Our boy Dumont is coming up dirt-ier and dirtier."

"And the Maitland woman is looking shinier and shin-ier."

At that, Ty looked up alertly. "Who says?"

Paul flipped him a letter stapled to a memo form. Ty did a double take at the seal stamped into the corner of the expensive stationery. He whistled through his teeth. "From the governor's wife?"

"The First Lady of Texas is pleased to offer herself as a character witness for Ms. Beth Maitland, whose generous contributions to the child-care community of our state cannot be overstated," Paul recited.

"How does this outpouring of support strike you?" Ty asked, scanning the letter, which was addressed to the district attorney and had been copied to the mayor, the chief of police and the division.

"The family probably instigated it," Paul said, "but that doesn't mean it isn't sincere."

Ty laid the letter aside and nodded. "That's my take, too." He went on to tell Paul what he'd learned that day. Paul listened attentively, occasionally quirking an eyebrow or tossing out an astute observation. When Ty was done, Paul took his feet from the corner of his desk and leaned forward.

"Okay, so what's our next step?"

"We poke holes in Dumont's story so the truth can leak out," Ty said.

"You're sure that's the way the wind blows?"

Ty considered a moment, stilling himself emotionally and mentally in order to access the small voice that whispered through his soul. A picture of Beth Maitland sprang instantly to mind, her long, thick, coffee-brown hair froth-ing past her shoulders in layers of wavy curls. He saw the vibrant blue of her eyes, the elegant line of her nose, the slender oval of her face with its delicately pointed chin and wide, expressive mouth. Her perfect peaches-and-cream complexion invoked thoughts of warm, pale silk. He felt the definite urge to smile, as if an unexpected shaft of sunlight had broken through a gray and gloomy sky. That woman couldn't have killed anyone, and no one in his right mind would believe she had. Had Dumont set her up? His blood boiled at the very notion.

"Well?" Paul prodded.

Ty shook away the image and the emotions it evoked, aware that his small voice had developed a healthy libido. She was an extremely attractive woman, Beth Maitland, and he'd felt definite vibes around her. Something told him that she was as strongly attracted to him as he was to her, not that he could let that matter. She was an official suspect in a high-profile murder. He happened to think that she was innocent. "Let's get Dumont and Beth Maitland in here for another interview, together this time," he decided.

Paul rocked back in his chair, asking nonchalantly, "And which one do you want me to call?"

As casually as he could manage, Ty answered, "Doesn't matter. Dumont, I guess."

Paul winked and grinned. "Knew you'd say that."

Ty kept his face expressionless. "Yeah? Then why'd you ask?"

"Just to hear you admit that you want to speak to Beth Maitland yourself."

Ty snorted rudely. "I admit no such thing, and just because the woman is attractive doesn't mean she's my type, Jester."

"Why isn't she your type? Besides the obvious, that she's a suspect."

"She's rich," Ty answered succinctly.

"That doesn't make her like that chick your mom told me about," Paul argued, "the one from college who—"

"I know the one you're talking about!" Ty snapped, thinking he'd have to have a careful word with his mother.

It was unlike her to discuss his personal business even with his closest friends. "What did my mother tell you about her, anyway?"

Paul shrugged. "Just that she was from a prominent Houston family who didn't like the idea of their little debutante hooking up with a Native American."

A dirt-poor redskin, her daddy had called him, a breechclout gigolo without so much as his own tom-tom to his name. The insult still burned rancorously in his gut whenever he thought about it. He was very, very proud of his heritage. At the time, however, his erstwhile girlfriend's tearful wailing that her daddy was going to revoke her credit cards if she didn't stop seeing him had seemed the worse insult. He'd been stupid enough to think that, because she'd hopped into his bed every chance she got, she'd loved him. He'd found out rather graphically how he'd stacked up against her plastic money and her society friends. It had been a brutal reality check, and one he wouldn't need again, but Paul didn't have to know that.

"She was nothing, that girl," Ty said evenly, "just a little passing infatuation. My mother shouldn't read so much into things."

"Your mother is a very wise woman," Paul responded.

"Well, her wisdom sometimes gets a little tangled up when it comes to her children," Ty remarked. "But if you tell her I said such a thing, I'll have to cut your nose off."

"Crow punishment for betrayal," Paul exclaimed delightedly. He loved hearing about the old lore and traditions.

Ty chuckled. "Maybe I'll have to strip the skin off the soles of your feet and stake them to a fire-ant hill. Punishment for trespassing in private territory."

Paul frowned, and Ty could almost see the wheels turning behind his eyes. "You made that up!" he finally declared. "The People never did any such thing."

"Who said it was Crow punishment?" Ty teased. "It's just my personal remedy for nosy partners."

"Oh, yeah? Well, have I ever told you my remedy for smart-aleck Indians?"

"Indian is an incorrect and unacceptable label," Ty said, deadpan.

"So sue me, native boy," Paul retorted, reaching into his desk drawer for a rubber band, which he shot from between his fingers. Ty dodged the harmless missile and pulled out his drawer to get at his weapons stash.

The serviceable gray-carpeted floor around their abutted desks was littered with red and green rubber bands, and the mood had lightened considerably by the time Ty finally looked up Beth Maitland's telephone number and made that call. The play had done nothing, however, to prevent the slow thickening of his blood that occurred when her light, musical voice brought back to mind her sexy image. He reminded himself that Beth Maitland was not a woman in whom he should feel the slightest interest. Now all he had to do was silence that whisper in his soul, the one that brought a vision of her to the mind's eye and promised that here was fire to melt the ice of his heart.

CHAPTER THREE

TY WAS COOL. He didn't blink an eye when Beth Maitland sauntered in wearing tan suede slacks that showed off her long, slender legs and tight, round bottom. He said nothing about the matching fringed jacket that she wore over a tight, wine red knit shirt that left no doubt as to the strength of her feminine attributes. He did not compliment her suede half-boots, which matched her shirt in color, or comment upon the way she had twisted her long, lush hair into a plump, frothy roll skewered with a trio of silver-and-turquoise pins. He failed to remark that the open, turned-up collar of her shirt emphasized the creamy length of her slender neck, or that an expensive silver-and-turquoise beaded necklace called eye-catching attention to the deep crevice of her cleavage. To the casual observer, his fascination and appreciation would not have been unduly marked. Only he knew that she amazed him by looking even better than he remembered. Moreover, she possessed a quirky, natural style that was wholly her own, and being a man of a certain personal style himself, Ty could only applaud. Silently, of course.

He got to his feet and greeted her impersonally. "Ms. Maitland, thank you for coming."

She nodded and glanced past him to Brandon Dumont, her eyes going wide then clouding with confusion as she took in the small, dark woman next to him. Ty brushed back the sides of his suit coat and parked his hands at his waist, watching the byplay. Looking bored, Dumont pinched the crease of his navy slacks where one knee crossed the other. The Mexican woman next to him bowed her head and did not look up again, as if avoiding Beth Maitland's gaze. Beth tilted her head to one side, questioning Ty with her eyes. He smiled reassuringly, realized what he was doing and quickly blanked his face.

"You know Mr. Dumont," he said, "and my partner, Paul Jester." Paul was standing on the other side of the table, and he nodded at Beth. Ty went on. "You may also know Ms. Letitia Velasquez, Mr. Dumont's housekeeper."

Beth fixed the woman with a curious gaze. "Yes. Hello, Letitia. It's nice to see you again."

The housekeeper lifted a trembling smile in acknowledgment of the greeting, then quickly bowed her head again. Dumont frowned at the housekeeper but in no way acknowledged Beth Maitland. Paul pulled out the chair next to him at the table, leaving the end seat for Ty and keeping Dumont and the housekeeper on the opposite side. Beth walked around to the chair and gracefully lowered herself into the seat, smiling at Paul as he pushed the chair beneath her. She slipped the strap of a small, hand-tooled leather purse from her shoulder and placed the purse on the table in front of her. She looked across the table directly at Brandon Dumont.

"Hello, Brandon. How are you?"

"As well as can be expected," he said tonelessly without looking at her.

Beth glanced at Ty, then turned her gaze on the housekeeper. "Letitia," she said gently, "how is Frankie?"

Letitia Velasquez slowly lifted her head. "He is worried, Ms. Maitland," she answered just above a whisper.

Brandon Dumont suddenly jerked his head up and looked at Ty, demanding testily, "Can we get on with it, please?"

Ty froze the man with a cold, hard glare and watched with satisfaction as the color drained from his already pale face. Dumont reminded Ty of a banked fish, pale and slimy, but he supposed that he was attractive enough, with his soft good looks, trendy spiked haircut and expensive clothes. Ty suspected that his medium brown hair had been artfully highlighted and that the shocking blue of his eyes was achieved via colored contact lenses. The artifice disgusted Ty. He had no respect for this man, but he attempted to submerge that emotion in the determination to do his duty. He turned his gaze to Beth Maitland.

Calmly, Beth linked her hands and rested them atop her purse. She was the one Ty addressed. "Are we expecting your attorney?"

"No," she said. "He's in court today, but I'm perfectly willing to carry on without him."

Ty knew that he ought to be glad about that. Lawyers tended to gum up the works. But he didn't much like the idea of her being here on her own, not with Dumont dropping unexpected witnesses on them.

"Are you sure about that?" he asked. "Because we can reschedule."

Her generous mouth curved softly as she smiled at him, genuine blue eyes warm enough to speed up his heartbeat. Definite vibes. "It's all right," she said. "I want to get this over with. Besides, what do I have to fear? I didn't do anything wrong."

Dumont made a sound in the back of his throat, but when Ty looked at him, he was studying his fingernails. Ty pulled out his chair and straddled it.

"Okay." He flipped open the file folder he had placed on the table in front of his seat earlier, extracted a pen from his inside coat pocket and clicked the point down. "I had intended to go over your individual statements with you, Ms. Maitland and Mr. Dumont. See if we can't clear up some of the discrepancies. But the presence of Ms. Velasquez has changed the agenda."

"How so?" Beth asked, clearly puzzled.

Ty glanced at Paul, wondering if his partner disliked this

unexpected twist as much as he did, and chose his words carefully. "Ms. Maitland, during our last interview, you denied harassing Mr. Dumont and his wife, the deceased, did you not?"

Beth blinked. "Yes, I did. I do."

"You never called the Dumonts on the telephone to complain that they had ruined your life by getting married?"

"No, never."

"You didn't go to the Dumont home, demanding to speak with Brianne Dumont and making a scene?"

"Of course not!"

Ty glanced at Paul, who quickly spoke. "Ms. Velasquez says you did."

Beth's mouth fell open and her eyes went wide. She turned an incredulous gaze down the table. "Letitia?"

The housekeeper raised her head, tears streaming down her cheeks. "I'm sorry, Ms. Maitland. I say only what I must. I'm so sorry."

"No need to apologize, Letitia," Brandon Dumont said flatly. "Ms. Maitland knows what she's done."

"I know I did not harass or kill Brianne!" Beth exclaimed. "And you know it, too, Brandon Dumont!"

"Do I?" he replied coolly. "You were always fond of telling me what I knew and what I meant. Perhaps if you hadn't been, I wouldn't have left you for Brianne."

Ty saw that she was trembling, but when she turned her blue gaze on him, he realized that the emotion racking her body was pure anger. "He's lying! I broke up with him. He asked me to say that it was the other way around."

"And you never harassed the Dumonts?" Ty asked.

"Never!"

"But Ms. Velasquez swears that you did," Paul said.

Beth turned to the small woman huddled next to Dumont. "Letitia," she pleaded, "please don't do this. Please tell them the truth."

"That's exactly what she's doing," Dumont snapped.

The housekeeper broke into sobs. "I only say what I must," she repeated. "I only say what I must!"

"Can't you tell the poor woman is devastated to have to do this?" Dumont went on. He smiled maliciously at Beth and added, "She always did prefer you, you know."

Letitia Velasquez buried her face in her hands and sobbed brokenly.

"There, there," Dumont said, with the same inflection he'd use with a pesky fly.

Beth closed her eyes and said softly, "It's all right, Letitia. Whatever's going on, it'll be all right somehow."

"I don't want to say it!" Ms. Velasquez sobbed.

"You don't owe her any apologies or explanations!" Dumont growled at the woman. "You know what's at stake."

"That sounds like a veiled threat, Mr. Dumont," Ty said mildly.

"Don't be absurd," Dumont retorted. "I only meant that if Letitia does not do the right thing, a murder will go unpunished."

"Oh, no," Ty said. "We'll get to the bottom of this one. Never doubt it."

"I should think you've seen the bottom—as you put it—already," Dumont rejoined smoothly, but never once during the entire exchange did he look Ty in the eye.

"Some might think that," Ty replied noncommittally, but he'd suddenly had all of Brandon Dumont that he could stomach for one day—and he wasn't quite ready to give up on his original game plan just yet. He still might get some important personal questions answered if he played this right. He stashed his pen, flipped the folder closed and got to his feet, sweeping the folder up in his hand. "Paul, why don't you take Ms. Velasquez downstairs? Give her a minute to collect herself before the stenographer takes her statement."

Paul was already on his feet and moving around the end of the table to Letitia Velasquez's chair. "Come with me, ma'am."

The little housekeeper cast a worried look at Brandon Dumont, then got stoically to her feet, wiping tears from her face with one hand, her old-fashioned patent-leather purse clutched in the other. She glanced guiltily at Beth, then turned her head away and swiftly followed Paul from the room. Beth was glaring daggers at Dumont, who seemed amused. Ty gestured with his free hand toward the room beyond the door at his back.

"I'm going to grab a cup of coffee, then we'll get down to brass tacks. Can I bring anything for you two?"

Beth shook her head mutely. Dumont curled his lip in an expression of disdain, as if to imply that simple coffee was beneath him, and said sharply, "No, thank you."

Ty slipped out of the room, pulling the door almost closed. Catching the eye of one of his co-workers, he pantomimed drinking, then pressed his palms together in supplication and jerked his head at the interrogation room door. An understanding nod and quick movement in the direction of the coffeepot parked in an out-of-the-way corner was his answer. Ty stepped to one side of the door, put his back to the wall and waited.

Beth was the first one to speak. "Why are you doing this, Brandon?"

The smugness of Dumont's voice made Ty want to slap the cuffs on him. "Why, whatever do you mean, Beth dear?"

"Cut it out, Brandon. We both know you're trying to frame me for Brianne's murder."

"Trying to frame you?" Dumont echoed, slight emphasis on the first word. "Tsk, tsk, Beth, why don't you just accept your punishment like a good little Maitland and be done with it? Your family will get you off with minimal time, say ten or twenty years, which you'll probably serve in some walled country club. You know, it's positively unfair what the rich can get away with."

Beth seemed to ignore his taunts. "It's because I broke up with you, isn't it. Is your pride that monstrous? Is this my punishment for not loving you, Brandon?"

"Yet you agreed to marry me," he told her quickly.

"Yes," she answered slowly. "I wanted to be in love with you. I wanted you to be everything that you seemed then. But the image didn't hold, Brandon, and do you know why? It's that desperation in you, that grasping, frantic desperation. Eventually it seeps through the cool, handsome veneer and makes the other person feel...used, a means to an end."

"Used?" Dumont snarled. "You amused yourself with me, then tossed me aside like so much trash."

Ty's ears pricked, and he straightened away from the wall. So Beth Maitland had ended the relationship, just as she claimed. He had felt inclined to believe her before; now he knew she was telling the truth. Too bad what he'd just heard wouldn't be admissible in court. His co-worker approached with the cup of coffee, and Ty signaled him to silence before he drew near enough to place the cup in Ty's hand. Ty mouthed, "Thanks," and turned his ear to the door as the other detective tiptoed away.

"I guess I should have ignored the fact that you cheated on me with Brianne," Beth was saying.

"That was your own fault, and you know it," Dumont argued. "A man has to have satisfaction."

Ty had heard enough. Any more and he risked his case. Eavesdropping without a court order was a tricky business when it came to gathering evidence. He opened the door and walked in. Dumont shifted gears as smoothly as butter melted, saying to Beth in an aggrieved tone, "I loved Brianne. I adored her. I couldn't help myself. But I'm sorry that I cheated on you, especially if that's why you killed her."

Beth rolled her eyes. She looked at Ty and said calmly, "I didn't kill Brianne Dumont, and he damned well knows it."

"All I know is that my wife was found dead—in your office—after you threatened her."

"Threatened her?" Ty repeated sharply, plunking down the file folder and placing the coffee next to it. He brought his hands to his hips and stared down the table at Dumont. "You never mentioned anything about threats before."

Dumont stiffened. "Well, what do you think all that harassment was about?" he demanded. "She wasn't just amusing herself!" He gestured at Beth.

"The way she amused herself with you?" Ty asked flatly, and Dumont visibly paled. "Suppose you explain that to me."

Dumont straightened in his chair. "Y-you were listening!"

"That's right. Now, let's hear it, Dumont. Which was it? Was she so crushed when you dumped her for another woman that she was moved to murder, or was she playing with you? In which case, it wouldn't make much sense for her to harass and murder your wife, would it?"

Dumont swallowed. Then he seemed to realize that he had been rattled, and his face mottled with rage. "You don't understand these Maitlands!" he exclaimed. "They think they own the damned world and everything in it." He flung a hand at Beth. "She wasn't in love with me, but she wasn't through with me yet. She didn't want me to be with anyone else until she said so. I crossed her, and she got back at me."

It was a completely self-serving explanation, but Ty had nothing with which to counter it. Yet. He waved a hand at Brandon Dumont. "Anything else you want to tell me?"

Dumont subsided into his studied nonchalance. "Not at the moment."

"I'll call you if I need you," Ty told him dismissively.

Dumont glanced around the room, as if expecting to find someone or something else to keep him there. Realizing that he was being told to go, he got to his feet. "I'll show you where to meet Ms. Velasquez," Ty said.

Dumont lifted his chin and tugged at the bottom of his tweedy designer suit coat. "I, um, promised the poor woman I'd be at hand to support her," he said suggestively.

"That won't be necessary," Ty replied. "Detective Jester is taking care of her. Follow me, and I'll show you where you can wait." He turned toward the door. Dumont followed reluctantly, skirting the table and dragging his feet into the ward room. Ty walked him to the elevator, giving him much more explicit instructions than necessary on how to reach the public waiting area. He wanted to give Beth a chance to pull herself together, to think. A rattled suspect often said or did something to incriminate herself. Ty didn't want that. But what he did want from Beth Maitland was best left unacknowledged for both their sakes.

BETH PULLED a deep breath and put her head back. She had known, of course, but somehow it was still a shock to have it confirmed. Not that he had said anything particularly incriminating. No, Brandon was much too smart for that. He was, in fact, much smarter than she had given him credit for being. Well, she wouldn't make that mistake again. Neither would she be tamely led to the slaughter as dictated by his massive arrogance. Brandon Dumont was not going to get away with framing her for his wife's murder.

Ty Redstone entered the room, stopping just inside the door to study her with that blank, inscrutable expression of his. She wondered if it was part of his Native American heritage or a result of his police training. Probably some of both. It didn't completely obscure the powerful personal awareness of her that she sensed in him, or the surge of satisfaction that she felt as a result of it. Perhaps she sensed it because it was mutual. Ty Redstone was a devastatingly attractive man, sexually compelling. He reached behind him and pulled the door closed, and suddenly she felt at a distinct disadvantage. Impulsively, she shot to her feet, anxious to make him believe in her innocence.

"Save it," he said, beating her to it, "I'm not trying to prove that you murdered Brianne Dumont, because I'm not convinced you did. I'm just trying to get at the truth." He brushed back the sides of his suit coat and tucked his hands onto the slopes of his narrow hips.

Beth felt her knees wobble and stiffened them. "You believe me?" she asked incredulously.

He smiled self-deprecatingly. "Let's just say I have a nose for a frame-up and a very open mind."

Relief percolated inside her, making her feel suddenly giddy. "You believe that Brandon's framing me?"

Ty Redstone bowed his head, his inky hair sliding in thick, sleek clumps behind his ears. "Problem is, I can't prove it," he said matter-of-factly, stepping to the end of the table. "Yet." Beth didn't know she was going to do it until her arms were around his neck and she was leaning into him across the blunt corner of the table.

"Thank you! Oh, thank you! You don't know what a relief it is to—" She realized abruptly that he was standing with both arms raised, palms facing outward, the very antithesis of an embrace, while she wrapped herself around him. She realized, too, that his heart was slamming every bit as rapidly as her own. He was trying to keep his distance—and not completely succeeding.

Clearing his throat, he gingerly brought his hands to hers, gently disengaging her arms as he pushed her away.

"Sorry," she mumbled, very aware that he wasn't looking at her. Instead, he was focusing on the folder that he had laid on the end of the table.

"Sure. No biggie."

"I suppose that sort of thing happens all the time," she said, hearing the husky tenor of her voice.

"Uh, no, actually. That's, uh, that's a first."

She was oddly pleased. "Really?"

He nodded and flipped open the folder. A hand drifted up to rub at the corner of one eye. "I'm usually considered kind of, oh, unapproachable."

"Unapproachable?" she echoed disbelievingly. "You?"

He slid her a look around the tip of his finger. She sensed a challenge in it, a watchfulness, a measuring calculation. She shook her head. "Uh-uh. No, that's not how I'd describe you at all."

"No? And how would you describe me?"

Beth knew she was being audacious and didn't care. "Personable. Sexy. Drop-dead gorgeous."

His mouth dropped open. Then he coolly folded his arms and swept his gaze over her, up and down and up again. She was breathless by the time he said, "Not even my friends would describe me as *personable*." Amusement laced his tone. "I like my privacy too well for that."

"Do you?" Beth said, swaying close again. "I can understand that."

His dark eyes were focused intensely on hers, so compelling that she sensed, rather than saw, his smile. Then abruptly he pulled back again. "I bet you can. Hardly a day goes by that I don't find the name Maitland somewhere in my daily newspaper."

She wrinkled her nose, disappointed. "You get used to it after a while. Sort of."

He shook his head and broke the eye contact. "Not me. The press are all over this one, and it's driving me nuts."

She winced and rushed to apologize. "Look, I'm sorry about that. She really didn't do it on purpose, you know. They were going on and on about it, and she just sort of threw it out there."

His smooth, copper brow furrowed. "What are you talking about?"

"My mother. She gave your names to the press, yours and Detective Jester's."

Ty chuckled. "Ms. Maitland, the press has had my name and number for years. Your mother may have saved some newshound an extra phone call to find out who was handling the investigation, but that's all. Trust me on this."

Beth laughed. "Oh, I'm so glad. I was afraid we'd caused you all kinds of trouble."

"You have," he said flatly.

"Oh." Properly chastised—or at least pretending to be—she bowed her head, looking at him from beneath her brows.

"But not on purpose," he admitted. "I know that. Comes with the Maitland territory, I guess."

"I'm afraid it does," she answered unapologetically.

He nodded and straightened, bringing his hands to his hips once more. "Listen," he said after a moment of intense silence, "I don't want you to worry. We'll get to the truth."

"I'm not worried, I'm angry," she declared feelingly. "At first I just couldn't believe Brandon would do this to me, that he'd go this far. Now…" She looked at Ty openly, needing an answer. "He killed her, didn't he? He killed her to frame me."

Ty shook his head. "Ms. Maitland, we have no proof of that."

"Beth," she corrected automatically.

"What?"

"Call me Beth. There are a number of Ms. Maitlands. I'm Beth."

He shook his head again and picked up his thought. "We have no proof that Brandon Dumont killed his wife, and you're not to go around telling people that he did—or even that I suspect him of framing you for the murder. That will only alert him to the focus of our investigation and give him a chance to more deeply bury his trail. Do you understand, Ms. Maitland?"

"Beth," she repeated, and he sighed, pinching the bridge of his nose with one hand.

"Do you understand what I just told you, *Beth?*"

Pleased, she answered him primly. "Yes, I do, Ty." She leaned forward slightly. "I may call you Ty, may I not?"

His lips twitched with what could have been a smile. "I suppose so."

The light of interest fairly smoldered in his eyes, but he was working hard to suppress it. She didn't want him to suppress it. She wanted just the opposite. Placing both hands on the tabletop, she leaned closer still. "Now who's unapproachable?" she teased huskily. "I don't think you're unapproachable. I think you're a blasted magnet."

A slow grin spread across his face, and he leaned down, bringing his nose close to hers and flanking her hands with his. "And I suppose there's iron beneath that sweet, feminine exterior of yours."

"Must be," she murmured, feeling breathless, as if he might be about to kiss her. When his gaze dropped to her mouth, she felt a surge of exultation and tilted her head. Suddenly the door opened, and Paul Jester breezed in.

Ty jerked back from her as if she'd suddenly developed an offending odor. She glared at Jester and barely restrained herself from stamping her foot. Jester sent a surprised look between the two of them and quickly closed the door.

"Uh... I, uh, I got the Velasquez statement."

"Yeah, thanks," Ty said smoothly. He tapped his lower lip with his forefinger and turned to face his partner, face totally expressionless.

Beth could only marvel. He did that so well, covered so smoothly. It was like a mask that he could produce at will. She, on the other hand, was all too transparent, blatant even. She wondered what he thought of that.

"What do you think?" Ty asked Paul, ignoring her.

Paul glanced at Beth and carefully hedged. "About Velasquez? Uh, we'll have to check out a few things."

"You can speak freely, Detective Jester," Beth said, folding her arms. She glanced at Ty at the same time Jester did and added, "I've been given to understand that I'm no longer an actual suspect."

Jester lifted both eyebrows at Ty. "Yeah?"

For the first time, Ty appeared a tad flustered. He licked his lips, then said, "Let's say…not the chief suspect."

Jester split another gauging look between them, accepted the obvious and shrugged. "I didn't get much out of her," he said baldly. "She just kept saying that Ms. Maitland called often, sounded mad and stopped by sometimes to shout at everyone. She couldn't remember dates, and she kept apologizing, saying she didn't want to hurt Ms. Maitland but couldn't help it." He looked at Beth. "She begged me to help you, says she knows you're a good woman." He addressed Ty. "I can't help feeling that he's got something on her."

Ty looked at Beth. "What about that? You know any reason Ms. Velasquez could be coerced to give testimony against you?"

"It could have to do with Frankie," Beth suggested.

"Her son?" Jester clarified.

"Yes. I know Brandon helped him enter the country once after he'd been deported. I don't know how Brandon worked it. I just know that Letitia was weeping and thanking him one day. Her English was all jumbled together with Spanish, but it was all about Frankie. I know that."

"Okay. That's where we'll start then," Ty said.

"Maybe I should go with you," Beth suggested quickly. "My Spanish is pretty good, and—"

"No." It was a flat refusal, no room for compromise, and it hit her as patently unfair. It was her neck in the noose, after all.

"But—"

"No," he repeated. "Officially, you're still a suspect. I can't let you tag along on an investigation. Jester will take care of the Velasquez question."

"What about you?" she demanded.

He slid his hands into his pants pockets. "I want to take a look at Brianne Dumont's background."

"She had some socially prominent friends," Beth pointed out quickly. "I could—"

"No!" Ty reiterated strongly.

Beth felt like a little girl being scolded for requesting a cookie. She shot to her feet, arguing, "They won't tell you anything. They'll speak more readily to someone they know."

"What does that mean?"

"Just that I know these people. I know how their minds work. They'll talk to me."

"But not me," he said, "because I'm not one of the club."

"They'll talk to me because they know me," she argued.

"You're one of their own, you mean!" he accused, jerking his hands from his pockets to snap up the folder on the table.

Paul made a sound that told Beth she'd overstepped, but she wasn't sure how exactly. She glanced in his direction, then back to Ty. "Well, yes, if you want to put it that way."

A flash of temper lit those midnight eyes. The mask slipped away, revealing his disdain. "I may not get my name into the society pages, but I know what I'm doing."

"I didn't mean it that way. You're misreading me completely."

"Leave the detective work to the professionals, Ms. Maitland," he snapped. "Social standing doesn't figure into this in any way."

"I never said it did."

"No, but you meant it," he told her, striding toward the

door. He threw it open and slid a scathing look over one shoulder. "I know *exactly* what you said and *exactly* what you meant. Now, if you'll excuse us, we have work to do."

He was throwing her out. She considered, for a moment, digging in her heels, but a glance at Paul Jester told her that he wouldn't recommend it. Another time then. Coolly, she snatched her purse and lifted her chin.

"I trust you'll keep me informed, at least," she said regally, sweeping toward the door.

"We'll be in touch," was the cool reply.

She meant to walk out without a backward glance, but she couldn't do it, not after what had almost happened in this room only moments earlier. At the last second she stopped and turned, seeking his gaze with her own.

"Ty?" she said softly, imploringly.

For an instant, that icy disdain seemed to melt a little, but then he swept back the sides of his coat and parked his hands on his hips in a gesture of sheer implacability. "Go home, Ms. Maitland," he ordered, "and let us do our jobs."

Angrily, she whirled, fleeing a deep disappointment. But he was more than just wrong if he thought she was going to sit on her hands and wait for him to slowly dig up what she could uncover in a twinkle. It wasn't the only thing about which Ty Redstone was wrong, but it was the one in which she was going to rub his handsome nose.

CHAPTER FOUR

THE DOLL-LIKE COUPLE smiled with practiced civility and murmured patent responses. Sitting side by side on their immaculate sofa in their immaculate home, they looked like magazine cutouts, perfectly groomed, perfectly dressed, and they did everything in tandem, including smile and politely evade substantiative answers to direct questions. With some inborn sense of protocol and timing, the husband politely checked his watch twice before bringing a firm end to the interview, if the efforts of Detectives Redstone and Jester could be called such.

More like a waste of time, Ty thought glumly as Jester aimed their nondescript, department-issue sedan toward the next address on their list. So it had gone for days now. The interviewees were interchangeable. The results as well. *Nada.* They hadn't learned a darned thing. Brianne Dumont remained a cipher, a dead cipher, unfortunately. The answers to their questions were rote.

"I really couldn't say."

"I pay no attention to gossip and rumors."

"One doesn't like to pry into the private lives of others, you know."

"We were friends, but casual acquaintances more than intimates."

Brianne Dumont might have been a cardboard cutout for all the attention her "friends" seemed to have paid her. Undoubtedly she'd moved on the very fringes of the upper echelon of Austin society, but if she'd had another circle of intimate associates, they hadn't been discovered yet. Her co-workers might have been more forthcoming than her so-called friends, but the late Mrs. Dumont had held herself aloof, letting them all know that they were beneath her consideration socially. Those listed in her personal address book and calendar were saying the same thing, albeit very politely, about her. The gist of it seemed to be, "She was around a lot, but we didn't really know her and didn't care to."

As much as he hated to admit it, even to himself, Ty sensed that they were getting the royal runaround, just as Beth Maitland had predicted. What he wouldn't give for one lousy scum sucker in the mix. That sort always had something to fear from law enforcement and so could be pressured, shaken, fouled up. These society types had money, prestige and respectability to fall back upon; they wouldn't allow themselves to be intimidated by mere civil servants.

"Who's next?" Paul asked, after flashing his badge and guiding the sedan expertly through the guard gate of one of the city's more exclusive neighborhoods.

Ty checked his itinerary. "Name's Giselle Womack. According to Dumont, she and Brianne were roommates for a short while after college until Giselle married."

"Womack," Paul said thoughtfully. "Hmm. Wouldn't be any connection to Womack Industries, would there?"

Ty sighed. "Oh, yeah."

"All this money in the world," Paul said, shaking his head. "You'd think a little of it would fall on us, wouldn't you?"

"Speak for yourself," Ty said. "I don't much like what money does to people."

"Most of us don't have that prejudice," Paul quipped. "Personally, I'd like to see what a little of it could do to me." He slowed the sedan and turned it off the broad, tree-lined street onto the pebbled circular drive of a large Italianate house in cream stucco and white marble.

Paul whistled. Ty groaned. "Does the term 'exercise in futility' mean anything to you?"

His partner ignored that and nodded at a flashy yellow convertible parked in front of the door. "Suppose Mrs. Womack has company?"

"Shouldn't think so," Ty answered, opening his car door. "She knows we're coming."

Paul got out and walked around the front of the car. "Seems to me there'd be room in that four-car garage back there for family cars."

"Guess we'll see," Ty replied, his footsteps carrying him toward the front door. He pushed the bell and rolled his shoulders, adjusting the weight of his gun and the placement of the shoulder holster. The door opened, and a sullen, gray-haired maid in a beige uniform greeted them.

"Are you the police?"

"Detectives Jester and Redstone, ma'am."

"They're waiting on you. This way."

They? Ty glanced at Paul, then over his shoulder at the flashy yellow convertible with its clean white top. If Mrs. Womack had called her attorney in to hold her hand, that was one flamboyant advocate. He stepped into the opulent, tiled entry and followed the maid, Jester behind him. They were shown into a sunny solar room at the back of the house crammed with so many plants that the bamboo furnishings were all but hidden. Ty heard rushed whispers and giggling, but wasn't sure from where until the maid pushed back the frond of a particularly impressive potted palm and addressed someone Ty couldn't quite see, announcing baldly, "They're here."

She turned to Ty and Jester, letting the palm frond fall into place. "Ya'll want some coffee or something?"

"No, thank you."

She nodded sharply and plodded off. Ty traded glances

with Paul before he stepped around the potted palm—and looked straight into the smiling face of Beth Maitland. She set aside a cup and saucer and bounced off the short sofa where she was sitting next to a plastic-looking blonde. Her wide smile beamed with perfect white teeth. "Ty!" she exclaimed, holding out her hand as if greeting an old friend.

Exasperation warred with anger and no small amount of sheer delight. The woman took his breath away, and he was going to give her a tongue-lashing as soon as he got her out of here.

"Giselle," she gushed, "I want you to meet Ty Redstone and Paul Jester." She flipped a little wave at the woman sitting with crossed bare legs beside her. "Giselle Womack. That's Mrs. Harold Womack," Beth confided, amusement twinkling in her eyes as if they shared a private joke.

Ty tried to keep a straight face as he nodded at the young woman preening in her seat on the narrow sofa, but the picture of Harold Womack that sprang to mind made that difficult. Ty had done a little research on his interview subjects and had found more info on Harold Womack than most. One thing he'd come across was a newspaper photo taken at a charity golf tournament. He could see it now— Harold Womack, a full head shorter than the other men in the photo, bald as glass, sixty if he was a day, his belly hanging over his belt, a cigar clamped between his teeth as he prepared to swing a club at the ball on the ground. Ty had wondered at the time if the man could even see the ball for his belly. Now he wondered if old Harold hadn't bought himself a cute little trophy wife to help him hold age at bay.

Giselle Womack hadn't yet seen thirty, but her smooth face bore the signs of bad cosmetic surgery, a blunt, slightly scooped nose, the prominent jut of a too rounded chin, lips that looked as though they'd been stung by a peculiarly accurate bee. Her hair was a little too blond and big to be real, and unlike Beth's full, firm bust, Giselle's proudly displayed breasts looked hard and unnatural on her bony frame. Only the ostentatious diamonds glittering on the hand she held aloft for Ty's greeting seemed genuine. He wondered if he was supposed to shake that hand or kiss it. He settled for a quick press and a slight nod.

"I've heard so much about you, Ty," Giselle said breathily, fanning her shoulders to call attention to the cleavage displayed by the little knit dress she was wearing. At least, it would have been a dress on a ten-year-old; on her it was a long shirt two sizes too small. He forced a slight smile and glanced daggers at Beth from the corners of his eyes. Heard about him, had she? He could only guess what Beth Maitland had told her. Paul slid his hands into his pants pockets and rocked on his heels, indicating with a slight clearing of his throat that he was perfectly aware he was being left out of the welcome. Battling exasperation, Ty managed a polite reply.

"Nice to meet you, Mrs. Womack."

Mrs. Womack waved her diamonds and said, "Oh, honey, call me Giselle. We're not formal here. Are we, Beth?"

Beth folded her long legs and took her seat. "Not at all," she confirmed, and lifted a hand toward the chairs placed at either end of the rectangular glass table standing before the couch. Ty picked the chair closest to Beth, leaving Paul to cross in front of the table and gingerly take the chair next to Giselle Womack. Paul nodded affably and was pointedly ignored. He shot an amused look at Ty and settled back, prepared to be invisible.

Giselle leaned forward, allowing Ty yet another view of her cleavage, and said, "I think it's wonderful how you're helping Beth."

Helping Beth. As if he was a paid assistant. Ty ground his back teeth. "We're investigating the murder of Brianne Dumont."

"I'm dying to know," Giselle said, gushing. "Was she or wasn't she?"

Ty lifted both eyebrows. "I beg your pardon?"

"Hasn't anyone else told you?" Giselle fairly crowed. "I just knew someone would spill the beans."

By now Ty realized he wasn't going to get a straight answer from the blonde; she was too busy congratulating herself on being the one to manage the revelation. He turned to Beth Maitland. "Was she or wasn't she what?"

"Pregnant," Beth answered bluntly, a light dancing in those sky-blue eyes. "Brianne claimed that she was pregnant."

Claimed was the right word. Ty had seen the coroner's report. Brianne Dumont had not been pregnant at the time of her death—had *never* been pregnant—but he kept that bit of information to himself.

"And Brandon was fit to be tied, I can tell you," Giselle said in a conspiratorial tone.

"When was this?" Ty asked, realizing that he just might have been handed his first real break.

Giselle pursed her lips, considering. "Mmm, about a month before the elopement. Personally, I had my doubts, but then he married her, you know, so I had to wonder if it wasn't true."

"You're saying that Brandon Dumont married Brianne because she claimed to be pregnant with his child."

Giselle nodded. "Why else? Everyone knew he was engaged to Beth. He was practically shouting it from the rooftops. I asked Brianne what she was going to do, and she said, 'I'll tell you what I'm not going to do. I'm not going to be dropped like some long-distance phone company when a better rate plan comes along.' She said if the competition had been anyone but a Maitland, she wouldn't have had to—and I quote—'go so far.' It made me wonder, you know, if she did it on purpose—or if she wasn't pregnant at all, just saying she was to force his hand."

Ty looked at Paul, confirming that the other man would remain silent. Paul, after all, had read the coroner's report, too, but he didn't so much as raise an eyebrow. Ty turned to Giselle Womack. "Thank you, Mrs., uh, Giselle. I have just a few more questions for you."

Giselle Womack waved her jewel-laden hand. "Ask anything you want. I'll be glad to help dear Beth any way I can."

Ty got right down to it. "Would you say that anyone else knew about this supposed pregnancy?"

Giselle snorted laughter. "Honey, *everyone* knew. You can imagine the talk." Meaning everyone who was anyone in Austin, including those people he and Paul had interviewed just that morning, no doubt. Giselle Womack had probably spread the gossip. She glanced at Beth and backtracked a bit. "Well, not *everyone*. I mean, no one was going to say anything to dear Beth and her family." Dear Beth brushed imaginary lint off one knee and bowed her head, sliding a look at Ty from beneath her slender brows.

Ty swallowed the acrid taste of his own pride and forged ahead. "How was it that you learned of this supposed pregnancy?"

Paul had his notebook out and had been taking down everything that was said. He began scribbling furiously while Giselle rattled on about her relationship with Brianne Dumont, telling more than Ty wanted to know. How they met in college, who they dated, who they knew, how they shared expenses and an apartment—out of choice, of course, not because they *had* to or anything—and talked about the men they would marry one day.

"Looks and image were always important to Brianne," Giselle confessed, as if the very idea was ludicrous, despite her obvious attempts to change her appearance. She went on until Ty wanted to scream. Finally, he got to his feet.

"I think that's everything we need," he announced, cutting off the torrent of words.

A look of dismay crossed Giselle Womack's face. "Oh, but—"

Beth reached across and squeezed the woman's manicured hands so tightly that her long plastic nails clacked together. "Thank you so much, Giselle. I can't tell you how I appreciate this."

"Oh, it was my pleasure." Giselle simpered as Beth got to her feet. "You will call me for lunch now."

"Just as soon as I'm free of this unpleasantness," Beth promised. "And I'll tell my mother how anxious you are to serve on her charity board. I'm sure she'll be pleased."

"Well, it is my duty, you know," Giselle said, gazing at them from the couch. "Harry's always saying how we have to think of the less fortunate and put ourselves out there to help."

Ty couldn't help reflecting that getting her picture in the paper was doubtless Giselle's definition of putting herself out there. Probably her definition of doing her duty, too. He smiled and nodded as Beth assured Giselle that they didn't need to be shown out of the house, not that Giselle showed any signs of intending to do that. He was reasonably sure the maid had better things to do, if her employer's indolence was any indication.

Finally, they withdrew and strode quickly to the entry. Beth seemed to be bursting with energy, as if she might take flight the instant they were out of doors. Ty clamped a restraining hand on her arm, warning her silently that she wasn't getting away from him until he'd given her a piece of his mind. Before he could decide whether to scare her with possible charges of interfering with an investigation or scorch her ears, Paul's cell phone rang. Hurrying ahead of them, he pulled it from his coat pocket and took the call. Suddenly he bolted for the front door.

Ty and Beth looked at each other and ran after him,

catching up with him on the drive. "I've gotta go!" he yelled, waving his phone as he ran around the car to the driver's side. "Pauly fell and broke his arm! I've got to meet Nan at the hospital!"

"What happened?" Ty yelled, throwing wide his arms.

Paul shook his head, indicating that he didn't have the details. "Can you get where you need to go?"

Completely at a loss, Ty stood there. Not so Beth Maitland. She waved at Paul Jester and said, "He can take my car. You go on."

Not waiting for Ty's agreement, Paul yanked open the car door and got in, yelling, "I'll call when I know something!"

Ty rushed down the steps as Paul started the car. "Give Pauly a hug for me." Paul nodded and put the car in gear, backing it up to pull around Beth's convertible. "Tell him I'll bring him something special for his medicine bag!" Ty called, and Paul waved as he started forward and pulled away.

Beth stepped onto the drive beside him. "Is Pauly his son?"

Ty felt oddly agitated. "Yeah. Yeah, he's, um, four. And Bailey, their little girl, is two." He thought of adorable little Bailey. Had Paul's mother rushed to the house to stay with her, or was she on her way to the emergency room with her frantic mom and brother?

"Nan must be his wife's name, then."

"What? Oh. Yeah." Ty rubbed a hand against the back of his neck, wondering if he ought to check on Bailey, maybe follow Paul to the hospital. But which hospital? He'd forgotten to ask.

"What was that about a medicine bag?" Beth asked.

A second or two passed before he was able to wrap his mind around the answer. "Oh, it's a Crow thing."

"Crow?"

He gestured impatiently and snapped, "Indian."

She tilted her head as if intrigued. "You're Crow then?"

"Half Crow, half Tonkawa and Caddo," he answered absently.

"I'm not familiar with the Tonkawa and Caddo tribes," she said thoughtfully, engaging his interest for the first time since Paul's phone call. Suddenly he remembered that he was angry with her interference in his investigation—or supposed to be.

"Oh, like you're familiar with the Crows," he said snidely, surprised at his own pettiness.

"No, not really," she answered lightly, shivering in the cool breeze that ruffled the tree branches. She folded her arms. "Was it Joseph Walker who said the Crows were the most beautiful people on the face of the earth?"

Ty stared at her. She had surprised him. He felt himself softening as he reached for her arm and turned her toward the flashy yellow convertible. "Where's your coat?"

"In the car."

He tried the passenger side door and found it open. "Give me your keys and get in."

She didn't argue, just slid into the creamy white seat and popped open her little black handbag. After extracting the keys on a bracelet-size gold ring, she handed them over without a word. Dangerously pleased, Ty closed her door and walked around the back of the car, picking out the right key on the ring. Nestled among the keys was a gold B studded with what looked like diamonds, a fine reminder that the rich were different from everyone else. Their values were skewed by all that money and influence, and he'd do well not to forget it. Steeling himself against the effect Beth Maitland seemed to have on him, he got behind the steering wheel and slid the key into the ignition switch, trying not to be impressed with the automobile.

The engine rumbled powerfully to life and immediately sank into a contented purr. Ty figured it was time to set Ms. Maitland straight about a few things, but then he looked at her. She was stunningly beautiful in black denim against a field of cream white leather, as at ease as if they did this sort of thing every day. Something happened inside his chest—had his heart flopped over?—and every harsh word he'd formulated vacated his mind. He opened his mouth and heard himself asking conversationally, "So what do you know about Joseph Walker?" *Good move, Redstone,* he chided himself.

"I know he may well have been the greatest of the mountain men," she answered smoothly.

He smiled and reached for the gearshift in the console between them. "You think so, do you?" *Skating on thin ice, buddy. Just remember, she's a suspect. And rich.*

"I do," she answered. "He was an honorable, skilled and wise man. Handsome, talented, strong. And he had a great respect for the native cultures."

Ty aimed the car down the drive and secretly exulted in the surge of power that met his physical commands. "You've done some reading about the period, I see."

"Yes," she said, "just recently, as a matter of fact."

"Oh, really? I minored in history in college, so I know something about the period myself."

She shifted in her seat as he turned onto the empty street. "*I* minored in history in college."

"No kidding?"

She was beaming at him. "Well, that's something else we have in common, isn't it?"

"Something else?" he echoed.

"Besides the investigation, I mean."

Whoa. He swerved to the curb and brought the car to a complete stop. Leaning toward her, he bridged the gap between their seats with his arm. "You are *not* part of this investigation. You're a suspect, for pity's sake!"

Her eyes took on a large, wounded look. "I thought you believed me."

"I do. But formally you're still a suspect."

"Oh, *formally*," she said dismissively. "What difference does that make?"

"Technically it makes all the difference," he began, but she dismissed that, too.

"Technically, formally, those are just words. The truth is what matters. And I think we got a little piece of that today, don't you?"

"Yes, but—"

"I got her to tell it," she insisted. "Giselle wouldn't have said anything to you if I hadn't spread a little Maitland influence on her."

His pride pricked, Ty retorted, "You don't know that!"

"Did anyone else you spoke with today mention that Brianne was pregnant?" she insisted.

"Claimed to be pregnant," he corrected unthinkingly, "but that's beside the point."

She seized on his slip like a hungry dog snagging a bone. "Claimed? It was a lie, wasn't it? Wasn't it?"

He grimaced, wanting to kick himself. Why couldn't he think when he was around this woman? "It was a manner of speech. You used it yourself."

"I knew it!" She collapsed into her seat, her mind obviously churning. "And when he found out she lied, he killed her," she muttered. "Brianne used the lie of pregnancy to try to break us up and get him to marry her. That's why I got the gossip."

"What gossip? How did you hear it?" he asked, suddenly aware that he'd neglected that line of questioning.

"Giselle. She's been trying to cultivate a relationship with us ever since she married Harry. What she doesn't know is that my mother can't stand Harry Womack. But Giselle seems to believe that Harry's money gives her entrée to every house in town—and to an extent, it does."

"But not the Maitland house," Ty surmised.

She didn't bother confirming, just went on with her story. "Giselle called me at work one day, like we're really friends or something, and said that she just couldn't live with herself if she didn't let me know that Brandon and Brianne were having an affair. I always figured that Brianne put her up to it, because they were roomies at one point, you know.''

''So you took it on yourself to question her today,'' Ty said, realizing that he should have expected this.

''I knew you would get to her sooner or later,'' Beth said plaintively. ''I thought I'd just save you a little time. When she told me you'd called for an appointment, I figured I might as well grease the skids, so to speak.''

Ty shook his head. ''Do you have any idea how many ways you could have blown that interview, not to mention the case?''

''But I didn't!'' she exclaimed. ''She'd never have told you what she told me if I hadn't played buddy-buddy with her.''

The fact that she was probably right only stoked Ty's temper. ''That's beside the point.''

''That's entirely the point! You need me!''

''I need you to get out of my way!'' he yelled, not that it seemed to matter one whit.

''I can't just sit on my hands hoping someone else will prove my innocence!'' she yelled right back. ''What if it was you accused of murder? Would you sit at home with your hands folded and do nothing?''

He didn't dare answer that. Closing his eyes, he strove for a reasonable tone. ''Beth, you cannot be involved in this investigation.''

''I *am* involved in this investigation,'' she corrected him. ''I'm right at the center of it, and not because I want to be.'' She had a point, unfortunately. But she wasn't through, not by a long shot. ''Ty, I need to *do* something. I can't go back to work until this is resolved, and I'll go insane if I have to sit around watching soap operas all day. I have to try to clear myself.''

He shook his head, more swayed by her argument than he wanted to admit. "It's just not possible."

"Why not? You were going to question Brandon in front of me the other day. Why is that all right, and this isn't?"

Exasperated, he resorted to obstinance. "No. You'll just get in the way."

"I won't!"

"It could jeopardize the case."

"It could *make* the case! Look at what happened today."

"Beth, we're dealing with murder here," he argued desperately. "If Dumont did this, he laid his plans very carefully, and he did it meaning to hurt you. I can't take the chance."

Suddenly she was touching him, her slender hand gently cupping his cheek and jaw. He melted inside like butter in the warm summer sun and was, conversely, hard as stone elsewhere.

"Ty, please," she implored. "If I'm really in danger, then won't I be safer with you than out on my own?"

He couldn't seem to get enough air to make a coherent answer. Maybe it was the sudden vision he had of Beth in his bed. Somehow he managed to speak. "You'll be safest at home."

"But I can't stay there and do nothing!" she repeated. "Please, Ty. Please let me go with you."

Her mouth was driving him crazy, those luscious coral lips forming the syllables of her words. Was that the same lipstick she'd worn the other day? No, he didn't think so. He tried to clear his head and come up with a smart answer. His stomach rumbled, providing inspiration. "Fine. I'm just going to lunch now."

She broke into a smile. "Lunch? Oh, good, I'm famished." She dropped her hand and settled into her seat. "Where did you have in mind?"

"I—" He broke off, realizing he'd just invited her to lunch. Man, he was really keeping his distance, wasn't he?

What a rock. If he was smart, he'd drive straight to the office and turn her keys over to her with a firm dismissal. Apparently he wasn't as smart as that. "I don't have anyplace specific in mind."

"I know a wonderful little diner," she said, smiling broadly. "It's called Austin Eats. Do you know it?"

A diner? For a Maitland? He started to shake his head. "No, I...oh, wait, that's the place next to the clinic, isn't it?"

"That's the one."

It really was a diner, and fairly close. "Austin Eats, it is," he said, mildly surprised. This could be a good thing, he told himself as he started the car moving once more. He could explain it all again, carefully this time, unemotionally, professionally. She was an intelligent woman. She'd understand, eventually, that he couldn't have her tagging along on interviews. Then, when this was all over, maybe— No. He slammed the door on that thought abruptly. He wouldn't make the same mistake twice. No matter how strongly attracted he was. He'd learned his lesson about rich, socially prominent young women a long time ago. He needed no reminders. Usually.

He shifted in his seat, knowing he was in trouble. Big trouble.

CHAPTER FIVE

BETH SMILED and waved at her friend Mary Jane Potter, who was carrying dirty dishes from the large, curving counter toward the kitchen. The new waitress, Sara, had already taken their order. As usual, the place was popping with lunchtime trade. Mary Jane jerked her head toward Ty and waggled her eyebrows suggestively. Beth couldn't help laughing. Ty was an absolute doll, a true hunk, so gorgeous he made her eyes ache. When she'd touched him in the car, it had felt as though a bolt of lightning had struck her. She shivered just thinking about it.

Ty was on the phone. He'd called Paul as soon as they'd ordered and sat with his head bowed and his hand over one ear as he spoke into his cell phone. Sara delivered their coffee with a smile, tucked a wisp of long blond hair into the net pinned to the back of her head and hurried off to greet a pair of newcomers who took the counter seats just vacated by a couple of nurses from the clinic. Sara was something of an enigma, an amnesiac so wholesomely pretty and sweet that it was hard to imagine she could have suffered any event traumatic enough to damage her memory. Beth couldn't help searching her soft blue eyes every time she saw her for any sign of trouble, but she'd never discerned so much as a hint of anything out of the ordinary. Poor woman. Someone somewhere had to be missing her. Ty finished his call and pocketed the phone.

"Is Paul's little boy all right?" Beth asked.

"Sounds like a pretty nasty break. The little imp climbed

onto the refrigerator to get at a cookie jar and jumped off when he heard his mother coming. But he'll be okay. They'll be putting his arm in a cast soon. And I don't think he'll be climbing onto the refrigerator again.''

"I certainly hope not. He sounds precocious.''

Ty grinned. "Yeah, you could say that. A real vivid imagination, that boy has.''

"You sound fond of him.''

"Oh, yeah. He's a real cute kid. Reminds me of my baby brother, frankly. And that little sister of his! Oh, man, she wraps me right around her baby finger every time. Just like my own kid sister.''

Beth laughed, intrigued by the thought of Ty Redstone beguiled by a pair of kids. "I love children,'' she said.

"Which would explain why you do what you do.''

She tilted her head, studying him. "What explains you? Why did you go into law enforcement?''

He shrugged and looked away. "Why not?''

She knew he was trying to evade the question and wasn't about to let him. "Was it a boyhood dream? An accident of fate? What?''

He picked up his coffee cup and sipped the black brew, making a sound of approval. She followed suit, well aware that Austin Eats boasted the finest coffee in town.

"Well? Why won't you tell me?''

He chuckled. "Okay, okay. But it sounds more dramatic than it is.''

"So tell me,'' she urged, propping her chin on the heel of her hand, her elbow braced against the countertop.

He took his time, obviously choosing his words carefully. "My father grew up on the Crow reservation in Montana. He didn't have a lot of experience with white culture. My mother, on the other hand, grew up in Oklahoma and had little experience with reservation culture. They met when she went up with a friend to visit family on the reservation. She spent the summer there, and they married, but she wasn't happy with life on the reservation. There weren't many opportunities, and some of Dad's friends were pretty heavy drinkers. Anyway, he didn't want her to be unhappy, so he went back to Oklahoma with her and got a job as a mechanic. He had a gift for working on cars.'' Ty paused to sip his coffee.

"What happened?" Beth pressed, delighted to be hearing about his family.

"Before long my father took over the whole shop," Ty went on. "His boss just turned it over to him, all but the books. Then one day the cops waltzed in and locked up the place. Before we even knew what it was all about, Dad was charged with receiving stolen property. The owner, who had been responsible for the so-called maintenance contracts that kept the business humming all those years, claimed ignorance. In reality, he'd been operating a stolen car ring and moving the vehicles through a wrecking yard where Dad got lots of his parts. Only it was Dad who the cops nailed as the ringleader. Suddenly my father was in prison and my family was living on food stamps.''

"Oh, Ty, that's awful!" Beth said. "But I'd have thought that would burn you on law enforcement for all time.''

He shook his head. "No, the police were just doing their job. One of them, a guy named Fisher, came to believe Dad was innocent, and he spent his free time trying to prove it. Even after my father was killed by another inmate in a fight, Fish didn't give up, and eventually he got the goods on the man who framed my father.''

"The shop owner."

"That's right. My father's employer. By the time he got caught, though, I'd graduated from college and gotten hired as a part-time deputy. I was with Fish when we made the collar. The best part was when the creep broke and admitted everything he'd done to my dad.''

"I imagine you had something to do with that," Beth mused softly.

Ty picked up his cup. "Oh, yeah." She knew that was all he was going to say on that subject.

"So it was this Fish and what happened to your father that inspired you to enter law enforcement?"

He took another drink and set the cup in the saucer. "That's right."

"How did you wind up in Austin?"

"Went to college here."

"UT?"

"Yep."

"Me, too."

He chuckled. "I was long gone by the time you hit campus, I'm sure."

"Oh? How old are you?"

"Thirty."

"I'm—"

"Twenty-five," he finished for her. "I know."

Beth smiled. "Gee, we have lots in common, don't we?"

"Not so much," he said, turning his cup in the hollow of the saucer. "Anyway," he went on, deftly changing the subject, "it didn't take me long to realize that the opportunities for advancement in law enforcement were pretty slim in a small town in Oklahoma. I mean, Fish had been in his job for twenty years, and that was all right for him, but I had a college education, and I got restless pretty quickly. So I figured, why not try my hand in Austin?"

"And here you are," she said, sensing that he'd moved quickly through the ranks.

"And here I am," he agreed, just as Sara placed salads in front of them.

Beth picked up her fork. "I'm glad," she told him impulsively. He slid her an enigmatic look, as if not quite trusting what he'd heard. She smiled and added cheekily,

"I wouldn't want anyone else investigating me for murder."

He chuckled and plunged a fork into his salad. For a time, they ate in companionable silence. Then Beth thought to ask about his family. "I think we have more in common than you believe," she said. "Family, for instance. I already know you have a younger brother and sister whom you obviously love. What you said told me that. Where are they now?"

"My mother lives alone outside of Austin," he said. "She's a country girl at heart and never remarried. My sister elected to attend college on the Crow reservation in Montana where our father was born and met her husband there. They both teach at that college now, and our younger brother is one of their students."

Beth imagined that she heard a certain tension in his voice when he mentioned his brother, but she couldn't be sure. "What are their names? How old are they? What are they like?" she asked.

He answered immediately. "My mother's name is Naomi. She's fifty, small, intuitive, strong. Deirdre is twenty-seven, tall, beautiful, brilliant. Cob's not twenty yet. In lots of ways, he's the one who suffered most after our father went away. I'm not sure he even remembers him. I tried to be a strong male role model for him, but I guess I was too young to do a good job of it."

"Sounds like you're worried about him."

"He's my brother," Ty said simply.

Beth smiled and nodded. "I understand. I feel the same way about my brothers. And sisters. Family's very important."

"Yes, it is."

"You see, we have more in common than you think."

He shook his head ruefully and went back to his meal. By the time she'd finished her grilled cheese sandwich, he'd scarfed down a big bowl of chili laced with fiery hot salsa, and Beth felt that she knew Ty Redstone fairly well. She found much to admire in him besides his good looks. He was a loving, dutiful son and concerned older brother, not to mention a good cop. And he excited her in ways no other man ever had.

Her reasons for wanting in on the investigation were perfectly valid, as far as she was concerned, but had they not been, she knew that she'd have looked for a way to get next to Ty Redstone. He was just too delicious to pass up, and whether he wanted to believe it or not, they had a lot of shared interests. Maybe being accused of murder wasn't the worst thing that had ever happened to her, after all.

TY SHOOK HIS HEAD stubbornly. What the hell was wrong with him, anyway? Why had he told her what was on his agenda? This woman's presence seemed to send his good sense begging. She turned his brain to mush—and the rest of him to steel. He couldn't believe he was this hot for her. She was not the sort of woman he would normally choose. Why hadn't he taken the keys from her again, driven himself to the office and walked away? Instead, he'd docilely gotten into her car on the passenger side—and argued for the last ten minutes about whether or not she was going to accompany him during his interview with Frankie Velasquez, the son of Brandon Dumont's housekeeper.

"I can help," she said for the dozenth time.

"I don't need your help. Your social connections are of no use here."

"Do you speak Spanish?"

"A little."

"Because Frankie speaks minimal English," she said, and he kicked himself for not thinking of that. He could always request a formal interpreter, but that would mean bringing Velasquez into the interrogation unit, and he didn't want to do that yet for several reasons. Maybe Jorge Mendoza would be free to accompany him to the interview. No,

Jorge was working that domestic violence mess that blew up last night.

"My Spanish is fluent," Beth said suggestively, and Ty groaned, sinking down in his seat.

"You're trying to get me fired, aren't you?"

"No! I want to help!"

He bent his head and cupped his hand over his brow. He wasn't really thinking of taking her along, was he? "I lost my mind somewhere," he moaned.

"Frankie knows me," she went on, moving unerringly toward her goal. "He'll talk to me. I know it."

Ty moaned. Why was he even fighting? He knew he was going to take her along. He threw up his hands in surrender. "All right, all right, all right." She clapped her hands, like a little girl getting a new doll. "But I ask the questions," he insisted. "You are translating, nothing more, nothing less. Got that?"

She was already starting the car. "Got it."

He closed his eyes and told himself it would be okay. Everything was going to work out just fine. He'd be in control of the whole situation the entire time. Just like he was in control now.

Yeah, right. And his mother was really the Queen of England. He didn't seem to be in control of anything since he'd met Beth Maitland, not even his thoughts. Worse yet, he liked it. He liked her. He liked being with her, even if it did border on sexual torture. No doubt about it, he needed his head examined—not to mention other less intelligent parts of his anatomy.

FRANKIE VELASQUEZ looked desperately at Beth and exclaimed, *"Yo no comprendo."* Exasperated, Beth repeated the question slowly. Impatiently, Ty broke in.

"Look, either he knows why his mother would lie for Dumont or he doesn't."

Beth ignored him and continued to speak softly and

slowly to the nervous young Mexican. He looked about nineteen, though his papers put his age at twenty-three, papers that Ty was pretty sure were fakes. The kid was shaking in his boots, his hands crushing the handle of the rake he'd been using to gather leaves. They'd tracked him down through his employer, a local gardener who maintained yards all over town, and the moment Ty flashed his badge, the kid got a hunted look that had intensified as the interview progressed. Ty was reasonably sure that if Beth hadn't been with him, the kid would have turned tail and run for the hills. He wasn't even ticked about it anymore. Much. His priority was to get the job done, to get at the truth, and if Beth's presence was going to facilitate that, so be it. He was quickly losing patience, however.

It was darned cold out. The sun had disappeared behind an overcast sky, and the wind had kicked up. The way Beth was huddled inside her waist-length black leather jacket, Ty knew that she was chilled to the bone. Frankie Velasquez wore nothing more with his jeans than a stained sweatshirt over a couple of ragged T-shirts. Ty figured that he was the only one sensibly dressed, and even he was cold. Finally, he had had enough. He seized Beth by the arm to let her know that he meant business.

"Get in the car."

"Wait a minute. He'll talk to me, I know it."

"Maybe so, but you're freezing out here." He pointed a stern finger at Frankie Velasquez. "You. Get in the car." The kid turned pale.

"No, no. Frankie no do wrong."

Ty looked at Beth. "Tell him to get in the car."

"He thinks you're arresting him."

"Well, tell him I'm not!" Ty snapped.

Beth began patiently explaining the situation to Frankie, who was obviously reluctant to believe her. Muttering under his breath, Ty seized them both by the arm and propelled them toward the car. Frankie dropped the rake and dragged his feet, babbling incoherently while Beth tried to calm him and Ty's temper boiled. Reaching the car, Ty yanked the passenger door open and slapped the seat back forward. The cramped back seat looked decidedly uninviting, but he pushed Frankie through the narrow opening anyway, then handed Beth into the front seat and walked around to the driver's side while Beth again began to calm Velasquez.

Ty examined what it was that bothered him about Frankie Velasquez and Beth Maitland. For one thing, he had not been prepared for the familiarity the two shared. The way Frankie's eyes had lit up when he'd spotted Beth had instantly grated on Ty, but he hadn't really gotten irritated until he'd seen the way she so patiently and repeatedly tried to reassure the guy at the risk of her comfort and health. Ty concluded in disgust that he was jealous—of a shaking kid in raggedy clothes. Disgustedly, he dropped into the seat and slammed the door, twisting sideways to face Beth, who was speaking softly and soothingly to the young man in the back seat.

"Will you leave off that?" Ty growled.

Beth looked at him in surprise. "What?"

"You're an interpreter, remember? You tell him exactly what I say, hear me? Exactly."

She folded her arms, clearly miffed. "Fine."

Ty turned his head to glare into the back seat. "Cut the crap," he ordered, ignoring Beth's gasp. "Do it," he told her. "Translate it."

She did so tersely. Frankie began to shake his head, but Ty didn't back off.

"Your mother lied for Brandon Dumont." He paused to let Beth translate. Frankie bowed his head. "I *will* find out why." The kid began to writhe as Beth spoke in Spanish. "You tell me what you know, and I'll try to keep you out of it."

"*Madre de Dios,*" Frankie whispered, crossing himself

and staring out the window. He began to speak in broken spurts, and Beth translated.

"He says, 'It's all my fault. It's all my fault. What can I do? I was stupid. My friend said it was his father's car. The police said we stole it. My papers were gone. They deported me. My mother begged Señor Dumont to help. He got new papers so I could come home. It will kill her if they send me away. What can we do?'"

Ty lifted a hand to stop the flow of words. "Enough," he said roughly. "I can't hear any more of this, not yet. In fact..." He looked at Beth meaningfully. "I don't think we've even had this conversation yet. I don't speak Spanish, so I don't really know what was said. Understand?"

Beth nodded, knowing exactly what he meant. "Officially, you only know what I tell you."

"And you're going to tell me just enough to go to my supervisor and ask for immunity for Frankie and his mother."

"So they can testify without getting into trouble."

"I have to check out his story first. If he's really a car thief, I can't do much."

"He's no thief!" Beth exclaimed. "Look at him. He wouldn't steal air!"

"I said *if.* Work with me on this, will you?"

She subsided quickly, nodding. "Okay. I'm sorry. Can I tell him he has nothing to fear?"

"Don't ask me. I don't know what's going on. I can't understand a word."

Beth smiled and reached for his hand. She held it all the time she was speaking to Frankie Velasquez, and Ty found that he didn't mind the gentle way she handled the young man nearly so much as he had before.

By the time Beth had reassured Frankie and Ty had let him out of the car, the weather was turning ugly. With rain falling and the temperature dropping, the streets were bound to ice over, a deadly situation. As Ty drove the convertible toward headquarters and his own transportation, he worried about Beth driving home in this speed mobile. She talked the whole way about what Velasquez had told them and how Ty had to protect the boy, but Ty was too pre-occupied to pay her much heed. He couldn't figure out why he had such a problem with her. What made her so different from all the other women he knew? He turned into the parking lot where his Jeep awaited him and brought the convertible to a stop behind it.

"So what do you think?" Beth asked, and Ty shrugged, draping his arm over the steering wheel as he turned to face her. "Okay, then," she said brightly, "I'll do it."

Obviously he'd missed something important. "Do what?"

"Run naked through the streets."

"What?"

"Well, do you have a better idea?" she asked reasonably.

He did, as a matter of fact, and it was tying knots in his groin. He screwed up his face and demanded, "What the hell are you talking about?"

Her mouth twitched, his first indication that she was teasing. "Giving the press something else to write about."

Better she should run naked in his bed and the press should go hang themselves, he thought. Barely subduing a chuckle, he said, "That would sure do it."

"So you're in agreement then?"

"Lady, you do something like that, and I personally will lock you up."

"With or without my clothes?" she quipped. He gave her a quelling look, and she stuck out her bottom lip in an exaggerated pout. Ty suddenly felt as if a tight metal band had been wrapped around his ribs. He had to blink to make his brain work and then clear his throat to speak in an embarrassingly hoarse voice.

"Uh, you...you better get home. The streets are icing."

"Ty," she said softly, "don't do that. Don't turn it off like that. Please."

He stared out the windshield, trying to find a way to discuss what shouldn't be discussed. He couldn't do it. Best to ignore it and hope it went away. Like the flu.

"I'll follow you," he said flatly. "Make sure you get there okay."

She sighed and muttered, "You don't have to do that. I'll be fine."

"I said I'll follow you!" It came out more sharply than he'd intended, and he immediately softened his tone. "I want to make sure you're safe."

She lifted blue eyes gone smoky gray to meet his gaze, a gentle smile curving her lovely mouth, and then she leaned slowly forward and pressed that mouth to his. He had time to move away, but somehow time did not translate into action. He didn't even close his eyes. Or breathe. He was too busy trying to keep his hands off her. Finally, she straightened away from him. He was hard as stone and perspiring as if the car were a luxurious sweat lodge with steam rising from fired rocks. She tilted her head, offering him more of the same, and in that moment he experienced something he'd never known before—sheer panic.

He nearly broke his ankle getting out of the car, slipping on the slick pavement. Beth, in contrast, let herself out calmly and walked around to take the driver's seat with nothing more than a censorial glare in his direction. Ty was cocooned inside his four-wheel-drive SUV before he could get a good breath, and he didn't really breathe easily until the convertible turned safely into the drive of the Maitland mansion some twenty agonizing minutes later, and even then he knew that it wasn't going to last. Beth Maitland had set a fire in him that he was very sure he couldn't put out alone.

TY PARKED THE SEDAN and got out, taking measure of the front entrance of the Maitland Maternity Clinic. The little ice storm of two days ago had dissipated by the following morning, leaving broken tree limbs, a few downed power lines and dozens of fender benders in its wake. Apparently it was one of those auto accidents that had necessitated Beth's temporary return to the day-care center at Maitland Maternity. According to the butler at the Maitland mansion, she was covering for one of the day-care providers who was trying to get her car in running order after it was hit during the ice storm.

As he walked across the parking lot to the clinic entrance, he mentally ticked off all the reasons he should not be doing this. She was officially a suspect in a murder case. She was a rich society flake who'd likely forget his name once the case was closed. She was headstrong, stubborn, unreasonable, impulsive and too sexy by half. She had kissed him, turned his life upside down, invaded his dreams, made him want things he couldn't—shouldn't—have. Just spending time with her was dangerous to his peace of mind, his heart and, yes, his career. But here he was anyway.

The instant he stepped into the lobby, he knew something was wrong. He shrugged beneath his shoulder harness, assuring himself that his weapon was within easy reach, not that he was likely to draw his gun. The lobby was full of people. He hadn't seen Beth, but he was sure she was there, along with Megan Maitland, Michael Lord, who was the head of Maitland security, and a few others Ty couldn't identify, including a uniformed guard standing face to face with a big man in jeans, flannel shirt and a dark blue down-filled vest. It was this man upon whom Ty's attention was focused.

"By God," the man was shouting. "I want my wife and I want her now! You sons of bitches got no right to keep her away from me!"

Ty evaluated the situation. He'd heard that some men

went wild with worry when their wives were in labor and delivery, but this seemed like more than fear to him. If not, he'd have to take his hat off to Michael Lord for dealing with such incidents on a daily basis, while Ty hadn't calmed a crazy since his days on patrol. Not that he'd forgotten how. The man was burly, but with enough gut to mark him as a heavy drinker. His hair had been shaved and was growing back as blond stubble. A prison cut? Skinhead? Militia? Or just bad taste? One thing was certain, the fellow had poor manners, using that language in front of ladies. Quickly, Ty palmed his badge in his left hand and took up the appropriate stance a couple yards behind the man, feet planted wide apart, arms loose.

"Anything I can do?" he said loudly, letting it be known by the tone of his voice that he was taking control of the situation without being belligerent about it. The crazy was beyond such subtleties. He spun on his heel and strode stiffly to Ty, shoving his face up close, hands balled into hard fists. His round chin and flat cheeks wore the same stubble that bristled atop his head. Black eyes drilled Ty.

"Who the hell do you think you are? Better keep your nose out of my business if you know what's good for you." The man curled his lip in a sneer, looking Ty up and down. "Damn tom-tom thumper. Almost took you for a wetback, but you dress too good. White-man wanna-be...well, you just back off or I'll have to damage that pretty face."

Ty moved quickly, grabbing one thick wrist and wrenching it up and around, spinning the man where he stood and taking him up on tiptoe. With the other hand, he shoved his badge in the man's sputtering face. "Not white man, just *the* man," he said, ignoring the crazy's ineffectual struggles.

"Let me go! They've got my wife. Ask 'em! They're hiding her. Ask Jake Maitland where he's got her."

Ty wrenched the arm a little higher, saying calmly, "Can't hear you, tough guy." He looked at the uniformed guard. "Call for a patrol car, why don't you? Tell them I asked for it."

The guard nodded and reached for the telephone on his desk, but Megan Maitland rushed forward. "No. Wait." Ty cocked his head at Michael Lord, trusting him to see the necessity of locking this one up, but Lord lifted a quelling hand and bent his ear to Megan Maitland.

The troublemaker in Ty's grasp slumped forward to lessen the pressure on his arm, gasping, "I got a right to see my own wife no matter what she says."

"Not if she says no," Ty told him smartly, "and no doubt that's the case."

The man gnashed his teeth and trembled with rage. Michael Lord nodded resignedly and moved toward Ty. "Toss him out and let him go."

"Aw, come on, let me haul him in," Ty argued with feigned disappointment.

"Mrs. Maitland says to let him go."

"You sure?"

Michael glared at the troublemaker. "This time," he said significantly. "You come around here again, and I'll bust your head."

"And I'll help him," Ty said, turning the man toward the entrance. "Be a nice change from beating that tom-tom." Ty marched him through the doors and onto the walkway, then shoved him away.

The man stumbled, righted himself and turned, bawling, "Jake Maitland's got my wife, and no man keeps me from what's mine!"

"Sure, sure, beat it, you loon, before I call the white coat brigade."

The man shook his fist at the clinic door. "You ain't heard the last of me, you damned Maitlands!"

Ty reached into his coat for no more reason than to slide his shield into the inside pocket, but the guy seemed to think he was pulling a gun, judging by the way he took to his heels. Chuckling, Ty watched the tough guy run until he disappeared around a corner. Then he turned and walked inside the clinic.

The next thing he knew, Beth had wrapped herself around him like a good down comforter. Ty rocked on his heels, stunned—and pleased—by the energy and warmth of her greeting, a very public greeting. "Oh, Ty!" She tilted her head and whispered huskily, "Thank goodness you came when you did!"

He meant to give her some pithy, smart retort, but it wouldn't have meant much since he couldn't seem to stop himself from lifting his arms and folding them around her, despite the obviously rapt audience. *Damn,* he thought, standing there with Beth's supple body pressed to his, their arms locked around each other in an embrace that felt too right to be real, *who's the actual loony?* He knew better than to let himself care about this woman. He knew the dangers in such easy displays of affection. And he knew that he'd played the hero just for this, for her. He didn't even have sense enough to run from the trouble. Instead he stood here holding it against him. And was happy to do it.

Who was he kidding? He wanted her, had never been this eager for a woman before, and he meant to have her, at least once. Why else had he tucked that condom into his pocket a couple days ago, and why was he standing here grinning like a cat with a feather in his mouth? Another thought occurred, and it rocked him right down to the soles of his feet. What if once wasn't enough?

Heaven and all the ancestors help him.

CHAPTER SIX

"ARE YOU ALL RIGHT?" Beth asked anxiously. It was a stupid question. She'd seen everything that had happened. Ty had tossed Eckart out on his ear, figuratively speaking, and had hardly rumpled his coat doing so. But she couldn't help feeling anxious on his behalf.

"Of course, I'm all right," Ty answered smoothly. An instant later, he dropped his arms and stepped back. Flicking a gaze at their onlookers, he cleared his throat and adjusted the already perfect knot of his busily patterned bronze, brown and silver tie. He tucked a strand of black hair behind one ear and glanced at Michael. "So who was that guy?"

"His name is Vincent Eckart," Michael said, and Ty wrote it on the small pad he carried in his breast pocket.

"What's the deal with his wife? He seems to think you're hiding her."

Jake Maitland stepped from behind a wall at the end of a hallway near the elevator bank and sauntered closer. "It so happens that I am," he admitted evenly.

Beth watched Ty take Jake's measure before closing his notebook and sliding it, along with his pen, into his shirt pocket. "Can't imagine why," he said in a sarcastic tone.

"Oh, he's a real pleasant fellow, all right," Jake quipped.

"I hope you have her someplace safe," Ty said, "because I don't think you've seen the last of that real pleasant fellow."

"I'm sure you're right," Jake agreed. He looked at Michael and said, "She's at Garrett's ranch."

Michael lifted both eyebrows, and Beth explained to Ty, "Garrett is Michael's brother."

"I know who Garrett Lord is," Ty said, looking at Michael and Jake. But of course he did, she told herself ruefully. He had been investigating her, after all. "I suggest you get some extra security in on this," he told Michael. "You really should've let me arrest the guy."

"That was my doing, Detective Redstone," Megan said, stepping forward. "Perhaps it was foolish of me, but we've had more than our fair share of negative publicity lately, and Chelsea Markum is already trying to get the scoop on Jake's friend."

Beth cringed inwardly, knowing that she was responsible for a lot of what had been printed and reported recently.

"But you're right about the extra security," Michael said.

"Maybe you have someone in mind, Michael?" Jake asked.

Michael replied immediately, "Max Jamison."

"I know Max," Ty said. "The two of you went through the academy together, didn't you?"

Michael nodded. "I wondered if you remembered me."

"Austin lost two good officers when you and Jamison moved on," Ty said matter-of-factly.

"Thanks," Michael replied.

"And thanks for tossing out Eckart," Jake added.

"I was just about to do it myself," Michael said, "but you saved me the trouble."

"My pleasure." Ty split a glance between Michael and Jake. "I imagine you'd have managed without me, though."

Beth noticed that Jake was staring pointedly at her when he said to Ty, "Lucky thing you came along when you did."

So even her family sensed what was happening between her and Ty, Beth realized, or rather what both of them wanted to happen, even if Ty was too stubborn to admit it.

A sheepish look came over him at Jake's subtle insinuation and he muttered, "Uh, yeah, I, uh, was in the neighborhood...so anyway, it's a good thing I stopped in." He narrowed his eyes at Beth, adding in an undertone, "Can we talk?"

"Is this about Beth's case?" Megan demanded, and Ty telegraphed a message to Beth with his eyes. He didn't want anyone else in on this.

Beth quickly took care of it. "This is personal, Mother. I'm sure you understand."

Ty lifted a hand to the back of his neck, and Michael and Jake pretended not to notice as Megan did what shrewd mothers everywhere do so well—sized up the situation and made a decision about the welfare and safety of her child in the hands of a near stranger. Apparently satisfied, she nodded briskly and visibly thawed, extending one slender hand in a jangle of bracelets. "In that case, I have work to do. Thank you again, Detective Redstone."

"No problem," Ty mumbled. Jake clapped him on the shoulder, grinning, and walked away.

"Thanks, man," Michael said, already on the move.

Ty seemed increasingly uncomfortable. He dropped a wary look on Beth as she took his arm and led him toward the back hallway. Once out of sight and sound of the lobby, she stopped and asked, "Why are you here?"

Thoughtfully, Ty rubbed at the corner of his right eye. "Dumont's come up with an alibi for the time of his wife's murder."

Beth caught her breath and leaned against the wall. "Blast him."

"Now don't get shaken over this," Ty said comfortingly. "I didn't say it was an airtight alibi. I know the guy he's claiming can place him at the time, a bartender with a sheet spanning decades. I'm on my way over there now to give him a rattle."

"I'm coming with you," Beth said firmly, and to her surprise, Ty didn't argue.

He looked away for a moment, seemed to puzzle over something, and finally said, "Can you get away now?"

"Just give me a minute," she said, and he nodded.

"Okay. Listen, there's something else you ought to know."

"What?"

"This bartender, Gustopherson, he's been up twice for forgery, specializing in fake documents for illegal aliens."

Beth caught her breath. "Frankie Velasquez."

Ty shrugged. "It would seem so. Jester's checking out that end of it. Off the record for now."

Beth took a deep breath. Was this case coming together for her, or apart? "Want to take my car?" she asked.

"Not to the part of town we're heading into," Ty said dourly. "I've got a department-issue sedan out front. I'll drive around to the back door and pick you up there in a minute or two."

She nodded. "I'll be quick." He walked to the lobby, shaking his head and muttering about having lost his everlasting mind. Beth smiled and hurried toward the daycare center and her office. She really needn't have come in, but it was hard to stay away when she had nothing else to keep her occupied. She was surprised to find her mother waiting for her in the sparsely furnished room. After the discovery of Brianne's body, Beth had decided to have the place redecorated to dispel the memory of the murder, and it was down to the bare bones of desk, two chairs and built-in bookshelf and coat closet while she decided what to do with it.

"He's quite a man, Detective Redstone," Megan said the moment Beth walked through the door. Beth couldn't help grinning as she hurried behind her desk and pulled her handbag out of a bottom drawer. "But this is about the case, isn't it?"

Beth bit her lip, deciding how much to tell her mother. She knew how Megan was likely to take it, the wild child as sleuth. On the other hand, her mother deserved the truth. Finally, she admitted, "He knows I'm innocent, and I'm helping him prove it."

"Do you think that's wise, dear?" Megan worried aloud.

"I've been of help, Mother. Really, I have. Even Ty says so."

"But is it safe, Beth?"

"Ty won't let anything happen to me."

"Seems to me that Ty Redstone is turning into something of a champion for your cause," Megan mused. "It also seems to me that he's taking a chance by doing so."

Beth paused in the act of extracting her keys from her purse. "How so?"

"You may be blind to your own safety, darling, but what about Ty? He's undoubtedly breaking rules by including you in this investigation. What if his superiors find out what he's doing? It could be trouble for him. Why don't you let him handle it alone?"

For a long moment, Beth considered her mother's words and finally shook her head. "Ty knows what he's doing. If he didn't think this was the best course, he wouldn't take it."

"But think of the danger," Megan urged. "Beth, we're talking murder here."

"We're also talking about clearing my name," Beth replied, "*my* name, and as far as my personal safety goes, you saw how he handled that situation just now. I'm safe with him, I know it."

Megan sighed. "All the same, I wish you'd stay out of it."

"I can't do that," Beth said firmly. "I'll go insane if I have to wander around the house doing nothing while Ty's out there investigating on his own. I'll just have to be very careful that I don't do anything that could reflect badly on him.''

Her mother leaned forward. ''Are you sure that's all there is to it?'' she asked gently. ''There are better ways to get to know a man, Beth.''

''Not this one,'' Beth said flatly, knowing it was true.

With a sigh, Megan shook her head. ''Obviously, I'm not going to change your mind.''

''No, you aren't.''

''Is there anything I can do to help, then?''

Beth dangled her car keys. ''Drive yourself home in my car this evening if I'm not back by the time you're ready to leave.''

''I was thinking more along the lines of hiring a private investigator.''

Knowing instinctively that Ty would pull back if challenged in such a way, Beth shook her head adamantly. ''No, Mom. Promise me. Promise me!''

Megan sighed and took the keys. ''Fine. You'll call if you're going to be late?''

''Of course.'' Beth moved around the desk and kissed her mother's smooth cheek. ''Thanks, Mom.''

''I hope you know what you're doing,'' Megan whispered urgently, and Beth smiled.

''That'd be a first, don't you think?'' When Megan blanched, Beth added solemnly, ''Trust me on this, Mother. Please.''

Megan nodded, but her smile remained wistful as Beth hurried from the room.

TY LOOKED at the dive he was about to enter and then at the woman beside him. The two did not fit. A converted storefront, the bar boasted windows painted black and, in one instance, covered. The street address had been drawn in big, wobbly letters on the raw wood of the boarded-over window, and a small, broken plastic sign hanging over the door proclaimed Bar. It was the lowest of the low, and he had brought Beth Maitland here.

"Maybe this isn't such a good idea, after all," he muttered, having not just second thoughts but third and fourth.

"Nonsense. It'll be all right," she said confidently, a certain eagerness lighting her lovely smile.

"Maybe you'd better wait in the car," he suggested.

She peered down the vacant sidewalk. A row of trash cans in the alley behind them rattled as two vagrants dug through them. "You really think so?"

Ty glanced around worriedly and admitted to himself that she would likely be safer with him than alone in a car. "Probably not," he admitted. "The whole area's pretty seedy."

"Doesn't look like the sort of place Brandon would hang out in," she observed, "not the Brandon I knew. But then, I didn't really know him at all, did I?"

"I don't think anyone really knows that guy," Ty replied. "What made you hook up with him in the first place?"

She scrunched up her face in an exaggerated wince. "I don't know. We met at a party. He was good-looking, intelligent. He tried so hard to charm me, and he made it plain right away that he was interested in more than just a good time."

"You know that's what most people say about you, don't you? That you're always after the good time?"

Beth sighed. She had known, of course, that her reputation would precede her, but those who knew her best understood that beneath the easygoing, fun-loving exterior was a woman capable of a serious relationship. She'd hoped that Ty Redstone would see that for himself. "A girl can have just so much fun," she said. "I'm real good at that, frankly, but everyone wants something more eventually. I mean, I always wanted a real relationship, but it wasn't an immediate concern, you know. Then somehow it just started to seem like it was never going to happen. Maybe it was all these marriages taking place in my family lately...R.J., Ellie, Abby... And there was Brandon. I thought, 'Why not?' Didn't take me long to figure *that* out. Too bad I didn't just dump him before I found out about Brianne.''

"Ain't that the truth," Ty agreed.

"I felt responsible," she explained. "I thought I was going to break his heart. That was when I still thought he had one." She looked at him with those big baby blues and asked softly, "Do you understand?"

He nodded, but in truth he was more concerned with understanding his own lack of sense. It was all right there in that stunning face. He saw that face everywhere, chin tilted stubbornly, nose in the air, mouth smiling, eyes sparkling, smoldering. He had watched emotion dance across it, shock, a hint of fear, resignation, anger, compassion, concern, mischief, interest, flirtation, desire, trust, all of it supported by that quick, witty intelligence. And he'd brought that face here. What had he been thinking?

But that was precisely the point—he hadn't been thinking. If he really thought about what he was doing, he'd have to examine the fact that he wanted this woman so badly he couldn't sleep nights or walk straight, and where that would lead him, he was afraid to go. Besides, right now was not the time for self-analysis. He had a job to do, and he was still strong enough to put that first.

"Okay," he said, squaring his shoulders, "you stick close and let me do the talking for once. Will you do that?"

Beth nodded.

Ty looked her over, took in the long, loose skirt, Western boots, belted-over blouse and accessories with a critical eye. "Take off the jewelry," he ordered. Quickly, she stripped off the turquoise and silver necklace and bracelets. "Better hide the combs, too," he decided, and she plucked free the matching combs, shoving them in the pocket of her skirt as her hair tumbled about her shoulders. She shook her head and thrust her fingers through the thick, wavy mane. Ty watched, fascinated, as tendrils began curling about her face in the damp, cool air.

"Anything else?" she asked.

He couldn't help himself. "Yeah, get ugly, will you? You're too beautiful by half to take into a gutter joint like this."

The smile that curved her luscious mouth and smoldered in her blue eyes punched him straight in the groin. "Only half?" she teased, taking his hand in both of hers and leaning into his arm.

"You don't need me to tell you how beautiful you are," he said softly, doing just that.

"I think maybe I do," she replied in a husky voice.

Her hands felt cool around his. "Why do I get the feeling I'm playing with fire?" he murmured, staring at her.

"Because you are."

He wondered where he could find an asbestos overcoat, because he was definitely going to need it. He swallowed and said, "Let's get it done." She nodded, and he turned toward the black-painted glass door. Thinking? Hell, he wasn't thinking at all anymore. He'd thought all he was going to and was operating on pure instinct with this woman now. The warrior way, his mother would say, but he wasn't sure it was anything other than pure self-indulgence.

"We're going in here like we own the place, understand?" he coached under his breath. "Anybody eyes you, you tell him to go to hell, but do it standing next to me."

"No problem," she assured him as the door swung open beneath his hand and they stepped into a dark netherworld of smoke, liquor and the cracking of pool balls.

Ty took measure of the room as he strode to the bar. A pair of bikers hovered over the single pool table. An overweight businessman dressed unseasonably in a short-sleeved shirt and a cheap, clip-on tie fed quarters into a video game machine. A thin, elderly woman with dirty gray hair straggling about her face slumped over one end of the bar, an empty shot glass close at hand, while a middle-aged man with a huge belly, scraggly ponytail and suspenders scooped crushed ice over the long necks stacked in a rectangular cooler behind the bar. He glanced in their direction with obvious interest, wrote them off as lost or slumming and went back to packing ice around the bottles of beer.

Ty shoved aside a metal stool with a cracked vinyl seat and stood at the bar, careful not to touch anything, Beth at his side and slightly behind him. The bartender leered at her, and she sent him straight to hell without saying a word, her glare spiked with disdain. Ty almost laughed. The bartender frowned and finally deigned to speak to them.

"What'll you have?"

"Information," Ty answered succinctly.

The big belly turned away, revealing a thin, mousy ponytail clubbed at the nape of a thick neck. "Fresh out."

"You haven't heard the questions yet."

"Don't matter."

"Are you Gustopherson?"

"Who wants to know?"

Calmly, Ty reached into his pocket and extracted his badge, which he plunked down on the bar. "Detective Ty Redstone. I'll ask again. Are you Gustopherson?"

The bartender glanced down, grimaced and snarled, "I don't have to talk to you."

Ty looked at Beth, trusting her to play along. "Is that what I asked him? I don't think that's what I asked him."

"Nope. You were just asking if he's Gustopherson," she said gamely, and turned her head to watch the players at the pool table.

"That's what I thought." He smiled at the man in the

fly-specked mirror behind the bar. "You want to talk to me now, or you need persuading?"

The man's reply, in front of a lady, made Ty's blood boil.

"Persuading it is," Ty replied through his teeth. Hopping onto the bar rail, he reached across the sticky counter, grabbed the ponytail and yanked. The smart-aleck stumbled, toppling backward far enough for Ty to hook an arm around his neck. The other hand he crammed into the back pocket of a pair of very grimy jeans. Extracting the wallet he found there, he flipped it open on the bar, asking Beth, "What does it say?"

She leaned down to read the print on the driver's license through the murky plastic while the bartender gurgled beneath Ty's tightening arm. Ty glared a daggered warning via the mirror at the bikers looking up from the pool table. "Anthony Gustopherson," she announced, as the bikers glanced at the badge on the bar and decided they need not get involved in whatever was going on. The old woman at the end of the bar snorted and turned her head away, while the businessman never took his eyes from his game.

Ty shoved the bartender away, then scooped up the wallet and tossed it at him before hopping off the bar rail and straightening the hang of his coat and tie. "Now let's start over," he ordered evenly. "Forged any documents for illegal aliens lately, Gus?"

Angry but cowed, Gustopherson growled a reply. "I don't know what you're talking about."

"Sure you do," Ty said cheerfully, abruptly tossing out the name. "Frankie Velasquez."

The big-bellied bartender suddenly looked hunted but stubbornly insisted, "Never heard of him."

"Sure you have. You made him a set of docs a few years ago, and a man named Brandon Dumont paid you for them."

Gustopherson relaxed and went into his bluff. "Dumont.

Dumont. That sounds familiar, but I never did no documents for him. I gave that up long ago. I served my time and learned my lesson, got me a good job here.''

"Oh, yeah, this is top rung," Ty said sarcastically, "serving booze to bums. Now suppose you tell me how you know Brandon Dumont."

The bartender snapped his fingers. "He's that guy what managed my mother's investments," he said without the least credibility. "Yeah, I know him. Good man."

"You never had a mother, Gus," Ty told him, letting him know that he wasn't buying the act. "You were hatched under a rock."

Gustopherson bristled but doggedly stuck to his script. "I saw Dumont not too long ago, in fact."

"I bet you did," Ty interjected.

"He dropped by one evening. We had some loose ends to tie up. My mom died last year, see."

Ty chuckled. "You're in the wrong business, Gus. You ought to be writing fairy tales. Or did Dumont write this one? Yeah, I bet he did. How long did it take you to memorize your part?"

"Think what you like, pig," Gustopherson shot back, growing more agitated. "It's my story, and you can't prove otherwise."

"Let me guess what night Dumont happened to drop by," Ty said, needling, and named the date of the murder.

Gustopherson smirked. "See. You didn't have to go hassling me, after all."

"You know," Ty said, picking up his badge and pocketing it, "if you were Crow, your name would be Too Dumb to Blink Without Instruction."

"Hey, you got no call to insult me, red man!"

"It's Redstone, Detective Redstone, and I'm not insulting you, Gus. I'm just stating facts. While I'm at it, let me tell you something else. Brandon Dumont isn't as smart as he thinks he is, either, and right now I've got a man digging through every financial record Dumont's had his sticky fingers on since he hit Austin. You better pray we find something with your mother's name on it, and while you're at it, go for a real miracle and pray that we can't connect you to Frank Velasquez—unless you're looking forward to spending the rest of your life in prison."

Gustopherson had paled visibly. "Y-you can't prove anything."

"You better hope," Ty interrupted. "Ever heard of three times and you're out? It's a little felony policy we have here in Texas. I checked your sheet. You go down this time, you go down for good."

"Now wait a minute!" Gustopherson blustered. "I—I could be wrong about my mother. It might have been another relative!"

"You'll have to do better than that, Gus, if you're going to cut a deal with the D.A. Now you think about it and get back to me."

With that, Ty snagged Beth's hand and pulled her tight against his side as he strode for the door. Behind him, the agitated bartender beat the bar with a dirty towel before grabbing the phone. Satisfied, Ty shoved open the door and handed Beth through it, then stepped out of the cesspit. The sun had come out to bathe the dirty sidewalk in the clear, soft light of late afternoon. Ty turned his face up, feeling clean and hopeful.

"He'll break," Ty announced definitely. "We won't find any records to support his story. He'll contact Dumont and try to regroup, but the lie's already out there, and he knows we know it. He's got too much at stake to hold the line. He'll break, and then Dumont's alibi evaporates."

They weren't home yet, but they were definitely on the right track. Dumont had made a bad mistake trying to alibi himself. Too much cover, too much coincidence, too much explanation—all the bad guys eventually made the same mistakes. Gustopherson was the weak link in the chain of

Dumont's story, and soon he would snap. Ty felt the same surge of satisfaction he always did when his gut instincts were proven true and a case started to make the way he thought it would. Only this time it went deeper, was stronger, and suddenly he knew why he'd brought Beth along.

He'd wanted her here for this moment, this instant when the momentum started to shift and good gained strength over evil. He'd wanted her to see him make it happen, to understand what drove him to places like this, why he did what he did. He needed her to know him, to understand his job at its best and its worst.

It scared the daylights out of him, that need. It meant that he was getting in way over his head. They'd gone beyond simple seduction. He'd been telling himself that it was just sex. If he were honest with himself, he would have to say that he'd made up his mind about that part of it days ago. This was something else, something he couldn't, didn't want to name. At the same time, elation filled him, the kind of thing that happens when you ignore your fear and leap out of an airplane with nothing more than a folded piece of silk between the freedom of heaven and pounding yourself a foot deep into the hard, cold earth. The kind of thing that happens when you meet your fate. It was exactly then that he faced what he was about to do, and it wasn't the smart thing, not this time. But he was going to do it, anyway. He couldn't make himself do anything else. Just this once, he was going to go with the flow and see where it took him. Afterward, he'd worry about where he'd gotten himself and try to find his way back.

BETH WAS FLYING. Going in at Ty's back, watching him work, feeling the adrenaline rush that fueled his love of the job all added up to an exhilarating experience. She was flying. She was also confused. She hadn't served the slightest purpose in being here with him. In fact, she could have been much more hindrance than help. So why had he brought her along? Even if the case was finally beginning to move her way, he was under no obligation to tell her, let alone include her in the action. Why let her in now when he'd fought to keep her out before, giving in only grudgingly when she'd proved that she could be of assistance? She could think of only one reason, and it bubbled in her blood like champagne.

She had to stop and think how she really felt about it. This had nothing to do with being accused of murder and everything to do with what danced in the air between them whenever they were together. She'd been aware for a while now that he and his partner were turning over every leaf in every corner of her already rather public life. That was to be expected, and he had demonstrated his knowledge of her personal affairs. What she wondered now was if he thought her promiscuous.

She was perfectly aware that she sometimes got up to some risqué hijinks. Her siblings were fond of calling her the wild child. Nevertheless, she was careful about intimacy. She'd made a couple mistakes in college, read a guy wrong, believed him more serious than he was, but she'd been very careful since then. She'd learned to play the game; she'd even learned to *like* the game, but she was careful to keep it light, not to go too far. She would flirt, and she would tease, but she was smart enough not to go beyond that. Until Brandon, she hadn't ever had a truly serious relationship because she hadn't found anyone with whom she wanted to have one.

And now, all at once, here was Ty, compelling her to do more than flirt, to take risks she'd never before taken, to hope that what lay behind the flirtation was solid and strong. But what did *he* hope? Where did he want to go besides the obvious? Did he think that she jumped into bed with everyone at whom she batted her eyes? She wasn't sure she could bear it if he did. She wasn't sure she could walk away without finding out, either. So what next?

They stood on the sidewalk, each seeming uncertain. Beth bit her lip, wondering what to say. Ty cleared his throat.

"I, um, I should take you home."

"I know."

"I don't want to, though."

"I don't want you to."

He nodded, and they began to walk side by side down the street. She was shaking inside, and at the same time, her skin felt too tight. Suddenly she couldn't stand it anymore, couldn't go any farther.

"Ty, you should know something. I—I mean, I want you to know something."

He stopped and turned to face her. "Yes?"

"I...I never slept with Brandon."

He tilted his head. "No?"

"No."

"Why not?"

She thought that over. There was just one reason. "I didn't want to."

He didn't seem surprised. "That's what he meant about you not meeting his needs, how he justified going to Brianne."

"That's right." Embarrassed, she turned away and moved at a clip down the sidewalk. She hadn't gone five feet when his hand clamped on her shoulder and spun her around.

"Wait a minute."

She ducked her head, blinking sudden tears. "I'm sorry. I don't know what's wrong with me. I've been under a lot of stress."

"No kidding," he said dryly.

"I—I guess I'm just relieved that you believe me and that Brandon's alibi didn't change that."

He pulled in a deep breath. "Maybe I should take you home, after all."

She looked up suddenly. "No! No, I...need to be with you right now. Just you."

He closed his eyes, then he made a sympathetic sound and wrapped his arms around her, whispering something she didn't understand.

"What?"

"Uh, Isakawuate, Old Man Coyote, the Trickster."

She smiled through her tears. "You think a Crow deity is playing tricks with my mind?"

"Isakawuate is just his Crow name," he explained gently, brushing at her tears with his fingertips. "All the Plains tribes and most of the others believe in the Trickster, as well, and give him their own names. But you're not the one I think he's fooling with."

"No?"

He shook his head solemnly. "The old boy's been after me for a while now. We're practically on speaking terms."

"Suppose you could sic him on Brandon?" she asked teasingly.

Nodding, he curled a finger beneath her chin. "It's going to be okay. We're going to take this case one step at a time. Just be patient and trust me."

"Oh, I do," she said, gripping the sides of his overcoat. "You have to know I do."

With one hand he smoothed the hair from her face. "I'm not sure you should."

"I am." And she was, oddly enough.

At her words, he pulled her close, tucked her head beneath his chin. After a time he said, "I want to show you something."

"All right," she whispered.

He held her a moment longer, massaging the back of her neck with his warm, nimble hand. "You should understand

that it's private, something I don't show everyone, someplace I don't take everyone.''

Knowing intuitively what would happen if she agreed to
go with him, she whispered against his throat, "Thank
you.''

He squeezed her tightly, then turned her gently toward
the car. Arm in arm, her head on his shoulder, they walked
down the sidewalk.

CHAPTER SEVEN

NEITHER SAID A WORD on the drive across town. He kept shifting in his seat, but she didn't think it was doubt making him so antsy. Her heart was pounding twice as hard as usual, as if her blood had thickened and had to be pushed with great force through her veins. She felt hot, sluggish in a way she couldn't explain. When they pulled into the parking lot of an apartment complex beside the river, she was interested but not surprised.

As he got out and walked around to open her car door, she sat very still, examining her doubts and fears. She didn't find any that could overcome the compulsion she felt to follow this path to its end. On the contrary, despite the risks, she very much wanted what was going to happen. How ironic. She'd wanted to take these risks with Brandon and hadn't been able to make herself do it. With Ty, she couldn't seem to help herself, even though he'd made her no promises and probably wouldn't. She hoped he realized that none had been asked for. She stepped out of the car.

He closed the door and took her hand, and they walked past the modest two-story building, across the brown, dormant grass toward the river. On the gentle slope of the broad bank, just above the sandy beach, stood a tall hickory tree. It was there, beneath those sheltering branches, bare of their leaves, Ty stopped and filled his lungs with the crisp air. He blew it out again. "Too cold?"

She shook her head and sat on a little shelf formed by a curving root, legs folded to one side beneath her skirt. Ty hitched up his pant legs and sat next to her, knees drawn up, arms balanced atop them. After a moment, he lifted his arm and looped it around her. She scooted close and laid her head on his shoulder. He rested his cheek against the top of her head and tightened his arm.

"I spend a lot of time out here," he said.

Beth looked at the blue, blue water in the waning sunlight. "I can see why," she replied, watching the sparkle of the light on the water.

They sat in silence after that, feeling the pull between them grow stronger until the sky turned rosy and the sphere of the sun sank in the west, lining the buildings in painfully bright red-gold. It was breathtaking, that sunset, but it was Ty who made her body tighten in a dozen places, Ty for whom her heart beat like a slow, steady drum. She knew that he was giving them time to change their minds and she knew, too, that she wouldn't.

Shadows crept along the bank, elongating the skeletons of the trees. Conversely, the surface of the water shimmered with white light. She watched and wondered if his pragmatic self would win, if she would have to console herself with the cold comfort of the strength of the temptation she posed and the length of the war he waged against it. Finally, Ty lifted his head, snatched a twig from the ground, tossed it away. He took a long, last look at the river and got up, pulling her with him.

"Let's go in," he said softly, and suddenly every nerve ending in her body was clamoring. She looked at him, seeing her desire reflected in his dark eyes, and found that her throat had closed. She nodded, letting him know that she hadn't, wouldn't, change her mind.

His hand fell away from hers as they turned and moved up the slope, and she sensed that he didn't touch her because he couldn't trust himself, because he was as eager as she, and privacy still lay some distance away. She wanted to run in that direction, if only she knew which way. Fortunately, the apartment was on the near end of the ground floor. She looked over her shoulder at the river as he unlocked the door. A smattering of city lights had replaced the dazzling display of the sun on the water's surface. Beth smiled and stepped through the open door, her heart singing, pulse racing. No turning back now for either of them. No turning back whatever happened.

TRY AS HE MIGHT, Ty couldn't talk himself out of this, and yet he was surprisingly uncomfortable, aware that his little apartment was not what she was used to. She looked around with obvious interest as he slid her sweater down her arms and hung it in the tiny coat closet with his overcoat and a collection of other garments he was always meaning to go through. That done, he tamped his impatience and stood with her on the slightly elevated landing that served as entry, corridor and dining area where it widened next to his minuscule kitchen. He tried to see the place with her eyes, the sand-colored tile of the landing and the knobby carpet of the same color in the sunken living area. He'd thought it a joke, the sunken part being about four inches down from the landing. Still, it helped to differentiate between the two and provided a good display area for his things.

Plain white walls, pale woodwork, a small, prefab fireplace fronted with sand-colored stone at the far end of the living area in no way detracted from the objects in the room. Ty looked critically at the hide shields, quivers, parfleches, paintings and beaded breastplates grouped along his walls. A small replica of a war bonnet in a glass case stood in a place of honor in one corner, along with a flute and drum and pipe. Quilled ceremonial moccasins sat beside the door, with an unstrung bow and a pair of tied arrows. Painted baskets, larger drums and hide rugs and robes, along with an assortment of cooking pots and other everyday items, were scattered around the laced hide sofa and chair for which he'd spent two full months' pay.

"Uh, most of these things are copies," he said quickly, not wanting her to get the wrong impression. "The originals, those things given to me by my grandmother, Lucinda Redstone, or Warrior's Wife, belong to the People and are in the Absaroke Museum in Montana."

"Absaroke?" she repeated.

"It means the Sparrowhawk People, the true name from before time, before we made the name of our enemies' disdain feared and honored."

"The name Crow," she said carefully, "for Absaroke."

"Yes."

She nodded and moved into the apartment, stepping down into the living area, looking around her again. "This is amazing," she said. "Do you have a decorator?"

He barked laughter at the mere notion. "No! Does it look like I have a decorator?"

"Yes. It's all very…" She spied the painting on the easel behind the couch, and he lifted a self-conscious hand to the back of his neck. "Artistic," she added, the narrowing of her eyes indicating sudden insight.

Holding his breath, he stepped down as she moved to the easel and studied the painting in progress. He glanced at the small figures clustered about the symbols on the canvas. They were strictly representational, a personal blend of old and new, the abstract and the primitive. Would she see that, read the meaning in the picture, sense the spirit in the brush strokes and technique? He held his breath, knowing that this was what he'd brought her to see, that he somehow needed her to understand all that she could of their differences, what truly stood between them. She stared a long time, her eyes doing all the work, head and body perfectly still. Finally she blinked and drew in a deep breath.

"Unbelievable," she murmured softly. Spearing him with a daring gaze, she asked bluntly, "How long have you been working on this?"

A smile lifted the corners of his mouth. "I'm slow," he answered frankly. "A year, maybe longer. I keep making mistakes."

"This is a hide canvas," she observed, walking behind the easel.

"Just cowhide," he clarified, strolling closer.

"How did you prepare it?"

He chuckled. She was avid to know and understand everything, and that pleased him almost as much as the fact that she didn't seem out of place here. "It's a variation on an old technique," he said.

"Your paint?" she asked, eyes bright. "It almost looks like ink."

"Dyes mostly."

"You use an overlay technique?"

"That's right. Layers and layers of thin color until I get it right."

She faced him squarely. "You are the most fascinating man. You're like your painting, layers upon layers, complex, rich."

He lifted both brows doubtfully, a little embarrassed. "I don't know about that."

"I do. At first glance it's obvious that you're a citizen of two worlds, white and Native American, the best of both, I think."

He shook his head, smiling and walking closer. "I'm not sure that's possible. My brother, Cob, certainly doesn't think so. He thinks the white world and the native one are eternally at war, that one steals from the other and that trying to combine them effectively destroys both."

She tilted her head slightly, considering. "What do you think?"

"That it isn't so simple."

Turning a slow circle, she looked around her once more, drinking in every detail. Suddenly but subtly, everything shifted, as if a threshold had been crossed, a door closed.

Ty's pulse leaped, his heart sped. His entire being seemed to open and reach out for her, seeking contact. When finally she faced him, she put her hand to her waist and untied the cord belt that she wore, letting it fall away. He stood and watched, transfixed, as she brushed the overshirt from her shoulders, letting it slide down her arms.

Something swelled inside his chest, pushing against his ribs and forcing all the air out of his lungs. Reflexively, he searched for oxygen, and to his surprise, felt it flow sweetly into him, bringing an odd peace and a feeling of inevitability even as his body awoke to savage hunger. Why had he thought he could talk himself out of this? It was too late for that, had been too late since she'd first touched him.

Ty removed his suit coat, folded it and slung it over the back of the couch, his heart hammering. It was a moment of intense aliveness when body and mind and heart and spirit all rose to the same level of awareness. He unbuttoned his cuffs and rolled back his sleeves, and she smiled, a slow, soft smile that set him afire.

SHE WAS TREMBLING but not with fear or uncertainty. Need. Desire. Eagerness. As he moved toward her, his sleeves rolled back as if he had a job to do and meant to do it well, she felt her heart lurch with a giddy gladness. His gaze never left hers, his dark eyes deep and burning with purpose. He stopped only when the next step would have mowed her down, toppled her like a pin in a bowling lane. His long, wide, capable hands rose to cup her face, and still his gaze held hers.

Drawn like a starving waif to a banquet, she swayed forward, her breath quickening. Finally, his gaze shifted, swept over her face and hair and settled on her mouth. He bent his head and at the same time lifted her toward him. She rose eagerly on her toes. He feathered her lips with his, just once, then his right hand fell away from her face and his arm clamped around the small of her back, pulling her fully against him as he took possession of her mouth.

A sweetness poured into her, a honeyed warmth that filled the empty places she hadn't even known existed. She slid her arms around his neck, arched her back and opened for him. He pushed his hand into her hair, cupped the back of her head and let his tongue drift into her mouth, leisurely stroking and tasting along the way. Her heart was drumming by the time he finished his gentle exploration, straightened and lifted his head.

"Wrap your legs around me," he ordered huskily, reaching to hike up her skirt. His hands slid over bare skin and spread across her bottom, lifting her and warming the taut silk of her panties as she twined her legs about his waist. She felt a jolt of electricity arc upward from the apex of her thighs as she settled against his hardness. A slight smile curved his lips, a little smug, very male, telling her that he knew exactly what she was feeling. He carried her easily toward the bedroom, stepping up and across the landing.

No light burned there, but it was not yet dark enough to eclipse her vision. Still she managed only a cursory impression of the room, one of neatness, sand and cream and splashes of primary colors. A desk piled with books took up one whole corner, a tall dresser another. A floor lamp with a movable arm stood next to the big bed. He took her straight there, leaning down, grasped a corner of the bedcovers and ripped them back, tossing them over the end of the bed even as he set her on her feet and straightened.

He kissed her again as he tugged the hem of her T-shirt from the waistband of her skirt, then he stepped back and peeled the top up her torso and over her head, dropping it behind him. Quickly, he stripped off his shirt, revealing a firm, smooth expanse of male chest. Fingers trembling, Beth reached behind her for the closure of her bra. He helped her, sliding the straps from her shoulders. The small barrier fell away, and he rubbed his hands over her back, urging her gently forward. She laid herself against him, turning her face into the hollow of his throat. His face turned upward as he put his head back and filled his lungs with air.

Nothing had ever felt so good as that warm, male flesh against her naked breasts, and the strong arms that held her there.

After a long, quiet moment, one of his hands moved into her hair, tugging her head back to allow him access to her mouth. This was no gentle exploration but a plunging demand. Her body was burning with need when at last he broke away, quickly pushed her to sit on the edge of the bed and knelt to tug off her boots and socks. Standing, he pulled her with him and stepped out of his shoes as he searched for a way to release her skirt, his movements growing more and more urgent. She tried to help him and only complicated matters. Then she remembered that the waistband was elasticized in the back. Laughing nervously, she hooked her thumbs in the sides of the waistband and shoved the skirt down, slip and all, kicking them aside. A chuckle rumbled from his chest as he slipped a small packet from his pocket and tossed it onto the bed. A condom. Quickly, he stripped free of his remaining garments. Then he stepped back and looked at her, allowed her to look at him.

The air became heated, burning her lungs as she filled them with increasingly rapid breaths. He was amazing, long and strong and elegant, all hard muscle and skin like burnished copper. She was dizzy from trying to take in the sheer wealth of male beauty before her by the time he stepped forward and slowly went down on his haunches. He wrapped his hands around her ankles, then slid them up the backs of her legs. She thought her knees would buckle when he laid his face against her belly, his hot breath tickling her through the scrap of silk that was all that covered her. As his wide palms cupped her bottom, he lifted his head and looked at her.

"We shouldn't be doing this," he whispered, and she thought fleetingly of what her mother had said about his superiors at his job. Then his fingertips found the tiny elastic waistband of her panties and peeled them to the floor. Gently, he lifted her feet free of the garment one at a time, and her thoughts whirled inside her head as she gripped his shoulders. He rose and picked her up, hands around her waist, then laid her on the bed, straddling her with his knees. "But damned if I can stop," he said, reaching for the packet of protection.

When he had it on, she wrapped her arms around his neck and pulled him down to kiss her, marveling at how easily he held his weight above her. He did so for a long while, touching her only with his mouth at first. It was enough to make her lose her mind, need building to harsh urgency. Eventually he eased his weight to one side and began reducing her to a shivering, moaning mass of sensation with his hands. As much as she wanted to repay him in kind, she could do nothing but receive, and she soaked up each sensation like a sponge.

When at last he rolled his weight onto her and joined their bodies, it felt to her as if he filled every empty place inside of her, a few so raw and hungry that she wept at feeling whole for the first time in her life.

Afterward she lay in the dark against his side, utterly content in a way she had never before known, silently contemplating the rectangle of light that fell through the open door from the living room onto the bedroom floor. He had spread her hair across his chest, fanning and combing it with his fingers, his body warm against hers. She wanted nothing more than to drift off to sleep like this, but she knew she couldn't. Finally she found the strength to speak.

"I needed this." She smoothed a hand over his hairless chest. "I needed you."

He curled a finger beneath her chin and pushed her head back, looking into her face. "You needed what happened no more than I did." He smoothed her hair from her face, smiling.

"Every touch," she said, "every whisper was so perfect."

Arrogance infected that smile, and he bent his head to hers, kissing her gently. When he pulled back, however, his expression was solemn. "We've both been very foolish here tonight, you know."

"Why do you say that?" she asked uncertainly. Hadn't he felt what she had? Hadn't he loved it? Hadn't he felt her loving him? She did love everything about him, she realized, and wanted to tell him so, but uncertainty held her back.

He sighed and passed a hand over his eyes. After a moment he told her what she had to know. "I have a job to do, Beth, an important job. Your future depends on my doing it right. What we've already done threatens to compromise that. I can't allow myself to compound the threat."

She sat up, dragging the sheet he'd pulled over them with her. "So where do we go from here? What's next?"

He looked away. "I do my job and hope it turns out as it should."

"Meaning?"

"We prove your innocence, and no one gets hurt."

"And afterward?"

He looked her full in the face. "There is no afterward, Beth. I thought you knew that."

Shaken, she stared at him. "You're saying we can't do this again."

His gaze was full of regret, but was it for what had already happened or what couldn't happen again? "Yes."

She closed her eyes, willing back the tears, a little surprised that she could do so.

"Could your job be at risk over this?" she asked, too late.

He didn't answer, an answer in itself. Instead he sat up and swung his legs off the bed. "Don't worry about it. I knew what I was doing."

And that was that. What a fool she was! No promises, she'd told herself, but at least it should have been a beginning. Now he was telling her that it was an end. All the empty places inside her cried out again, but she suppressed them and waited in silence until he'd pulled on jeans, a loose sweater and cowboy boots without benefit of socks.

He came back to the bed and leaned over her. "I'm going to make a cup of coffee. Want some?"

"No, thanks."

Silently he cupped her face in his hands and plumbed the depths of her gaze. He looked so sad and so decided. Then he kissed her lingeringly, his mouth gentle, expert. He meant it to be the last time; she sensed it. Her heart cracked open and anger surged through. She was not the fool. He was! Did he really think he could just walk away now? Finally he tore his mouth from hers and strode from the room, leaving her bereft and confused and determined not to be.

TY LEANED both hands against the edge of the countertop and listened to the dribble of water leaking from the basket of the small coffeemaker. Perhaps he should ask to be taken off the case. But no. He didn't dare. He couldn't trust anyone to see beneath the surface facts. The case against Beth was too easy to make. Too much was at stake. He and Jester were the only ones with personal experience. Anyone else would be working from a written report. His insights would be only too easy to dismiss. How on earth could he make anyone understand?

Then again, how could he possibly explain what had happened here? What difference would it make to anyone else that their mutual need had called to his heart like the compelling song of a reed flute, that his body's response had been too powerful to resist? Like the urge to breathe when his lungs were empty of air, his natural instinct had been to pull her close and drive himself into her. But he couldn't let it happen again. It wasn't just his career at stake, it was the life of an innocent woman, a very beautiful, intelligent, incredibly sexy, innocent woman. A rich woman. A white woman.

The pot finished brewing the small amount of coffee he'd measured into it. He filled the cup he'd taken from the cabinet and sipped the scalding liquid, intending to stand right there and nurse the cup until it was empty. Somehow, though, he found himself wandering across the living room and into the bedroom. She was dressed, including the shirt and belt that had been left behind in the living area, and stood with her back to the door, pulling a small brush through her long, crackling hair. Her handbag lay open on the foot of his bed. He felt a sudden urge to tuck her into that bed and keep her there, safe, his. He shook his head.

Beth Maitland was not his; she would never be. Too much separated them. Even if the case were settled, her innocence proven, too much stood between them, things like money, position, culture. He'd learned that lesson only too well.

At the side of the bed, he stooped and picked up his pants from the floor. Carefully extracting everything from the pockets, he stowed it all in his jeans, folded the slacks and laid them aside. He usually took better care of his things. He usually had better sense than to get sexually involved with a suspect in a murder case, too.

"It isn't just the investigation, is it?" Beth asked intuitively.

Caught off guard, he could only stare at her in the half-light for a moment. "Isn't that enough?"

"You didn't answer the question."

"Maybe I don't understand the question," he said, turning to straighten the bed. She sat on the foot of it and forced him to look at her.

"Yes, you do. Because if you don't, then what we just had was sex and nothing more. And I don't believe that's what happened between us. I can't believe that."

"Beth," he began, trying to warn her away with the tone of his voice.

She shook her head vigorously. "You made love to me, Ty. You made incredible love to me in this bed. And now you say that it can never happen again. Why not, Ty? Once the investigation is over and my name is cleared, why can't we—"

He parked his hands at his waist. "It wouldn't work, Beth."

"You don't know that."

"I do know it. I know exactly what I'm talking about."

She got up from the bed and walked to him. With her hand on his upper arm, she turned him to face her. "How do you know, Ty?"

He opened his mouth to tell her, then closed it again, suddenly remembering the way her family had behaved that afternoon. It had been almost as if they'd welcomed the suggestion of something personal going on between him and Beth. He shook his head. Margo had been quite enthusiastic at first, too, but in the end he had been nothing more than a diversion for her. As soon as he'd become inconvenient, she'd cut him loose without a backward glance. Of course Beth's family was pleased with the idea of personal involvement between them; they wanted him on her side. For now.

"I just know," he insisted stubbornly.

Beth folded her arms, a mulish look on her pretty face. "Who was she?"

His first impulse was to turn his back and walk away; his second was to deny it. But he was no liar, and he'd never run away from anything in his life. He swallowed the burn of acid in the back of his throat. "Her name was Margo Morris."

Beth's mouth fell open. "Not Madam Margo."

Ty drew his brows together. "What are you talking about?"

"Well, her daddy did keep it out of the local papers," Beth mused, "but you're a police detective. Surely you saw a report or something."

"A report on Margo?" Ty asked. "For what?"

"Running a prostitution ring in Louisiana."

He felt his eyes go wide. "Must be the wrong Margo. I'm talking about Margo Morris of the Morris banking family."

"Founders of one of Austin's largest private financial institutions," Beth added.

"The royal family of snobbery," Ty said.

"You got that right," Beth agreed. "That's what made it so juicy. It was the subject of gossip for months."

"In your circles, maybe," Ty muttered. "Are you telling me that Margo was actually procuring?"

"They say she was running prostitutes out of a three-story antebellum mansion in the Garden District of New Orleans, with all the best people in town as clients."

"Of course," he retorted, thoroughly flummoxed, "who else?"

"I think it's rich," Beth admitted, "a kind of poetic justice. The Morrises believe they're so much better than everyone else. Even Margo, who was forever in trouble with her parents, thought she was above everyone. She's money mad, you know, so that's how they controlled her, always cutting off her allowance, until finally, I guess, she decided to make some money of her own."

Ty drew a hand down his face. "I can't believe this."

"And why is that, specifically?" Beth asked.

With a sigh, he rubbed the little muscle that began to tic

in the corner of his eye. "When I knew Margo—well, it was a long time ago, in college—I thought, because she was from a good family, you know, that she would never do anything illegal."

"Define 'good family,'" Beth said.

"You know what I mean," Ty grumbled, feeling off balance and foolish.

"Just how well did you know Margo?" Beth asked, a note of jealousy in her voice.

Ty cleared his throat, pleased, though he knew he had no right to be. "We were involved."

"In an affair."

"If you want to call it that."

"What would you call it?"

"I thought she was my girlfriend," he said through his teeth.

"You were in love with her," Beth accused.

"I thought she was my girlfriend!" he repeated more heatedly.

"For how long?" Beth demanded, sounding so proprietary that he wanted to smile.

He shrugged and ducked his head. "Eight, nine months, almost the whole school year, I guess."

"So what happened?"

He sighed, preferring not to talk about it yet knowing she wasn't going to leave it alone. "Her father threatened to cut off her allowance and take away her credit cards."

"And the dope dumped you because of that!" Beth exclaimed, throwing up her arms. "What an idiot!"

"According to her family," Ty responded softly, "an Indian whose father died in jail without a nickel to his name was not socially acceptable."

"To the Morrises, Prince Andrew wouldn't be socially acceptable as long as Prince Charles was available," Beth observed dryly. "How'd you get hooked up with a fruit-cake like her, anyway?"

Ty lifted a hand to the back of his neck. "She, uh, introduced herself one day."

"I'll bet she did," Beth muttered. "I'll bet you were the best-looking guy on campus, so naturally you were for her."

The best-looking guy on campus? "I don't know about that," Ty mumbled, grinning despite himself.

"How were you to know she'd already slept her way across Europe by then?" Beth exclaimed. "Which is why, after all those fancy boarding schools, her parents made her go to college so close to home."

"How do you know all this?" Ty asked, peeking at her from beneath his brow.

Beth rolled her eyes. "The rich are just like everyone else, Ty. They talk. They screw up, they get talked about. Actually, it's worse than that. You live and breathe, you get talked about, because the rich are often extremely covetous and jealous. You might think it's money that holds together that particular social circle, but the real glue is gossip and malice. They all want to know the dirt on everyone else so they can gloat."

"Everyone who matters," Ty corrected irritably.

"All right," Beth admitted. "Everyone who matters to them. But isn't it that way with most people?"

He frowned. "Maybe."

"Definitely," she said.

He shook his head. Was Margo really as unworthy as Beth implied? But of course she was, a woman capable of procuring prostitutes for money! And that was the woman who had burned him so badly? Or had he made more of the whole episode than had really been there? He didn't know what to think about it. He looked at Beth and saw so much more in her than he'd ever seen in Margo Morris. Quite without meaning to, he opened his arms, and she walked into them as easily as if she belonged there.

Folding her close, he whispered, "Margo meant nothing,

but that doesn't change who we are, Beth, our individual circumstances, our backgrounds.''

"I understand what you're saying," she told him, "but you're making too much of it."

"I don't think so."

"Just don't write us off for good, Ty," she pleaded.

He wrestled with her words for a moment. "I can't make you any promises, Beth. I can't even think about it, not now. The case has to come first. Proving your innocence and getting Dumont have to take precedence over everything else."

"I understand that."

"But do you understand that after Dumont there will be another case and another and another?"

"Yes, of course."

"I wonder," he said, searching her face. "I'm a cop, Beth. You could cover me in money, and I'd still be a cop. And a Native American."

"What are you saying?" she asked.

"No promises," he answered, backing away. "I'm saying no promises."

"For now," she insisted implacably.

He said nothing to that, and she turned to stride from the room, snatching her brush and her purse along the way. Before reluctantly following her, he looked at the rumpled bed once more, wondering how he was going to sleep there without her.

CHAPTER EIGHT

VALENTINE'S DAY. It was stupid to feel slighted and disappointed because he hadn't called or sent a gift. She hadn't expected it. She really hadn't. But somehow she couldn't help feeling hurt. When Ty had dropped her off at the mansion that night, he had said nothing about calling or keeping in touch or even thinking of her. He had promised to stop Brandon from getting away with murder and framing her in the process. He had accepted her farewell kiss with warmth and ease, but he hadn't returned it, and after he'd walked her to the door, he'd beat a hasty retreat. She hadn't heard from him since, and though that was only to be expected under the circumstances, she missed him and felt more than a twinge of resentment.

Given the bleak prospects for her romance, if such it could be called, Beth should have appreciated the family gathering arranged by her mother. It should have provided distraction and comfort. She loved it when the whole clan came together, and this year it was larger than ever, with so many new additions. But tonight she wanted to sit in her room and brood. Where was Ty? Was he alone? With another woman? Beth absently sipped the champagne that Harold, the Maitlands' butler and dear old family friend, had poured into her glass, and glanced dispiritedly around the room from her perch on the scrolled bench beneath the bay window. Anna accepted a glass from Harold and dropped onto the bench beside Beth.

Mitchell and Jake had their heads together in one corner.

Abby and Kyle snuggled together in a chair in front of the fireplace, whispering and laughing, while Ellie and Sloan sat side by side at one end of the long couch, holding hands, legs pressed together. R.J. stood with his arms looped loosely about Dana, her back to his chest, and as Beth watched, Dana laid her head on her husband's shoulder and smiled at him, the fingertips of one hand lightly caressing a tiny jeweled heart pendant around her slender neck. At the center of the room stood Megan with Connor and Janelle. All three were beaming, but Beth was too miserable to wonder why. Anna was not.

"Mom looks like the cat who found the cream," she observed softly.

Beth took another drink. "Mmm."

"You don't suppose it has anything to do with that rock on Janelle's finger, do you?" Anna asked wryly.

Beth roused herself enough to ask dumbly, "What rock?"

Anna leaned closer. "Diamond," she whispered, "at least three karats." Beth blinked at her, slowly putting it together. "Third finger, left hand," Anna added, looking at her oddly.

Immediately Beth looked away. So Janelle and Connor were going to get married. She would have been more pleased if Janelle would just get the stupid birth certificate, or better yet, have the DNA test. She'd promised recently that the paperwork was in the mail, but how she could possibly know that was beyond Beth. Whatever the reason, Beth was glad to still have baby Chase in the house.

She couldn't imagine what she'd do with herself without that sweet child to look after. His mother occasionally put in an appearance in the nursery, and she made all the right noises and gestures when she did, but she always handed the boy over to Beth without the slightest hesitation, and Beth couldn't figure that out. Something wasn't right, and Beth knew that at another time and under other circumstances, she'd have been itching to find out what. Just now, however, it seemed to be all she could do to haul herself out of bed in the morning.

"Sweetie, is something wrong?" Anna asked, a shadow of concern on her face.

"What could be wrong?" Beth replied obliquely. "Abby, Ellie and R.J. are happily paired up and in love, Connor and Janelle are obviously getting married, and I'm under investigation for murder. That sure ought to make for a happy Valentine's, don't you think?"

"Oh, honey, I'm sorry," Anna said, quickly squeezing her fingers. "It's so preposterous that I can't even wrap my mind around the idea of you harming anyone. Even the police will have to see that eventually. How is it going, by the way?"

Beth shrugged, avoiding the issue. When she thought of the investigation, she thought of Ty, and when she thought of Ty, she thought of the last time they were together—and then her heart broke all over again.

"Don't you worry," Anna urged. "Jake says that those two detectives seem to really know what they're doing."

"Could we not talk about this now?" Beth pleaded. "I really just want to forget about it for a while."

Anna slipped an arm around her younger sister's shoulders. "Of course." She lifted her champagne glass. "Tonight's for celebration."

Beth had her doubts about that, too, but she didn't say anything. She didn't have to. Megan chose that moment to step forward and claim their attention.

"Thank you, my darlings, for indulging your mother by being here when you could obviously be enjoying, shall we say, more private moments." The three couples in the room looked at one another knowingly. The others glanced around in bemused fashion, Mitchell and Jake rolling their eyes. Megan smiled and went on, holding her champagne glass before her. "I won't keep you long, I promise. But I have two very important announcements to make. The first, I think, is significant as an omen of things to come." She inclined her head slightly and said, "It is official. Every single invitation—that's *every* invitation—for the anniversary party has been accepted."

Ellie disengaged herself from Sloan long enough to clap, beaming. "Hear, hear!"

"Looks like we've weathered the storms and come out on the other side intact," Mitchell commented.

"Well done, Ellie and Mom," Abby said. "You've both worked so hard, putting out fires all over."

"It was Mother, not me," Ellie protested.

"Not a bit of it," Megan said, shaking her head. "The wonderful thing about Maitland Maternity is that it is a family concern. We've all had a hand in making it what it is today, even you, Anna, and you, Jake. Our reputation for excellence and caring is what has brought us through and what will carry us into the future. I'm terribly proud of all of you, and unspeakably grateful that our many friends and supporters have seen through the press barrage of ugly innuendo to the truth."

"To Maitland Maternity," Jake said, raising his glass.

"To the Maitland family," Connor countered, lifting his drink and stepping to Megan's side. He tossed off half his drink while the others sipped decorously. Beth stared at her near empty glass, feeling relief and gratitude mingled with misery. She had so feared that her situation would spoil the anniversary celebration for her mother; she ought to have been as happy as the rest of them that it hadn't, but somehow she couldn't feel more than a mere lightening of the pain clogged around her heart.

"And now for the grand announcement," Megan said, "and the reason why I called you all here on this, the lovers' holiday." She looked meaningfully at Connor, who reached out and curled an arm around Janelle's waist.

Janelle had dressed in a form-fitting, embarrassingly

short sheath that displayed a wealth of cleavage—very expensive and a little cheap at the same time, much like Janelle herself. She had a dreamy look on her face that didn't obscure her smugness. Out of respect for her mother, Beth suppressed the urge to get up and walk out of the room.

Connor, thankfully, made short work of it, saying baldly, "Janelle and I are getting married."

Anna, at least, had the warmth of heart to express delight. "Oh, that's wonderful!"

Jake muttered something about it being past time, but R.J. seemed happy enough with his own love to give Connor and Janelle the benefit of the doubt. "Congratulations, you two."

"All the best," his wife, Dana, added.

"Let's make it official," Abby's husband, Kyle, said, lifting his glass. "To Connor and Janelle."

"To Connor and Janelle," Megan repeated, the others quickly following suit. After they had all had a sip of champagne, Megan went on. "I don't think I need to tell anyone how delighted I am, and as my gift to you, Connor and Janelle, I'm going to pay for the wedding."

Connor chuckled delightedly, while Janelle gasped and clapped her hands over her mouth. *Doing it altogether too brown, my dear,* Beth thought mockingly. She'd have bet cash money that Janelle had been expecting that very thing. Oh, well, if it made her mother happy, so be it. Megan was still talking.

"Anna," she said, addressing her eldest daughter, "you will plan it for us, won't you?"

Anna jumped to her feet. "Just try and stop me." She looked excitedly from Connor to Janelle. "This is too romantic. What exactly would you like?"

"Well, the works, of course." Connor said, rocking on his heels. "Do it up right."

"We'll start with the guest list for the anniversary celebration," Megan said, "and go from there."

"So large?" Janelle gasped, her eyes wide. "Oh, no, please. Let's just keep it family."

Frowning, Connor looked at her. "Why? I want the whole world to know how proud I am to make you my wife."

Janelle leaned into him, smiling coyly. "Oh, darling, that's so sweet, but really, I just want a small family affair." She looked at Anna. "Very elegant, of course, but small." She cast a glance at Megan and added, "We have a child, after all. I don't want the press to have a field day with this. It might have ramifications for the clinic, and we've already embarrassed you enough."

"Nonsense!" Megan exclaimed. "I've told you that all of the invitations for the twenty-fifth-anniversary celebration have been accepted."

"Still," Janelle demurred, "I'd be more comfortable with a small family wedding."

"Oh, that's so sweet," Anna said, pressing her hands together.

"If that's what you want," Megan conceded, "what do you think of having it here?"

"Could we?" Janelle gushed as if she'd just been given the crown jewels.

"I promise you, we'll make it a very elegant affair," Anna proclaimed. "We'll talk later and set up an appointment."

Janelle looked around, fluttering her eyelashes as if blinking back tears, and exclaimed, "I just don't know how to thank you all. You've been so wonderful to me and my son."

"There, there, honey," Connor said, patting her back. "You're part of the family now. And family's number one with we Maitlands."

If anyone else thought that was a supremely presumptive thing for him to say, no one indicated it, but Beth couldn't stomach any more. She tossed back the remainder of her drink and stood, intending to take her leave.

It was Jake who stopped her. "Hey, Beth, while we're all together, why don't you fill us in on how the investigation is going?"

Her other siblings added their voices to his, and Megan, too. Even Janelle managed to sound concerned, though it appeared to be beyond Connor. Beth wanted to offer them reassurance, but she couldn't compromise Ty's position. "I, um, can't give you details, but it looks like Brandon is trying to frame me. He won't get away with it, though, because the police see what he's doing."

"That rotten SOB!" Mitchell exclaimed.

"He won't get away with it," Jake stated flatly.

"You're right about that," Megan said. "I'm happy to say that I've developed a good deal of confidence in Detectives Redstone and Jester." She looked straight at Beth, one brow arching slightly, and added, "Detective Redstone in particular seems to have taken a personal interest in getting at the truth."

"He's just doing his job," Beth mumbled.

"Frankly, I had my doubts about him at first," Jake said. "He made it clear at the beginning that he considered Beth his prime suspect, but I've since heard a lot of good things about his abilities and judgment. They say he has an uncanny sense for snooping out a liar."

"And that would be Dumont," Mitchell stated decisively.

"Well, I don't know about Detective Redstone's abilities," Anna said significantly, "but he's certainly a handsome devil."

Beth felt her face flame. It didn't help when Ellie added, "He's a much better prospect for our Beth than Brandon Dumont ever was."

"Oh, no," Beth denied, suddenly close to tears. "Don't

say that. Don't even think it! Ty…Detective Redstone is just doing his job. There's nothing personal between us."

"And he's wise to keep it that way until this is all over," Jake said helpfully.

"I agree," Megan said. "The less said about a romance brewing the better, for both Beth and Ty."

"There is no romance," Beth insisted, perilously close to tears. "Please. Excuse me. I have something to do." With that she shoved her empty wine flute into Anna's hands and fled before her tears could spill over. She heard the murmur of concerned voices behind her and knew that they'd all be worrying about her, but she was beyond caring. All she wanted was a moment of privacy in which to compose herself. Unfortunately, she turned from the door and ran straight into Harold.

"Oh, Miss Beth," he exclaimed, juggling something in his hands as he stepped back. "Are you all right?"

She looked away. "Yes, of course. I seem to have something in my eye. Pardon my clumsiness."

"Not at all. I was just coming to look for you," he said. "These just arrived."

For the first time, Beth gave him her full attention. He was holding a simple glass vase, with two long-stemmed red roses in it. A frothy bow had been tied around the neck of the vase and a card dangled from one end of the ribbon. Beth's heart leaped into her throat. Ty! She knew he couldn't ignore her, not after that afternoon. Taking the vase in her trembling hands, she quickly extracted the card from the little envelope and flipped it over.

"Wishing you a Happy Valentine's Day," it read. "We miss you." The note was signed, "Cheryl and Lizzie." Her assistants at the day-care center. Whirling, Beth burst into tears. Harold was instantly at her elbow.

"Miss Beth!"

"How very thoughtful of them," she wailed. "Thank you, Harold." She ran for the staircase and the safety of her room, the roses clutched against her chest. Never had a Valentine's Day felt so forlorn.

JANELLE SLUNG the fur-trimmed cloak about her shoulders and strode rapidly around the pool toward the guest house.

"Hold on!" Petey groused, hurrying to snag her by the shoulder and turn her around.

"Not now!" she said, seething, glancing in the direction of the house. True, everyone had dispersed after their announcement and Beth's melodramatic exit—honestly, that girl just couldn't bear for anyone else to be the center of attention—but you never knew who might be watching and listening.

"Just tell me why you nixed the big wedding," Petey grumbled, lowering his voice. "The real Connor would get a big wedding, not to mention a boatload of expensive gifts!"

"What are a few wedding gifts compared to the mother lode of the Maitland fortune when Megan announces you're her long-lost son?" Janelle insisted, turning away once more. It was too damned cold to stand out here explaining the facts of life to this ninny of a husband of hers.

"But what about our introduction to society?" Petey argued, hurrying along beside her. "I thought you wanted—"

Janelle stopped and rounded on him, relatively sure that the deepening night and the shrubbery would shield them from view of the house. Distance should manage the rest. "Will you just *think* for once? A Maitland society wedding would be big news. With all the press coverage of late, we can't risk it."

"But—"

"The real Connor could get wind of it," she told him irritably. "Or just reading his name in the paper could shake little Miss Amnesia out of her stupor. And why haven't you taken care of that?"

"I'm working on it," he whined. "A murder takes careful planning."

"It also takes guts," Janelle said, pushing her face close to his, lest he miss her implications.

His handsome but stupid face hardened. "I said I'd take care of it, and I will."

"Fine. You take care of the brat's mother, and I'll take care of the wedding."

"Whatever you say," he mumbled.

Janelle turned on her heel and strode toward the guest house. Being married to this jerk was wearing thin on her, and here she was about to marry him for the second time! Wouldn't Megan and the others croak if they knew the truth of it! Any whisper of the truth could blow the whole deal—or worse—and there were already too many loose ends, namely the real Connor, and Lacy, the baby's mother. If that nutcase should regain her memory... Janelle shuddered at the possibility. They had to be careful. They not only stood to lose the Maitland millions but would almost certainly wind up in jail if they were discovered. Why didn't Petey realize that?

Still, the big lug had his uses, and so did this so-called Maitland wedding. She had no choice but to play this thing through. True, they were walking a tightrope, but her balance had always been good, even if Petey's was a little uncertain. As if to prove it, he grumbled sullenly that he'd been thinking a lot about those wedding gifts.

Janelle rolled her eyes. "Will you shut up about the wedding gifts! The family will be very generous, count on it. Besides, what the hell do we need with half a dozen soup tureens when we're so close to wiggling our happy fingers in cold, hard cash?"

Petey seemed to take her point. He was quiet for a long time. They were standing at the guest house door before he looked at her and blankly inquired, "What's a soup tureen?"

Thoroughly disgusted, Janelle went inside and slammed the door in his face. Really, how was a woman supposed to get ahead in this world, get a share of what was rightfully hers, when she had to think for two people all the time? She was definitely earning her share of the family fortune the hard way. Once she had it, she just might cut old Petey free.

TY SMILED at the woman sitting across the table from him and watched with pleasure as she opened the gift he'd brought for her. She turned back the flaps on the top of the box and lifted out the item inside.

"A four-cup coffeepot," she announced unnecessarily. "Thank you, son. It's a very thoughtful gift."

"Not very traditional for Valentine's Day," he admitted, "but you've been saying that the big pot takes up too much room, and since you've cut back on your caffeine and all..."

"It's a perfect gift for me on Valentine's or anytime," Naomi insisted, rising from the table to carry the little coffeemaker to the counter. "But if you're going to mark this day, shouldn't you be doing it with a girlfriend? It's a lover's day."

Ty sighed inwardly, but his voice was light when he said nonchalantly, "I don't have a girlfriend."

"And I don't have a husband," she said, "so you feared this day would be sad for me. Don't you see that I fear the same for you?"

Ty blinked, so aware of the aura of love that surrounded her he seemed to see it. Even after all these years, she loved his father with a constancy that time and death could not dim. He was awed by that love and a little frightened by it. He wasn't sure he dared risk a love like that.

Naomi turned from the counter and faced him, her small, knobby hands folded at her waist. A petite, bony woman with straight, chin-length hair heavily streaked with silver

about her smooth, narrow face, she managed to look somehow ancient and young at the same time. Her lips wore
their customary semi-smile, while her black-as-pitch eyes
registered far more than they could possibly see.

"What about that woman who works with you?" she
asked incisively.

He shrugged and looked away. "That was weeks ago.
She's seeing some guy in Vice now."

"You could have kept that from happening," his mother
said evenly. "Why didn't you?"

Inwardly he squirmed. Outwardly he merely inclined his
head. "She's not Native, Mother. She didn't understand."

"You could have taught her."

"Maybe," he said, "if I had wanted to."

Naomi sighed and strolled to the table, sitting in her rickety wooden chair. "You are surrounded by a spirit of loneliness, Ty," she observed softly. "It's time you opened
your heart. You want to. I sense it. Why haven't you?"

Ty studied the back of his hand on the scarred tabletop.
Slowly, realization slipped in. He had come here not so
much to mark the day but to tell her about what had happened with Beth. He could do so, he knew, without fear of
censure, misunderstanding or disappointment. Turning over
his hand, he studied his palm and began to talk about Beth
Maitland.

"I've never felt anything like it," he said, "but it's foolish and dangerous for both of us. I must let it be over."

His mother smiled, a gentle curving of her mouth, while
her eyes seemed to look inward. "When your father went
to jail," she said gently, "people said to me, 'Let it go.'
They thought I should divorce him and find another man
to take care of me and my babies, but it wasn't possible
because it was not finished between us. When he died there,
they said, 'Now you can love again,' but I knew that I
couldn't. Still it was not finished between us. It isn't finished between us even now. It will never be finished be-

tween us. When I die, he will be there, waiting for me. He's a part of my spirit, a part of my heart. If Beth Maitland is for you what your father is for me, you will never be able to let it be over."

Ty bowed his head, thinking. "I have no choice. We both have too much at stake."

"Perhaps just now it seems so," Naomi said, "but if she is the one, you'll look around soon and realize that nothing else matters, that you cannot be who you are without loving her."

He shook his head. "It's not that easy. I must protect her, whatever the cost. She could go to jail for something she didn't do."

"As your father did," Naomi replied. "It didn't stop me from loving him, Ty, or him me. Do what you must, son, but do not believe that you can stop your heart from loving her if she is the one your heart has chosen."

Ty gulped. These were not words of comfort to him. He was not sure he wanted it to be Beth Maitland. Why not some gentle Tonkawa girl like his mother? Why could he not love a woman like that? Then again, why love at all? Life was so much less complicated without love, especially love for a woman like Beth Maitland. Yes, it was better to choose not to love.

Unfortunately, he wasn't sure the choice was his to make. If his mother was right, and she usually was, the heart did the choosing, and all a man could do then was...let it be. But how could he when so much was at stake, when there were so many differences between them? Sighing, he put aside the confusion and smiled at his mother, saying, "Perhaps you could make me some coffee in that new pot."

"It will keep you awake," she warned him, rising.

His smile waned. "I haven't been sleeping much lately anyway," he admitted. Naomi cupped a comforting hand over his shoulder, then turned to do as he suggested.

CHAPTER NINE

HE SHOULDN'T be doing this. Without a doubt, Ty knew he
shouldn't be standing on the doorstep of the Maitland mansion, night coming on, his heart fluttering in anticipation of
seeing her again. But she had a right to know what was
happening. And he did so want to see her. That didn't
change the fact, however, that he shouldn't be here.

"Next time pick up the telephone, Redstone," he muttered even as he rang the doorbell. He listened to the re-
sounding bong that echoed inside the great, cavernous
house and was not surprised when the door opened immediately, since the watchman at the gate on the edge of
the property had alerted the house to his arrival. The butler—Harold, Ty believed his name was—nodded in welcome before stepping back and swinging the door wide.

"Allow me to take your coat, Detective."

It wasn't really a request, and Ty was irritated with himself because he felt so utterly compelled to comply. Uneasy,
he shrugged out of his duster-length overcoat and rocked
on his heels, hands clasped behind him. "Thank you. Is
Miss Beth in?"

The butler inclined his head. "Certainly. This way
please." With that he executed a neat turn and strode across
the broad, magnificent foyer, confident that Ty would follow. Ty glanced around as he did so, remarking to himself
silently that the place looked like a damned museum. A
double door was thrown open, revealing a small, elegantly

appointed parlor where three feminine figures sat before the fire. One of them catapulted out of her chair.

"Ty!"

She looked stunning in wide, wine-red satin pants and a matching shirt. Her long, curly hair was caught loosely at the collar with a ruffled, elasticized band that would slide free with the slightest tug of his hand. His mouth went dry at the thought of that hair spread across his bare chest. He cleared his throat and managed a belated reply.

"Hello. Pardon my interruption."

Megan Maitland had twisted around in her chair, a snifter in one elegant hand. "No pardon necessary, Detective. Could I interest you in a warming drink? It's an especially good cognac, if I do say so myself."

He swallowed and forced his eyes away from Beth. "No, thank you, ma'am. I'm driving, and seeing as this is official business of a sort, I wouldn't be comfortable."

"I understand," Megan said, nodding. "You're a man of principle, Detective. I appreciate that."

Principle, he thought. *Yeah, right.* The kind of principle that let a cop take an official suspect to bed. While he was mentally kicking himself, Beth gestured at the third woman in the room. She was so like Beth and yet so very different, with her short, neat hair and no-nonsense demeanor.

"I believe you know my sister Ellie."

"Ah, yes. We have spoken."

"The night of the murder," Ellie clarified rather tartly. "You gave me to understand that my sister was your prime suspect."

Ty nodded unapologetically. "You gave me to understand that an impartial investigation would determine otherwise. You were right."

Ellie relaxed in her chair. "Glad to hear it."

Beth was wringing her hands. "Official business, you said. What's happened?"

Uncomfortably, Ty glanced around and Megan Maitland

seemed to take it as a plea for privacy. She drained the remaining drops of her cognac, set aside the snifter and rose smoothly to her feet, gesturing at Ellie. "You'll pardon us, Detective, I'm sure."

He nodded, aware of Ellie studying him blatantly as if making up her mind whether or not to leave him alone with her twin. Finally she rose from her wing chair and moved to follow her mother toward the door. As she passed Beth, she murmured, "Official business, my eye."

Ducking her head, Beth looked away. Ty watched the women walk out of the room before asking, "What was that about?"

Beth shook her head, steeling herself against the hope that rose within her at the sight of him. "Doesn't matter. What is it you've come for?"

Ty sighed inwardly. She wasn't even going to ask him to sit down. And he couldn't blame her. He made short work of what he had come to say. "The D.A. and Immigration have agreed to grant Letitia and Frankie Velasquez immunity from prosecution and deportation if they testify against Brandon Dumont with significant product."

"Significant product," she echoed. "What does that mean?"

"It means that if their information helps prove Dumont's guilt in a crime, they won't be punished for any involvement on their part."

"In other words, Letitia can admit that Brandon forced her to lie about me harassing Brianne by threatening to turn Frankie over to Immigration for deportation."

"That's correct."

"But what about Frankie? He's in this country illegally."

Ty nodded his understanding of her concern. "If Frankie can give us the forger who put together his phony papers and I can get the truth out about that joyriding charge, Immigration is willing to overlook the illegal papers and reinstate his green card. And if the forger is the bartender Gustopherson, which I'm sure he is, that'll give us leverage on him.''

Beth closed her eyes, whispering, "Thank God."

"Frankie's not in the clear yet," Ty warned, "but I have six months to make—or rather, unmake—the auto theft charge after the yield of Frankie's testimony."

"The yield?"

"After we determine whether or not Frankie's testimony does what we expect it to."

"I see."

"It's good news, Beth," Ty assured her, "for everyone except Dumont and Gustopherson, if he's the forger, and I can't believe he isn't."

She lowered herself onto the arm of the chair, apparently overcome with relief. "What then?" she wanted to know.

"Well, if it pans out the way we expect, we'll be able to pressure Gustopherson to give up Dumont's alibi."

"And then it's all over?" she asked in a tremulous voice.

Ty took a deep breath, preparing them both for what he had to say. "No. It's not over. It punches holes in Dumont's story and casts doubt on your involvement, but it doesn't prove Dumont killed his wife and deliberately tried to frame you. He can always claim that Brianne swore you were harassing her and he didn't want to see you get away with it."

Only when the bleak disappointment swept over her face did he realize how pale and thin she looked. Obviously this was taking a greater toll on her than he'd realized. Her tired, forlorn expression tore at him, and he felt compelled to help her somehow. Quite without intending to, he found himself stepping forward, opening his arms. She launched herself at him, flung her arms around his chest.

"It'll be okay," he promised. "We're getting there. We'll get him. You have to believe that."

"I know," she whispered. "It's the waiting, the long,

empty days. If it weren't for having baby Chase in the house, I'd lose my mind. If only I could do something myself!''

He hadn't intended to mention this just now, but if it would help her feel that she was contributing to the investigation, then why not? "Tell you what you can do," he said, "you can volunteer to have your personal things searched.''

She lifted her head. "What for?''

"If I told you that, it could compromise the search.''

"Don't you need a court order for that kind of thing?'' she asked.

"Not if you give your permission, and frankly, it'll look better for you if you do.''

"But you can't tell me what you're looking for?''

"No.''

"I see.'' She bit her lip.

"Beth, I wouldn't ask if it wasn't important.''

"I know that,'' she said, "just as I know that you wouldn't purposefully do anything to hurt me.''

He winced at that word *purposefully*. "Do you want to talk it over with your mother or an attorney?''

She shook her head. "No. This is my decision. When do you want to do it?''

"Right now?'' He slipped his cell phone from his suit coat pocket. "Jester can be here in ten. The forensic team in twenty.''

"Is that really necessary?'' she asked, sounding confused.

"I can't do it on my own,'' he explained. "That's the rule. It safeguards the evidence—not that we'll find any.''

She nodded reluctantly. "I know you don't want the cognac, but how about coffee?''

"Coffee would be great.''

"I'll have to inform Mother and ask Harold to fix a

tray.'' She gestured toward one of the chairs before the fire. ''Make your calls. I'll be right back.''

She left him, returning only minutes later to take the chair next to him. ''So how have you been?'' she asked softly, not quite meeting his gaze.

He sat forward, elbows on knees, willing her to really look at him. Was this wan appearance a result of the investigation or something else? Instinct told him that it was something else, and he was almost ashamed at the gladness he felt at the thought that she had suffered as greatly from the hopelessness of their situation as he had.

''I've been busy,'' he said. ''How about you?''

''*Not* busy,'' she enunciated carefully, still not looking at him. ''Bored. Lonely.'' She did look up then, a pleading in her eyes that he could not deny. Suddenly words that he'd meant to keep to himself were tumbling out of his mouth.

''I've missed you!''

Her blue eyes sheened with tears. ''I've missed you, too.''

''I wanted to be with you Valentine's,'' he admitted, bemused by the husky tenor of his voice, ''but I spent it with my mom instead.''

''Your mom?'' Dashing the tears from her eyes, she slipped from her chair to kneel by his feet. '' Oh, Ty! I've been so unhappy.''

Those words were like knives in the heart for Ty. He closed his eyes. ''I'm so sorry. This is all my fault. I should never have—'' She silenced him with two fingers pressed against his lips. He looked at her, so beautiful, delineated by firelight, her hair a barely tamed nimbus of smoky brown.

''Ty Redstone, if you're about to apologize for making love to me,'' she scolded softly, ''well, you'd just better not, that's all. I won't have it.''

A feeling like ripe sunshine burst inside him, clean,

bright, sweet and luscious. How could he stay away from this woman when she had this effect on him? Reaching down, he pulled her onto his lap.

"What am I going to do with you?" he asked, settling back and wrapping his arms around her. "I can't be with you. I can't be without you."

Beth slipped her arms around his neck. "We have the next few minutes."

He didn't argue. He should have, but he didn't. With her mouth on his, how could he? He lifted his left hand to the nape of her neck, invading her hair with his fingers as he tilted his head, drinking deeply of her kiss. Her lips were soft, the tip of her tongue as sweet as nectar; with his tongue, he coaxed hers into his mouth, welcomed her delicate exploration. His right hand slid from her waist to cup the fullness of her breast. He had suckled that breast and dreamed of it since, of the small sounds she had made when he'd taken the rosy nipple into his mouth and drawn on it. Touching her through her clothing was not enough. He slid his hand beneath the hem of her blouse, and she framed her face with his hands, plunging her sweet tongue deeply into his mouth. It was then, thankfully, that Harold knocked on the door.

Ty groaned. Breaking the kiss, Beth huffed a sigh of deep regret, then slowly rose from Ty's lap and reclaimed her chair. Ty couldn't help smiling. She was looking more like his Beth, her chin held at a confident angle as she called for the butler to come into the room. Harold wheeled in a cart and parked it between Beth's chair and Ty's.

"I took the liberty of preparing a plate of cookies," the butler announced.

Beth shot him a knowing, amused look. "What a nice surprise."

"Will that be all then, miss?"

"Yes, thank you, Harold."

He nodded and left the room.

"Harold thinks I haven't been eating enough," she confessed softly.

Ty inclined his head, looking her over. She had felt fragile and light in his arms. "I suspect Harold's right," he said.

She shot him a chiding look. "That's the problem with servants, they see more than they should."

Servants. Ty felt a sinking sensation. Once again he became intensely aware of his surroundings and felt more uncomfortable than ever.

Beth noticed. "What?" she asked, pouring coffee from a sparkling silver pot.

Ty cleared his throat and crossed his legs. "I'm, uh, I'm just not used to the idea of servants."

"I know it must seem strange to you," she said, passing the coffee cup to him on a saucer, "but Harold is more like family than a servant, even if he is paid rather well."

"Really? How well?" Ty asked absently, lifting his cup to his mouth. The yearly figure Beth named so casually almost had him spewing coffee. Instead, he swallowed the hot stuff, gasping afterward for cooling air. "Beth, that man makes more money than I do!" he exclaimed, returning the cup and saucer to the cart with a plunk.

"Well, he's probably been on the job a lot longer than you have," Beth said placatingly.

"That's not the point!" Ty exclaimed. "Beth, your servants make more money than I do."

"Harold also makes more money than *I* do," she said, "which is why I don't pay his salary. My mother does. And what has this got to do with anything?"

Ty pushed a hand through his hair. "I just...I don't belong in this world."

"No one's asking you to."

"But it's all you know!" he argued.

"It is not," she retorted. "I went to college. I've had my own apartment, paid my own bills. I was perfectly happy that way. I only moved back home at Mom's request. Now that Ellie's married, it's just me here, but I don't expect to live here forever."

He shook his head and blurted, "Beth, I can't give you this kind of life!"

She sat back in her chair and drew up her long legs, curling them beside her, a smile curving her lips. "Why would you say that?"

Suddenly he realized how much he'd revealed of what he'd been feeling, how deeply she'd gotten to him. Disgusted with himself, he said the only thing he could. "Because it's true!"

"So what? Why does it matter?"

"Because it does, that's all."

"Yet you say we can't be together," she challenged. "Have you changed your mind about that?"

"No, I...not now."

"Does that mean we'll be together later?"

His mind seemed to be whirling. "I didn't say that."

She stirred cream into her cup and slapped down the spoon. "So what difference does it make what kind of life we could have together?" she snapped.

He opened his mouth and closed it again. She was right. It shouldn't matter. It didn't. Except... Damn! She had him thinking of marriage. How did she do that? He rubbed a hand over his chin and jaw, feeling a bit like a wild animal caught in a snare. "I, um, I'm just trying to explain that you can't expect...rather, why we can't plan..."

The knock at the door sounded like salvation to Ty. He put a hand over his mouth in case something else tried to fall out of it, something even more dangerous than what he'd already let slip.

"Detective Jester, miss," Harold announced, and Ty silently blessed Paul for making such a quick trip. Beth rose and offered Paul her hand.

"Hello, Detective Jester. Would you like a cup of coffee? It's fresh."

Paul rubbed his hands together as he came toward the fire. "I think there's time for a cuppa joe," he said heartily.

"Could you bring another cup, Harold?" Beth asked.

"Right away, miss."

Might as well earn that fat salary, Ty thought sourly, scooping up his cup.

Beth directed Paul to a chair and offered him some cookies from a covered plate before doing the same to Ty.

"This is cozy," Paul remarked innocently, munching cookies. "Fire feels good. They're saying it might get down to freezing again tonight."

Ty nodded, his mouth full of cinnamony crunch. Harold returned almost immediately with the extra cup and saucer, and within moments they were all three chatting before the fire. Beth asked after Pauly and was regaled with stories of nursing an adventurous boy with a broken arm. Ty noted that Paul didn't seem at all ill at ease in this palatial room, but then Paul wasn't personally involved with Beth Maitland.

Paul kept casting curious glances at Ty, and Ty knew that he was wondering why the search was being made now, at this time of night. Fortunately, the forensics team arrived moments later. Harold announced them, and Ty stood at once. The anxious expression on Beth's face made him say, "You can come if you want, but you can't interfere."

"I won't get in the way," she promised, rising. "What do you want to see first?"

Ty cleared his throat. "Forensics will do the public rooms and grounds. I thought Paul and I would handle the private quarters."

She blinked, then shrugged. "All right. Upstairs."

They followed her out of the room and up the broad, sweeping staircase, down a hall and then another, and finally she threw open the door to a bedchamber roughly the size of his apartment. Everything was done in white and mint green and immaculately kept. Ty stepped in first, wishing suddenly that Paul was anywhere else but here. He took a deep breath and moved into the room.

"Anything in particular you want to see?" Beth asked uncertainly.

"The closet," Paul answered, and she pointed to a pair of double doors. "Let's start there," he said to Ty, taking out a pair of plastic gloves. Ty pulled out his own gloves, wincing at the necessity as he opened the small packet he habitually carried on his person.

Paul opened the closet doors, an overhead light flickering on automatically. The place was immense, a warren of racks and shelves and bins. It looked like a department store had been crammed into a boutique. He traded a wry look with Paul and went inside.

It felt strange pawing through Beth's things, but the search went far more smoothly than Ty had expected after viewing the extent of her wardrobe. Everything was organized with neat precision, each garment bagged and grouped with like garments. They made a very thorough search. Finding nothing, they moved into the bedroom and closed the doors.

"Do you have clothing anywhere else?" Ty asked. Beth pointed to a bank of drawers built into one wall.

They went at it systematically, carefully lifting out the silken, frilly undergarments and nightgowns. It was all Ty could do to keep from caressing the intimate lingerie or ordering Paul out of the room before he could do the same. He hated the thought of another man fingering the clothing she wore next to her skin, and when he came across the very pair of panties he'd removed from her body himself, he almost lost the ability to breathe. By the time the last drawer had been searched, Ty was a basket case, trembling and suffocating, his heart beating much too rapidly.

They went on to look through the remaining pieces of furniture, finding each drawer and cubbyhole neat and organized. They didn't find so much as a dust bunny under the bed or behind the drapes covering the deeply set windows.

"What's behind those doors?" Ty asked, pointing to first one, then another, in opposite walls.

"That one's the bath. The other connects to my sister's old room."

"You take the sister's room," Ty said to Paul, moving to the bath.

The bathroom was as clean as a surgery, all white and fern green. The deep, wide tub was ringed with frothy plants. The shower, Ty noted with gulping interest, was constructed of glass as clear as air. He could imagine her showering there all too well. It didn't take long to determine that he wasn't going to find what they were looking for there.

"We'll need to see the laundry," Paul told her, having finished with Ellie's room.

"I'll take you down there now."

Ty left her bedroom with great relief, following Beth and Paul. They went down the stairs into a back hall and down another flight of steps, this one less opulent, to a cavernous basement laundry. There were two washers and two dryers, two ironing boards, one equipped with a steamer that hung from the ceiling, and a dry-cleaning machine. Tables stood along the walls. Empty hangers hung on rolling racks. Wheeled baskets sat lined up, ready for use. A drip-dry line had been stretched across one end of the room, a rubber mat below it. Beth led them to the bank of bins on the opposite wall where clothing came down the laundry chutes.

Paul began at one end and Ty at the other. Carefully, they went through everything. Afterward, Ty made a list of the rooms yet to search, and Paul went off to assign specific ones to the forensic team, while Ty followed Beth upstairs to the nursery.

Beth dismissed the night nurse, and they stood together over the crib, waiting for Paul to join them.

"I'm sorry we have to wake him," Ty whispered, staring at the soft bundle slumbering so peacefully. He looked like a child's doll, pink-cheeked and plump-mouthed.

"Oh, it's all right," Beth answered softly, pulling the covers over one tiny foot that had worked its way free. "He'd soon be waking for his bottle anyway." She moved to the tiny kitchen nook and began preparing the formula. By the time Paul arrived, it was ready.

Very gently, Beth leaned over and patted the baby awake. He stretched, tiny fists raised above his head, back arching with amazing suppleness. Finally, the little eyes blinked open. "Hello, my love," Beth crooned, gathering the tiny body into her hands. "Come and let me hold you. That's my sweet boy." The babe smiled at her and latched on to a lock of her hair.

Ty's heart turned over. Of course she would be good at this, he told himself. It was her job. But he was mesmerized by how perfectly suited to the role of mother this incredibly sexy woman seemed to be. She carried the babe to the rocker and sat down with him, producing the bottle as the little one began to fuss.

Paul turned on the light and started the search. Ty felt sure his partner wasn't going to find what they were looking for here, and by the time Paul had finished, Beth had the baby fed and asleep again. They slipped out as the nurse came in.

An hour or more later, the three of them stood in the parlor where they'd begun. Forensics had since given it a thorough going-over.

"That about covers it," Paul announced.

"Can you tell me now what you were looking for?" Beth asked.

Ty looked at Paul, and Paul took it upon himself to answer. "According to forensics, Brianne Dumont was strangled with a thin silk cord, possibly from a garment, a hooded jacket or a pair of pants."

"I have both," Beth said unflinchingly.

"Yes, we know," Ty replied softly, "but according to the fibers found by forensics, your things are the wrong colors, and all the cords are right where they should be."

Paul winked at her and tugged off his plastic gloves. "We'll apply for a search warrant for Brandon Dumont's house first thing tomorrow morning."

Beth folded her arms and bit her lip thoughtfully. "He wouldn't be that careless."

"Probably not," Ty agreed, "but we still have to look."

"And who knows, we could get lucky," Paul said. "At least we didn't find the cord or the garment missing it here."

By the worried look on Beth's face Ty could tell she found little comfort in that. "Step by step," he reminded her. "We'll get there."

She smiled tremulously and swept her hand down his arm. "Thank you. Oh, and you, too, Detective Jester."

"No problem," Paul said. "Here to serve. It's part of the motto."

"Motto?" Beth repeated.

"To serve and protect," Ty clarified. "It's the motto stenciled on nearly every door of nearly every police cruiser nearly everywhere."

"Ah." She smiled again. "Well, if Detective Jester's here to serve, may I assume that you're here to protect?"

Ty bowed his head. He hadn't protected her thus far. In fact, he'd put her in jeopardy in more ways than one, taking her to that dive to interview Gustopherson and then taking her to bed. From here on in, he vowed silently, he *would* protect her, whatever the personal cost.

"Can I offer you gentlemen more coffee before you go?" she asked, sparing him a reply.

"No, thanks," Ty answered for them both, "but we appreciate the offer."

"All right then. I'll walk you out."

Ty followed her through the house, Paul bringing up the rear. At the front door, Harold stood waiting with their coats. Paul slipped out ahead of Ty, saying that he'd see his partner first thing tomorrow morning, but Beth snagged Ty's sleeve, delaying him until they were alone in the foyer.

"When will I see you again?" she asked softly.

He laid a hand over her cheek, cupping the delicate bones with his palm. "I don't know, but I'll call." He brushed his fingertips across her lips, denying himself the pleasure of kissing her, and turned away. How had it happened? he asked himself as he slowly descended the steps to his car. And what on earth was he going to do now that he'd fallen hopelessly in love with Beth Maitland?

CHAPTER TEN

BETH RECEIVED several phone calls from Ty during the next days, and much of the news was good. Letitia Velasquez and her son, Frankie, revealed all in two long interviews. Brandon had indeed supplied Frankie's phony immigration papers. Better yet, Frankie had picked them up from the bartender Gustopherson himself, and both Gustopherson and Brandon had been handsomely paid by Frankie and Letitia. Then Brandon had threatened to make an anonymous phone call to the authorities about Frankie if Letitia didn't back up his lies concerning Beth's supposed harassment of Brianne.

Ty had enough to arrest Gustopherson and Dumont on charges of providing and trafficking in false immigration papers. It was decided, however, to keep Dumont in the dark and use the forgery charge to pressure Gustopherson to tell the truth about Dumont's whereabouts at the time of the murder. To that end, Letitia was advised to develop a sudden desperate need to visit her sister in Houston, requiring Frankie to drive her there. The next step would be to bring Gustopherson in. Once in police custody, he would be confronted with the Velasquez charges. The subject of Brandon Dumont's alibi for the evening of his wife's murder would be brought up. If Gustopherson made a grab at the dangled bait—and Ty felt certain he would, since they'd already proved he'd lied to them about his mother having business with Dumont—then Dumont's alibi would evaporate.

Not all the news was hopeful, however. A very thorough search of Dumont's home had failed to turn up a garment with a missing silk cord, and authorities in California were balking at an unofficial request to search the late Mrs. Dumont's possessions, which Brandon had boxed and shipped to her brother with unseemly haste the day after her murder. They were a long way from home free.

Still, it did Beth good to talk to Ty. Their telephone conversations rambled on several minutes after the official update was delivered, and she discovered a surprising intimacy in this. Plus, she learned to read the nuances of his voice. He invariably dropped his tone into the lower ranges when the conversation became personal, and a touch of huskiness could transport her to those delicious moments in his bed. Sometimes she identified a rough wistfulness that squeezed her heart with gladness, for surely it meant that he wanted to be with her as much as she wanted to be with him. And then there was the sound of his laughter when she teased, and the bright edge of affection, and even the somberness of reluctance when it came time to say goodbye. Yes, it did her good to hear his voice. She replayed every word and tone endlessly, even when the subject was strictly business, but no one was more shocked than she when Harold cleared his throat one lonely evening and announced that Detective Redstone was waiting to see her.

She dropped the book with which she'd been entertaining herself, unfolded her legs from the comfy chaise before the fire and fairly sprinted into the foyer. Ty had shed his coat, revealing a brown sweater and wondrously snug jeans worn over cowboy boots. He turned at the sound of her footsteps. A sudden smile lit his face, and excitement fairly radiated from him.

"Can we talk?" he asked, his voice dropping into that husky, intimate range she had come to know so well.

She availed herself of his hand and nodded, flashing a

look at Harold. "Can we get you anything?" she asked of Ty. "Coffee? Something to eat?"

"Not a thing," he answered positively, his gaze locked on hers.

He didn't want them to be disturbed, and hope tingled through her. She dismissed the butler with a wave of her hand. "Thank you, Harold. I'll show Detective Redstone into the small parlor. If we need anything we'll ring."

"Very good, miss."

She caught the skirt of her long, blue silk caftan in one hand and kept his hand in her other as she hurried to the parlor, the soles of her slippers slapping against the marble floor until she reached the carpet. After they entered the room, she released him long enough to push the doors closed.

"What's happened?" she gasped, whirling to face him.

He took a step toward her, caught both her hands in his. "We arrested Gustopherson today. He told all. Dumont used the same threat with him that he did with the Velasquezes. Gustopherson would either provide the alibi or he, Dumont, would make an anonymous phone call to the cops and blow his forgery gig wide open."

She had expected it, and yet knowing it had happened was sweet, indeed. Momentarily she closed her eyes in thanks, then thought to ask, "What happens to Gustopherson now?"

"He took a deal on the forgery with stipulation. He testifies against Dumont and gets seven to twelve years." Ty shrugged and added, "He'll be out in four, tops, but everyone's satisfied. There's something else, too."

This, Beth sensed, was the true source of his excitement. "What is it?"

"The California cops came through. One of the guys in our office has a buddy on the job out there." He snapped his fingers. "A personal phone call and suddenly they're as cooperative as all get out."

"What exactly does that mean?" Beth asked, heart pounding.

"They've searched Brianne's things," Ty said. "The boxes Dumont had packed were still sealed." He paused, adding drama to the moment, then said, "They found a hooded silk jacket with the cord missing—a cord of the right color and size."

Beth squeezed his hands. "Oh, thank God!"

"Now, it doesn't prove that Dumont used that cord to kill her," he added, cautiously, "but it sure raises some interesting questions. For instance, how would *you* have gotten your hands on something that belonged to Brianne? We already have Letitia's testimony that you did not harass, call or drop in on Brianne, so that's out. But how did it get to the scene? Why would *she* have carried it with her to your supposed meeting? It doesn't make sense. Unless someone else who had access to that cord picked it up to use as a murder weapon."

"And Brandon had the access," Beth concluded flatly.

"Bingo."

She put her head back against the door and smiled. "I always knew he did it, and you kept promising me that you'd get to the truth, and now it's finally beginning to happen."

"Nothing is set in stone," Ty cautioned, "but it's looking better and better." He rubbed at the corner of one eye and muttered, "If I just had some way to tie Dumont to the murder, some piece of forensic, anything."

"What if we confront him with the evidence?" Beth suggested desperately. They were so close. *So close.* "Maybe he would cave in and admit everything."

"Do you really think so?" Ty asked doubtfully.

She bit her lip, wanting to say yes, knowing it wasn't so. Finally she shook her head, pushed away from the door and strode toward the chaise and the fire, prepared to mull over this problem.

Harold had helped her rearrange the furniture, pushing away the three wing chairs she and her mother and sister had occupied the last time Ty had been here, so the chaise could be shoved close to the fire. Resigned to spending the evening alone since her mother was dining with Ellie and Sloan and the twins, Beth had eaten a sandwich, then indulged herself with a glass of red wine, a bar of chocolate and a book on the chaise before the fire. Preoccupied, she dropped onto the comfy, tufted chaise and twisted to the side, draping an arm over the low, scrolled back.

"No, Brandon won't confess," she concluded. "He'd gloat if he could get away with it, though." The seed of an idea began to germinate, but before she could concentrate on it fully, Ty changed the subject.

"What is that you're wearing?"

He had followed her to the chaise, and she glanced up in surprise before looking at herself, holding out her arms so that the long dolman sleeves fanned out. The front zipper had been slightly pulled open, revealing the rounded slopes of her unfettered breasts. The skirt had skewed around, causing the long slit in one side to part all the way to the thigh. She sat up straight and tugged her clothing into place. "It's a caftan," she explained a little defensively, "sort of a housedress."

"Some housedress," he said, "I thought it was an evening gown when I saw it in your closet."

It was impossible to miss the husky tone of desire in his voice. Suddenly the fire on the hearth wasn't the only blaze going.

"It's hardly more formal than a bathrobe," she commented, trying to cover her breathlessness with a little laugh.

He said nothing for a moment, just stood there staring at her. When next he spoke, his voice was as soft as the silk she wore, and she felt it just as keenly against her skin. "It suits you," he said. "Everything does, though. I keep asking myself if this world holds anything lovelier than you."

The compliment washed over her, dangerously seductive. She tried to make light of it, though her heart was beating so hard and fast she could barely think. "Keep talking like that and I'll take it off," she quipped in a sultry drawl.

His eyes widened, and then he grinned. "Promises, promises."

She stared at him, trying to decide if what she thought was happening was really happening. Then he quirked an eyebrow, as if to ask whether or not she was going to make good on her threat, and gladness poured through her. Slowly she rose to her feet, her gaze welded to his. Reaching up, she plucked free the barrette that held her hair in a loose chignon and dropped it to the floor. Then her hand fell to the zipper, and she began pulling it smoothly down until the dress was open to the knees. Next, she shrugged the dress off her shoulders and let it fall into a puddle at her feet, leaving her standing in front of him in nothing more than panties and a pair of flat, mule-type slippers, her hair tumbling about her face and bare shoulders.

He ate her with his eyes, a slight smile curving his mouth, and then he pulled his sweater over his head and dropped it on the arm of a chair. With one hand he reached for the snap on the waistband of his jeans, and with the other he reached for her, bringing her hard against him.

"I need my head examined," he confessed, but he was smiling wide when he said it.

"Well, let me examine it for you," she teased, grinning as she ran a hand up his thigh.

He danced away, chuckling. "I think I need to do some examining myself." His dark eyes swept over her as he began slipping free the buttons on his fly.

A small, distant sound had Beth glancing toward the door. "I'd better lock it," she said, rushing to do just that, her hands covering her naked breasts as the air grew cooler away from the fire. By the time she'd turned back, he was sitting on the chaise, pants open, stripping off his boots and socks. She skimmed off her shoes and started toward him as he stood and slid a tiny foil package from his front pocket. Quickly, he dropped the packet onto the chaise, shoved down his jeans and underwear and stepped out of them. Then he lifted a hand to her. She clasped her palm to his, and he pulled her into his arms.

"All the way over here tonight, I was scheming fever-ishly how to get you alone," he confessed, pressing his forehead to hers.

"You'd only have to ask," she told him bluntly.

"That both pleases and terrifies me, Beth," he said hon-estly, lifting his head. "We're taking such a chance. We could compromise your case."

She didn't want to hear that, didn't want to think about it. Deliberately, she dropped her gaze to his mouth. "Are you going to make love to me or talk?" she demanded.

That mouth curled into a grin. "Neither," he said, drop-ping onto the chaise and peeling her panties down her legs. She stepped out of them, and he swivelled on his rump, pulling her on top of him as he settled on the chaise. "You're going to make love to me this time."

She straddled him, smiling hotly. "Oh, yeah?"

"Yeah." He clasped one wrist and turned up her palm, slapping the condom into it. Laughing softly, she tore the foil with her teeth and listened to him groan as she fitted him with the sheath. He was trembling and breathing hard by the time she was done. He combed his fingers through her hair and cupped her face with his hands. "Quick," he urged. "I need it quick, Beth."

She pressed her mouth to his, braced her hands against the back of the chaise and shifted forward on her knees, positioning herself. He dropped his hands to her waist and pushed her down, moaning into the hollow of her mouth as she took him inside her body. Then he filled his hands with her breasts as she began to move over him, giving them both what they wanted, needed, as the storm built and spun around them.

He came before her, throwing his hips upward and his head back, gritting his teeth. She never stopped moving, but he seemed hardly aware of it as he gasped an apology. "I'm sorry. It was too much!"

"No," she managed to moan, her ears roaring. He shifted, lifting her breasts and seizing one nipple between his teeth. The roar became a howl that crashed over her in waves. She didn't realize she'd cried out until she surfaced some moments later and found that he'd clamped a hand over her mouth. He was kissing her neck and biting it in a lavish show of affection, one arm wrapped about her waist. She laughed deep in her throat, marvelously replete.

That was when the door handle rattled and her mother's urgent voice cried, "Beth! Are you all right? Beth!"

Both their heads zipped around, eyes going to the door.

"Beth? Beth!"

In sudden panic, both scrambled for clothes.

"I'm all right, Mother!" she called, stabbing her feet into her panties and yanking them up—backward. Ty tossed her the dress and shimmied into his jeans, cramming his shorts into his pocket as he reached for his sweater.

"I heard a cry," her mother said through the door, rattling the knob again.

"I'm all right, Mother!" Beth repeated loudly. "Just a minute, please!"

As she threw on her dress and Ty snatched his socks, Beth heard someone else, probably Harold, on the other side of the door with Megan. She prayed that he would keep her mother occupied for a few more seconds, at least. While cramming her feet into her shoes, she spied the barrette on the floor. She plucked it up and quickly began gathering her hair.

"Hurry!" she warned Ty.

"I am hurrying!" he retorted, struggling with his socks. "I knew this was a mistake. Hell and damnation, why did I do it? Why?"

Beth wrapped her hair on top of her head, clipped the barrette over it and dropped her hands to her hips. "Because you couldn't help yourself," she whispered fiercely, irritated with his refusal to admit the obvious. "You want me. You're in love with me! Why don't you admit it?"

He glared at her, working on the buttons of his fly, and she saw that he still had to pull on his boots. She hurried to the door, waving away her irritation and ordering needlessly, "Stay here!"

He muttered something under his breath, which she chose to ignore. Reaching the door, she paused to take a calming breath, lifted her chin, then released the lock and opened the door just wide enough to push through it, causing her mother to back up. Beth pulled the door closed firmly behind her and kept her hand on the knob, pasting a taut smile on her face.

Megan Maitland stood with folded arms, one toe tapping impatiently. Beth recognized the flash of fire in those blue eyes and mentally gulped.

"Mother. I wasn't expecting you...so soon."

Megan Maitland tilted her head, staring at her daughter. "Obviously," she said, and Beth bit her lip. Megan slid her hands to her hips. "Harold just told me that Ty Redstone is in there."

"Uh, yes."

"I didn't know that when I heard you yell. What was I to think?"

Beth's heart lurched, but she lifted her chin a notch higher. "I'm sorry if I worried you. It was nothing."

Megan rolled her eyes. "I know exactly what it was, young lady, and I don't appreciate it, not here under my roof, in the family room, for pity's sake!"

"It wasn't planned," she said softly.

Megan swiped a hand across her brow agitatedly, her slender fingers moving on to smooth the elegant line of her upswept hair. "That gives me no peace of mind. I wonder if you even know what you're doing?"

"I love him, Mother."

"You said *that* about Brandon Dumont," Megan pointed out gently.

"This is different," Beth said without the slightest qualm. "I wanted to love Brandon and couldn't. I can't help loving Ty."

Her mother stared at her for a moment, blue eyes plumbing blue eyes; then she sighed and melted. "Do you know what chances you are taking, both of you?"

Beth nodded. "It doesn't seem to stop us, though."

"That's what worries me," Megan said bluntly.

"I don't know what else to tell you, Mother," Beth admitted apologetically. "If it's any consolation, Ty has been as worried as you."

"I suppose I should be comforted by that, but somehow I'm not." Megan shook her head. "You've always been impulsive, dear, but never heedless. Now you're telling me that, despite the risks, you can't help yourself, and neither, apparently, can your young man. I'm afraid for you, Beth."

"I'm afraid for me, too," Beth confessed. "I'm afraid that I'm going to lose Ty, either to his own nobility or Brandon's lies."

Megan's expression softened. "Try to be sensible," she cautioned, but Beth knew herself too well to make any promises along that line.

"I'm not sure I can be."

"I don't want you hurt!" Megan said sternly. "And I don't want him hurt, either."

Beth smiled wanly. "Neither do I," she whispered. "I can promise you this much, Mother. I'll never willingly do anything to hurt Ty."

Megan sighed and leaned forward to kiss her daughter's

cheek. "All the more reason to behave yourselves," she admonished, but the warmth in her eyes belied the tone of her voice. She offered a troubled smile, then turned and walked away.

Beth waited until her mother was halfway up the stairs before opening the door and slipping inside. A fully dressed Ty was pacing in front of the chaise, one hand skimming the hair from his forehead.

"This cannot happen again!" he vowed the instant he saw her.

Feeling accused and emotionally battered, Beth sagged against the closed door. "You said that the last time."

"Well, this time I mean it!"

This was *not* how she wanted the evening to end, but she resented the censure in his voice. Couldn't he see that her heart was full to overflowing? Didn't he understand that she shared his worries and fears? "You came to me, Redstone," she said with more asperity than she intended. "Don't act as if I seduced you against your will."

"You stripped!" he accused.

"You dared me to!"

"Do you strip for everyone who dares you to?" he demanded angrily.

She narrowed her eyes, ready, willing and able to fight, if that was the way he wanted it. "No one's ever dared me to before," she said flippantly, hunching a shoulder.

He moved before she could register it and was standing with his hand clamped around her upper arm before she could look at him. He shook her slightly. "You ever take your clothes off for anyone but me, and I swear I'll..."

"You'll what?" she prodded, inwardly thrilled. "Arrest me? I don't think so, Ty. I don't think so at all."

He ground his teeth together, and suddenly she was miserably sorry for her taunting words. Regretfully, she lifted a hand to his heaving chest, and all the fight seemed to drain out of him, too. He pulled her against him, looped his arms about her loosely, his big hands warm against her back. He laid his forehead on hers and closed his eyes.

"What your mother must think of me," he said miserably.

"I don't care what she thinks."

He snorted at that. "The hell you don't. You said it yourself, remember? Family is every bit as important to you as it is to me."

"All right," she recanted, mumbling against his chest. "I do care, but I care for you more."

He groaned. "All the more reason this can't happen again," he said. "There's too much at stake for both of us. Help me, Beth. Help me do what I must."

"How can I?" she asked tremulously.

"Be strong," he whispered, but she felt that he said it as much to himself as to her.

She took a deep breath. "I can be strong," she said determinedly, "strong enough not to make love to you again until—"

"Until!" he exclaimed, breaking away to swing around angrily. "Until when, Beth? Until we're free to screw our brains out without fear of being caught at it? Because that's all I really have to offer you!"

She reached to the table behind her and found her book, then threw it at him. He ducked it easily, as she knew he would, and the book clunked harmlessly to the floor. She thought of throwing something else but decided she'd made her point since he was staring at her, mouth slightly ajar, as if she'd grown a second head. She folded her arms. "That's not true," she told him flatly, "and I won't let you believe it is. I mean it, Ty. I won't be responsible for my own actions if you say such a thing to me again!"

He opened his mouth, closed it, then opened his arms once more. She walked into them, weeping suddenly. "I'm sorry. I'm so sorry." He crooned words she didn't recognize, his native language, until she quieted and snuffled against his chest.

"No one's ever made me so mad as you do," she said.

"I know. I know. I shouldn't have been so crude."

"It wasn't that!" she exclaimed. "It's this stupid notion you have that I'm better than you, that I should expect better than you. I want to smack you every time you say it." She gripped fistfuls of his shirt. "Don't you understand? No one's better than you, especially not me."

He stroked her hair, gathered it into his fist and tugged her head back. "If that were true," he began softly, "if I was as good a man as I should be, I wouldn't be here now. I'd have managed to stay away."

"Ty, no," she pleaded.

"I can't let this happen again," he said firmly, "for your sake."

"But—"

His two fingers across her mouth silenced her. "We won't speak of *until* or *after,* because those times may never come for us, Beth. But you're right in one sense. I want you like I've never wanted anyone before or ever will again." He smiled wryly. "You're right about more than that, even, but it doesn't matter. We are what we are, Beth."

"You're a man, Ty," she told him plainly. "More man than any I've ever known. And I'm just a woman, nothing more, nothing less."

"I wish it was that simple," he said.

"It's as simple as you let it be, Ty," she replied, desperation and anger edging her voice. "As simple as *you* let it be."

He tilted his head, as if she were a puzzle he was trying to figure out, a picture he couldn't quite see. "Sweetheart, don't you understand that circumstances conspire against us? I am a poor man, a Native American cop. You're a rich, beautiful woman accused of a crime you didn't commit. I've already compromised your position and my own. I cannot let it continue. I will not. Much as I want to.''

His gaze switched to her mouth, and he bent his head to kiss her gently, lingeringly. She'd felt that kiss before, but it scored her even deeper this time, frightened her in a way it could not have done before. How often, after all, could he say goodbye until he really meant it? And how would she survive if she couldn't change his mind?

TY PROPPED HIS ELBOWS on his desk and let his head fall into his hands. It wasn't happening. He could feel it. Gustopherson seemed to want to pull it off, to wear the wire and get Dumont to admit to the alibi, but the man was as subtle as a raging bull and terrified on top of it. Jester knew it, too. The look he settled on Ty said it all.

"We could be giving Dumont too much credit," he said hopefully.

Ty nodded. "Yeah, and I could win the lottery without buying a ticket."

Jester flipped a hand in question. "You want to just forget the wire?"

Ty shook his head. "I don't see any better option, do you? Dumont didn't so much as blink when we confronted him."

"Maybe we're using the wrong bait," Paul ventured carefully, and Ty knew he was talking about substituting Beth for Gustopherson. A wild kind of anger rose in him, but he beat it back determinedly.

"I'm not even going to discuss this with you," he managed to say at last.

Paul sighed and lifted his hands pleadingly. "You're not being rational about this, old buddy. I understand that Dumont's a cool customer, that he has it in for her, but—"

"If you understood, you wouldn't be suggesting that we wire Beth and send her in to grill a murderer!" Ty interrupted. "For pity's sake, don't you think the woman's been through enough?"

Paul didn't bother to answer that. He knew better, apparently, than to beat a dead horse. He chose, instead, to offer empty comfort. It was all he had to offer since they'd come up on this brick wall. Without hard forensic evidence, they'd never make a conviction—unless Dumont confessed, and they both knew how likely that was.

"Maybe we're selling old Gus short," Paul said. "He might not get an outright confession, but he could get Dumont to implicate himself. And we've always got the trading-in-forged-documents charge."

"That would get Dumont time," Ty replied, "but it wouldn't clear Beth."

His partner's pale, guileless eyes studied him openly. "I'm not the D.A., but I can't believe it would go to trial. Any halfway decent lawyer would make a case against Dumont in her defense. The worst that could happen is that you and I will come off looking like goobers for not being able to settle the thing. I don't think it'll even go to court, though. She's a Maitland, after all. The powers that be are going to want an airtight case before they take a Maitland to trial."

Ty rubbed both hands over his face, weighing his words. Paul Jester looked like an overgrown cherub, but he was as sharp as a tack and deeply insightful. He was also Ty's partner and friend. In the end, Ty sighed and said, "I need her cleared, Paul."

Paul stared at him for a long time. "Okay," he said finally. "If that's the way it has to be, we'll just have to make it happen."

They were running out of options, Ty knew, and facing a permanent limbo that left him and Beth exactly nowhere. He would do anything—short of putting her in danger—to prove Beth's innocence. Unfortunately, he was fresh out of ideas. Maybe if he took a step back, tried another approach. "You a praying man, Paul?"

Those pale eyes flickered. "Yeah, I've been known to wing a fervent plea or two."

Ty got up and took his overcoat off the peg on the wall. "I'm taking some personal time. If anyone needs me, I'll be at my mother's, but I'd rather not be disturbed." He did not confirm that he was about to seek an ancient remedy for a troubled spirit. He didn't have to.

"To each his own," Paul murmured. "I reckon it wouldn't hurt to light a candle."

It wouldn't hurt, Ty thought glumly as he walked away, but would it help?

CHAPTER ELEVEN

"DETECTIVE JESTER." Beth glanced behind him, hoping, expecting to see Ty, and her disappointment must have shown.

"He's not with me, ma'am," the detective informed her bluntly. "I didn't even tell him I was coming, and I expect there'll be hell to pay when he finds out, but I had to have your read on something and figured Ty just might get in the way."

"I see." She didn't, actually, but at least Ty had not let Jester come alone. She gestured toward the leather chair placed at a slight angle before the matching couch where she sat in the library, a book on child care open at her side. "What is it that you need, Detective?"

He sat, brushing back the sides of the rumpled overcoat he'd obviously not allowed Harold to take, and leaned forward, elbows on his knees. "Well, it's like this. Dumont's been a brick wall, answers for everything, so we're wiring Gustopherson, the bartender, and sending him in to try to get Dumont to implicate himself."

Beth's first impulse was to laugh, her second was to groan in dismay. She did both without quite meaning to. "It won't work," she said. "Brandon's too smart. He'll never implicate himself, not to Gustopherson or anyone else he considers beneath him."

"I agree," Jester said flatly. "That's why I'm here."

Beth shook her head. "I don't understand. If you agree that it's doomed to failure, then why go through with it?"

Jester spread his hands. Beth couldn't help noticing how pale and square they were in comparison with Ty's. "Don't have any other option, at least not so far as Ty's concerned."

"But you think otherwise?" Beth probed.

"I'm hoping that *you* think otherwise," he answered obliquely, and she knew from the way he watched her that he was hoping for some definite response from her.

She crossed her legs, mulling it over. A wire. That meant a covert attempt to get Brandon to admit he had murdered Brianne and framed Beth for it. An undercover police operation. She imagined rooms full of sophisticated listening apparatus and armed officers on standby. What she couldn't imagine was Brandon spilling his guts without very good reason. In fact, the only inducement she could comprehend as being sufficient to loosen his tongue was the need to gloat. He wouldn't give that need free rein with anyone but her, since she was obviously the object of his malice. Otherwise, he wouldn't have worked so hard to frame her for Brianne's murder. She made a snap decision, one that required very little thought.

"I'll wear the wire."

Jester sat back, a small smile playing at the corners of his lips. "I thought you might say that."

"It's the only thing that makes sense," she told him, desperately trying to convince him. "Brandon hates me for breaking up with him. He blamed Brianne, but he also blames me because he knows Brianne was only a convenient excuse. He intended to pay us both back by murdering her and framing me for it. If anyone can make him implicate himself, I can, but only I can."

"You understand that this is not without risk?" Jester asked pointedly. "If Dumont hates you, as you say, and he discovers the wire, you could be in danger."

"But you won't let him harm me," she stated confidently.

He smiled. "I was thinking we'd do it at his office, so there are others around."

She sat up straight. "Yes, that makes sense. Even though the office is set off by itself, his secretary will be there."

"There are no guarantees," he warned her.

"I understand."

"And it could be dangerous."

"It's worth the risk," she assured him firmly.

Jester shifted uncomfortably, as if adjusting the fit of his coat across his shoulders. "You have to know something else."

"And that would be?"

He shifted again. Obviously, whatever it was weighed heavily on Detective Jester's shoulders. "Without a doubt, Ty is going to hit the roof when he hears this. In fact, I expect him to try to stop it."

"Because it puts me in danger, however slight," she surmised, and Paul Jester nodded.

"I actually hinted at something like this earlier, and he practically demolished me with that warrior look of his."

Beth smiled knowingly and not without a touch of sadness. "Can he stop it?"

"No. But he's not going to be happy with either of us."

He wasn't happy with her now, but that was beside the point. Would his anger over this be enough to put an end to the relationship? On the other hand, the relationship wasn't going anywhere as it was. She figured she might as well take this chance to clear her name and put an end to the nightmare and hope that Ty would come around. Still, she hesitated. She'd made so many mistakes already. Making love with him had exacerbated them. If only she hadn't convinced herself, even for a short time, that she could love Brandon! She hadn't realized just how stupid that was until she'd truly fallen in love with Ty. But could her timing have been any worse? And why hadn't she stopped what was happening between them, instead of recklessly plunging ahead. Now, after the intimacy of sharing her body with him, it hurt so badly to feel the distance between them. She couldn't help hoping he would call and being disappointed when he didn't. Every moment brought a sense of loss and emptiness. Perhaps if the murder investigation was over, Ty would be more open to loving her in return—if he wasn't so angry with her that he couldn't get past it.

And yet, what choice did she have? She could, very possibly, clear herself once and for all. Or she could agonize for months, maybe even years. Whatever happened afterward, be it sooner or later, was up to Ty.

"So what's it going to be?" Jester asked. "Do we risk it, or do we do it Ty's way?"

Beth took a deep breath. "We risk it."

The detective got to his feet. "I'll make the arrangements and get back to you."

"Do you think he'll be very angry?" Beth had to ask, rising also.

"Very," Paul answered flatly. "That's why I won't tell him about this until everything's set. I suggest you don't, either."

Beth's mouth thinned with bitter resignation. "Not to worry. I'm persona non grata these days. He doesn't seem to know I exist."

"Don't you believe it," Paul scoffed, "which is why he's going to want my guts for garters when he finds out about this. But don't worry. If everything goes as planned, he'll get over it."

"And if it doesn't?"

"Well, then," Paul answered softly, "I'll be looking for another partner—and you'll be on your own, kiddo."

"We'll just have to make it work then." Beth vowed.

"Yes, we will," Paul agreed, holding her gaze, "for his sake, I think, as much as yours." He gave her a small salute and walked away, insisting that he could see himself out. Beth hugged herself, thinking how well Paul Jester seemed to know Ty. She only hoped they were doing the right thing.

Within the hour she had devised no less than a dozen scenarios that would make Brandon Dumont admit his guilt—and win her another man's love.

"YOU'VE DONE *WHAT*?" Ty was on his feet, on the verge of going over the desk, before he could check his movement.

"Just calm down," Paul said in a tone guaranteed to put Ty over the edge.

"Are you out of your mind?" Ty demanded, throwing up his hands and beginning to pace the small area beside his and Jester's desks. "What on earth were you thinking? She can't go wired into Dumont's office! He could kill her before you could get a man into the room."

"He won't do that," Paul argued with irritating calm, "not in his office with his secretary just outside the door. That's why we chose that setting."

Ty heard the words but couldn't absorb them. He could only think of and speak to one worry. "It's too dangerous. I won't let her do it."

Paul sighed and folded his arms, rocking back in his chair. "Sorry, old buddy," he said gently, "but you don't have any say in the matter. I've submitted the plan to the cap'n and received his approval. It's all set up and ready to go."

"You did this without me?" Ty slammed a hand on the edge of his desk. "Damn you, Paul!"

His partner shook his head. "We didn't have any choice. You'd have shot us down."

Ty was reeling. "We? Us? You have a mouse in your pocket, man?"

Paul rocked his chair forward. "Naturally Beth Maitland was a part of the decision-making process."

"You and Beth," Ty said, anger reigniting as the implications fully sank in. "Beth was part of the decision-making process—" Ty thumped himself on the chest "—but *I* wasn't!"

"If you were rational about this—" Paul began wearily.

"Rational?" Ty threw up his hands again. "Rational? You call sending her in alone to get a confession out of a murderer *rational?*"

"Everyone agrees that it's our best shot."

"Everyone but me!" Ty retorted. "You're my partner! How could you go around me on this?"

"You left me no choice," Paul answered quietly, and even though Ty knew it was true, he couldn't accept what had been done, what was going to happen. He leaned against his desk, hands spread flat atop the blotter.

"I won't let you do this."

"We have to do it, Ty."

"No!"

Paul shook his head. "I'm sorry. You do what you have to—and I'll do the same. You'll thank me when it's over with."

"Thank you?" Ty stalked around the desk, reached down and hauled his unresisting partner, his friend, to his feet by his lapels. "This is my life we're talking about, Paul, *my* career, *my* future. If anything happens to her, it's all over. She has to come first. I have to stop you."

"Like I said," Paul replied mildly, "you do what you have to."

For an instant, Ty was disappointed. He'd have liked Paul to bristle, to hump up, to give him any excuse to put a fist in his baby face. Instead, he shamed Ty with his gentle, trusting demeanor. Ty released him and stepped back, struggling to control his volatile emotions.

"I need her safe," he exclaimed raggedly. "Don't you understand that I need her safe?"

"I understand," Paul said, and Ty saw that he did. It was all right there in those pale, guileless eyes. Ty shook his head. Had he imagined that he could keep the greatest truth of his life from his best friend and partner? He should have known better, and that realization made this betrayal all the more painful.

"If anything happens to her because of this," he said hoarsely, "we're through, you and me. We're finished."

Paul nodded and looked away, sliding his hands into his pants pockets. Ty wanted to shout, to scream, but he couldn't find any way to take the words back, for if he lost Beth, he lost Paul, too. How could he bear that? How could he bear it?

"I'm going to talk to the captain," he said, knowing it was useless but needing to try anyway. He stared at the silent Paul for another moment, then whirled away.

Behind him, Paul sighed, took his hands from his pockets and sat at his desk. Carefully, he turned over the small religious medal in his right hand. Then he closed his fist tight around it and shoved it into his pocket. His face was bleak as he pulled a file from a stack, flipped it open and began to read.

BETH PERCHED on the narrow bench seat running along one wall of the nondescript van and took slow, even breaths. Her pulse was racing, but she was determined not to show it. Paul Jester hovered over a captain's chair where a female technician wearing thick glasses and headphones sat. She concentrated on the laptop computer balanced on her knees and a beat-up reel-to-reel system at her feet. The van floor was a web of cables and wires, most of which Beth suspected were perfectly useless.

Minutes earlier, the technician had tossed Paul and the driver out of the van while she'd wired Beth, who'd been instructed to wear a blouse with simple buttons. After opening the plain white cotton blouse, the technician had clamped innocent-looking silver covers over each of the buttons. One of the covers was a microphone attached to a thin wire, which was glued to Beth's torso with flesh-colored cloth tape. It wrapped around her chest just below the band of her bra and followed her spine to the small of her back, where a tiny transmitter-receiver encased in a small, flexible pinkish tube was taped in place just beneath the waistband of her black jeans. With a red-and-black tweed cardigan over her shirt and a scarf tied jauntily at her neck, no one would ever be the wiser. At least that was the plan.

Beth had rolled up the sides of her hair and left the back to flow in crinkles and curls over her shoulders. The silver earrings and belt buckle that she wore complemented the button covers nicely. Her small handbag, which matched her black, western-style boots, contained a small canister of pepper spray, but she knew that the wire was her first and most important avenue of defense. She wasn't really frightened, just nervous. It would have helped to have Ty at her side. She'd promised herself she wouldn't ask, but she couldn't help herself when Paul turned and took a seat next to her.

"How you doing?"

"Okay," she answered. "I expected Ty to at least be here, though."

"Oh, he's around," Paul assured her entirely too lightly. "He's taking a last reconnoiter, making sure everyone's in place. You understand the setup? Want to go over it again?"

She shook her head. "He must be terribly angry. I expected him to try to talk me out of it."

Paul sighed. "The cap'n forbade it. The truth is, Ty threw such a fit that the cap'n put him on in-house suspension. He's been tied to a desk in the clerical department all week. I had to do some tall talking to get the cap'n to relent and let him come along."

A sudden lump filled Beth's throat. The last thing she wanted to do was to get Ty in trouble. She knew how important his career was to him. "I hope he'll forgive me," she murmured, and Paul clamped a strong hand on her shoulder.

"He will," Paul insisted. "It's me he'll likely hold responsible. I went behind his back, after all."

"I'm so sorry, Paul."

"Hey, not your worry. You just concentrate on the job at hand. Remember that you have to report movement. You have to let us know when you cross the street. Just speak naturally, like you're talking to yourself. That's our signal to swing into place. The van should pull up in front of the building about the same time you walk inside. Don't look for us. Just do your job, and we'll do ours. Got it?"

"Got it."

"Okay, let's take a walk."

He fished what looked like a hearing aid out of his pocket and twisted it into his ear, then slid open the side door of the van. The door hid the logo of the florist shop painted on the rear panel, so it didn't look particularly odd to a casual passerby when a couple stepped onto the sidewalk empty-handed. Paul took her elbow and turned her up the street, strolling casually by her side. When they reached the corner, he stopped and turned to face her.

"Okay," he said, as if speaking to her, "how's the com link? Any problems?" He glanced around, then looked at her. "Say something."

"Uh, wh-what should I say?"

"Excellent," he announced, speaking to the technician again. "Terrific." He reached for Beth's arm and turned her around the corner. "So, we're set. I'm going to stop up here and turn back. You go on around the next corner and cross the street. I'll be in the van. As soon as I get there, I'll radio the rest of the team and then I'll put you on the broad band so everyone can hear what's going on." He slid her a look out of the corner of his eye and added, "I promised Ty."

She looked down, grateful that Ty was at least within hearing distance and expressing some concern for her safety. Paul stopped and she turned to face him.

"You ready?"

"Ready," she confirmed confidently.

"Okay, let's go nail the lid on Dracula's coffin, eh?"

Laughter burst out of her at Paul's choice of image. "Shouldn't I be carrying a crucifix?"

"Good point," he said, jamming a hand into his pants pocket. He extracted a fistful of change—and something that he picked out carefully and handed to her. "My mom gave me this the day I joined the force—for protection, she said."

The medal in Beth's hand was worn almost smooth, giving the impression that it was well used, well loved. "I can't take this," she said.

"Hey, don't get me wrong. I expect it back when we're finished. Just consider it a little temporary insurance."

Beth grinned. "In that case, I'll take good care of it."

Paul nodded, and Beth leaned forward impulsively to kiss his cheek. His pale complexion instantly burned bright red. She slipped the medal into her pocket, feeling inexplicably calmer.

"No chances," Paul instructed, pointing a finger at her as he backed away. "He threatens you in any fashion, you get out of there, and say it so we'll know what's going down. Clear?"

"Clear," Beth said, starting off down the sidewalk alone.

Paul watched for a moment, then turned and headed swiftly the way he'd come.

She walked down the sidewalk, feeling the sunshine on her face. The air was crisp but utterly still here in this highrise canyon of steel and glass and concrete. Tires whirred on pavement as a luxury auto passed. A man in a gray suit carrying a briefcase and talking into a cell phone brushed past her without ever glancing up. Somewhere in the distance a delivery truck was backing up, its safety siren *whoop-whoop-whooping* into the near silence. Brakes screeched in another direction, so far away that she normally would not have even noticed.

She turned the corner and continued to the center of the block, where a crossing light facilitated rush hour traffic leaving the parking garage that linked the twin glass towers known as Lone Star Finance Central. Beth paused beside the light pole and pressed the crossing button, waiting for the walk light, despite a dearth of traffic in either direction. The light winked on.

"Crossing the street now," she announced cheerily as she stepped off the curb. A silver car coming from the opposite direction pulled to the curb in front of the office building, and a passenger hopped out. Beth recognized him instantly, despite the dark glasses and very expensive black suit. Jake. She almost said her brother's name, biting back the sound at the last instant. He hurried into the building without acknowledging her in any way.

She caught up to him in the foyer, where he leaned against a wall, his glasses parked on the tip of his nose and his arms folded. She opened her mouth to ask what he was doing there, but he lifted a finger to his lips and winked. Obviously he knew what was going on, and just as obviously he didn't want the police alerted to his presence. But how had he known? She hadn't told a soul, not even Ellie, for fear of worrying everyone. Of course. Ty.

A feeling of well-being suffused her. Ty was doing everything he could to protect her, even going so far as to bring in her brother to watch her back. Jake pushed his glasses onto his nose and shoved open the inner door for her. She walked briskly into the lobby, the heels of her boots tapping out a rapid staccato on the marble floor. They walked, seemingly apart, to the elevator bank in a small hallway off one end of the expansive lobby. Jake moved to the far wall and pushed the down button for an elevator.

Beth went to the opposite wall and pushed the up button. The down elevator came first and went on its way, empty. When the door to the up elevator closed, Jake was on it with her. He pushed the floor button above the one she chose. They rode in silence to the seventh floor, Jake pantomiming that he would come back down the stairs to be at hand if she needed him. Beth nodded her understanding, blew him a silent kiss and squared her shoulders just as the elevator slid to a halt. Jake folded his arms and pressed into the corner as the doors parted and she stepped off.

She walked down the hall and made a left turn, ignoring the bustle of bodies around her. Telephones rang, voices babbled, carts wheeled past pushed by secretaries or mail clerks. Brandon's office occupied the last suite at the end of a long hallway. He'd always said that he liked the privacy. Beth nodded at his secretary, a tall, cool blonde, through the glass wall. The secretary recognized her, of course, and was on the intercom before Beth walked through the door. A heartbeat later, the door to Brandon's office opened, and he appeared.

"Hello, Brandon," she said, for benefit of those listening. He gave her a hard look, then nodded at the secretary and stepped back, waving Beth through the door into the inner office.

She turned her shoulders as she slipped past him. "Thank you for seeing me."

He closed the door and leaned against it, sliding his hands into the pockets of his brown slacks. He wore a white shirt, and his silk tie had been loosened. His suit jacket hung on a brass coat tree across the room between the single window and a large armoire, which she knew hid a sink, bar and small closet with a mirrored door.

"Well, well," he said, "the princess herself."

The words were laced with such venom that Beth's hands began to tremble. She sat uninvited in the burgundy leather wing chair in front of his desk and placed her handbag in her lap. She adjusted her cardigan, flipping back its sides as if she were warm.

"Let me guess," he said, pushing away from the door. "You've come to offer an apology."

Beth gaped at him as he walked around the desk and sat in the expensive burgundy leather executive chair. "Why would I do that?"

"In hopes of getting out of this mess you're in, of course. Sorry I can't help you, however sweetly you plead."

Her heart was beating wildly, but she lifted her chin. "I'm not in a mess, Brandon, despite your best efforts."

"Oh, aren't you?" he scoffed, pressing his fingertips together as he leaned back and propped his elbows on the arms of the chair. "Not even a Maitland can get away with murder."

"You know I didn't kill Brianne."

"Do I?"

She ignored that. "And because I didn't do it, I don't have to worry about getting away with it," she said calmly.

He sat forward suddenly, his palms smashing down on the blotter sitting dead center on his desk. "You think you can get out of it just because you're a Maitland," he said, sneering.

"No, you think that," she replied smoothly. "You've always credited the Maitland name with powers it's never held."

"Then why are you here instead of sitting in jail?" he demanded, shoving himself to his feet. "They have more than enough evidence to arrest you!"

"You made sure of that, didn't you?" she prodded. "Don't bother to deny it. I know you set me up."

Silent, Brandon leaned his hands against the desktop, smiling smugly.

Despite the prickling sensation at the back of her neck, Beth forced herself to remain calm. "Why did you do it, Brandon? That's what I don't understand."

"Whatever's happening to you, Beth, you deserve," he said enigmatically.

"Why? Because I broke up with you?"

"Brianne didn't matter!" he exclaimed. "I told you that."

"It wasn't Brianne, and you know it," Beth persisted. "I'd have broken it off with you anyway. As hard as I tried, I couldn't be in love with you, and you can't forgive me for that, can you?"

"You think you're so smart," he growled, "but you're not. You're no match for me, and you never were. I only wanted you for your name and connections. Love be damned! But a man has needs. Everything would have been different if you weren't such a cold bitch."

Beth recoiled from the venomous expression on his face, but she didn't lose focus. "What do you mean?"

He ignored her question. "Did you ever intend to marry me?"

Quickly, she pondered her response and finally said softly, "In the beginning, yes."

He smacked a hand against the desktop. "Then why? Why wouldn't you sleep with me?"

Beth was not completely surprised by the question. He'd alluded to this before. "I—I wanted to wait for the wedding." They both knew it wasn't that simple. Something had held her back. Not so with Ty, obviously. She hoped that he was listening, that he understood.

"Your precious Maitland body is too good for me," Brandon said. "That's really what you think, isn't it? Isn't it?"

"No, I—"

"It's all your fault!" he roared. "If you'd satisfied me, I wouldn't have needed Brianne—and she couldn't have lied to me, threatened me!"

"Threatened you how?" Beth asked breathlessly.

Straightening, he strolled around the end of the desk to

lean against the corner, oddly calm. "You Maitlands," he said with a sneer. "Everything handed to you on a silver platter. You have no idea what it takes to get ahead in this world when you have no connections." He leaned forward slightly and confided, "I worked hard. I was careful. No one would ever have known, but Brianne had to stick her nose into my business. She knew I'd find out she'd lied about being pregnant, and she had to have a way to hold on to me. It's your fault. If you hadn't held back your precious Maitland body from me, I wouldn't have had to turn to her—and she never would have had reason to look at my records."

"And you wouldn't have had to kill her," Beth breathed, her heart beating so hard she was certain he could see it.

He smiled coldly, calmly, and folded his arms. She saw it then in his eyes, the cunning, the hatred, the satisfaction of having her at his mercy. Stark terror seized her. In that instant, suddenly she realized how greatly she'd underestimated the danger. She had to get out of there.

"I shouldn't have come here," she said shakily, rising to her feet. "I'm going now. I—I don't know what I hoped to accomplish. It's obvious you aren't going to be reasonable." She slung her purse strap over her shoulder and stepped toward the door.

Without warning he launched himself from the corner of the desk, zipping in front of her. With a flick of one hand, he locked the door.

"What are you doing?"

"It's all your fault," he said again, turning to face her, "and if the cops weren't so awed by your family influence, you'd be in jail now." He slipped his hand into the pocket of his pants. "First I arranged for her to go to your office. Then I slipped in through the private entrance you had shown me when we were still engaged. I knew you'd be busy turning off lights and shutting down the place. I had waited for you to perform those little chores so often, after all. I simply hid in the coat closet in your office, then when Brianne came in I slipped up behind her and strangled her." He smiled, and Beth's hand went involuntary to her throat. "I jumped back into the closet just before the cleaning lady arrived. Then in the pandemonium, I slipped away unseen. Simple, yet brilliant, don't you think? The thing was perfect, but you still haven't paid." He stepped forward menacingly and smiled, pulling his hand from his pocket. A blue silk cord, frayed at one end, dangled from it.

"I'll scream," she said loudly, backing up. "Your secretary—"

"Is much too well trained to get in the way." He finished her sentence for her. He took the cord in both hands and stretched it. "She left the moment I let you in."

Her mind racing, Beth realized that they were too far from the noisy main office for anyone to hear. She backed away, fumbling with the flap of her purse. "You won't get away with this."

He glanced at the armoire, smiling strangely as he moved toward her. "I'll just hide you, work late, take you down in the freight elevator. They'll think you ran to avoid prosecution."

"If the cops don't get you," she told him shakily, her hand closing around the pepper spray canister inside her purse, "my family will."

His eyes went wide, and he suddenly rushed her, roaring out his anger. She yanked the spray free, aimed it and pushed the button, turning her head away from the stinging mist, but Brandon ducked and came in low, throwing his arms around her waist and lifting her off her feet, slamming her into the wall behind her. The spray canister fell to the floor, useless. Holding her pinned with his body, he wrapped the cord around her neck and began to twist. She kicked and dug her hands free, flailing at him, but the cord bit inexorably into her neck. He slammed his shoulder into her midsection, driving the air out of her lungs, and she saw spots of black light.

"It's your fault," he growled, pushing her hard against the wall, twisting, twisting. "And now you die."

Oddly, she wasn't frightened. As blackness seeped in, she felt only anger—anger and regret. Oh, Ty. Somewhere in the distance she heard a sound, a boom, like something exploding, but she didn't try to identify it. Ty had been right. The danger was more real than she'd realized. But she'd done it for them. Would he understand that? It seemed terribly important that he did. In her mind, she saw him, his face hovering above her. He seemed to be shouting, but the incomprehensible words that she knew meant love were only whispers in the distance of another reality. And yet they comforted her. She smiled sadly. Too late.

Too late.

CHAPTER TWELVE

TY SAT on the hard plastic chair with his head in his hands, listening to the distant echo of the hospital intercom and the rapid click of heels on the shiny waxed floor.

"Where is she?" Megan Maitland's frantic voice demanded.

He lifted his head, straightened and sat back in his chair, utterly exhausted. Living a nightmare, having one's worst fears come true was tiring business.

Fortunately, Jake stepped forward to deal with his mother. "They're moving her into a room now," he said with urgent calmness. "She's sedated because they had to use a scope to be certain there were no tears or lesions in the esophagus. Apparently the scarf she was wearing around her neck protected her somewhat. You can see her in a few minutes."

Megan nodded, lines of worry etched between her brows. "You said Brandon did this. Where is he?"

"In jail, where he belongs."

"Thank God for that, at least. But I don't understand any of this. How did it happen?"

With a cough to clear his throat, Ty confessed tonelessly, "We sent her wired into his private office to get a confession for his wife's murder." He knew he should get to his feet. It was a courtesy that Megan Maitland both expected and deserved. He didn't dare, however, for fear that his legs wouldn't hold him.

Megan rounded on him with all the condemnation he expected. "You *what?*"

"I know it was risky," he admitted wearily.

"Risky! You nearly got her killed! My God, I thought you cared for her! What were you thinking?"

There was no point trying to defend himself. Ty knew she was right. This was all his fault. If he'd behaved professionally and kept the proper distance, Beth would never have agreed to anything so foolhardy. She'd done it for them. He'd known that from the beginning. Guilt lay at the pit of his stomach like a cold, slimy rock, a weight so heavy he staggered with it.

"Mother," Jake said placatingly, "you don't understand."

Ty shook his head, forestalling Jake's defense. "I'm sorry," he said uselessly. "You're right, Mrs. Maitland. I take full responsibility."

"Now wait a minute," Jake began, but Ty cut him off.

"If not for me, she wouldn't have gone in there. I don't blame you for being angry. All I can say is that I'm sorry."

Megan Maitland folded her arms primly. "Sorry just doesn't cut it, I'm afraid."

"You're quite right," Ty agreed, slumping in his chair. No show of manners or decorum could aid him. "I'll go in a bit. Leave you to take care of her."

Megan opened her mouth to speak, but Jake took her by the arm, rather firmly and steered her away. Ty would have stopped him if he'd been able, but he knew he had to save his energy for getting out of there. Sighing, he sat forward again, then pushed himself to his feet, using the arms of his chair. Putting one foot in front of the other took enormous strength, but stronger still was the need to go, to put distance between himself and the results of his poor judgment and obsession.

"WHAT HAPPENED? I don't remember much after Brandon attacked me."

Her voice rasped tellingly, but the doctor had assured her that no permanent damage had been done. Detective Jester rocked from one foot to another with embarrassment, looking down at the medal she had returned to him. Much good it had done her.

"Well, it was all Ty and your brother," he mumbled. "They got to you and took care of it. I'm real sorry, Ms. Maitland. I never counted on the secretary leaving like that."

"I know. I never thought she'd leave, either."

"Apparently Brandon worked it that way all the time. When he signaled her, she was to go. She looked at it as free time, but I think she must have known he was up to no good in that office of his."

"Most likely," Beth agreed. "But you can't blame her. He was the boss. She probably needed the job too badly to question him."

"That's what she says," Jester confirmed, pocketing the medal. "Still, I should have considered the possibility."

"You couldn't know," Beth said dismissively. "Now tell me what happened. How did I get out of there?"

"Like I said, it was all Ty and your brother. They were both in the stairwell down the hall. Ty was the first to realize what was happening, and they bolted to the rescue, only to find the door locked. Ty shot off the handle with his service revolver. Our team was there right behind them, but if not for their quick action...well, I don't want to think about it, frankly."

"Then don't," Beth said cheerily. "All's well that ends well."

"Yeah, well, that remains to be seen," Paul said, his tone alerting her. She already knew that something was wrong because Ty had not been to see her or returned her phone messages.

"What do you mean? It's Ty, isn't it?"

Paul nodded jerkily. "He was right, you know, about it being too risky. Oh, we got Dumont. You did good work in there, by the way, and you're completely in the clear, but we were lucky. It could have gone real bad."

Beth touched her throat, and for a moment she relived the terror of feeling the cord tight around her, cutting off her air. "I know it, but I'd do it again to clear my name."

"So you can be with Ty," Paul said bluntly.

"So I can be with Ty," she admitted freely. "I love him, you know."

"I figured as much. That's why I'm here now."

Beth frowned. "I don't understand."

"I don't fully understand, either, but somehow or other Ty blames himself for what happened in Dumont's office. He's put himself on leave, and the cap'n, well, he's covering his butt a bit on this—and mine, too, I guess—by letting Ty take the blame for what happened. It's not fair. It's not fair at all. Ty tried to talk us out of it, and the cap'n wouldn't have any of it. He wanted the case cleared, you see, preferably in your favor, but the relationship, between you and Ty, I mean, it gave the cap'n the pretext he needed."

"Ty's going to lose his job over this?" Beth's voice rasped painfully.

"Don't know as it'll come to that," Paul said, "unless Ty takes it into his head to make his leave permanent."

"What a muddle I've made of things!" Beth moaned, running a hand over her forehead.

"I muddled things pretty good myself," the detective admitted. "I figured how it was between the two of you, and I let that convince me that Ty was being too cautious. I wanted the same as you, I suppose, for the two of you to make it through this. Sending you in after Dumont seemed the surest way."

"It was the only way," Beth exclaimed. "You said it yourself."

"That may be, but the fact is that Ty tried to stop it and he's the one taking it on the chin now. Something has to be done."

Beth plucked at the bedcovers in frustration, wishing desperately that her mother had not taken her clothes with her. She couldn't very well go traipsing about town in a hospital gown and her bare feet. She didn't even have a coat! Blast Megan. Had she done this on purpose? "Where is Ty?"

"He's holed up out at his mother's place. Naomi hasn't even got a phone, and Ty's turned off his cell."

The decision was made without a second's thought. "Can you get me some clothes?" she asked.

Paul blinked at her. "Beg pardon?"

She yanked open the drawer in the bedside stand and removed her wallet. Unzipping the side compartment, she extracted several bills and thrust them toward the foot of the bed, where Paul Jester stood in stupefied silence. "Jeans, T-shirt, some sort of jacket. And shoes." He shuffled forward, arm slowly lifting as he reached for the money. "Hurry," she ordered, shoving the money into his hand. He nodded and headed toward the door, looking a little dazed. Then he grinned.

"Boy, you Maitlands don't fool around, do you?"

"Not when it comes to those we love," Beth said, and Ty Redstone was definitely at the top of her list. "I'd do anything for Ty, even go away and leave him alone if that would make him happiest."

"It wouldn't," Paul said flatly, and Beth smiled.

"I'm counting on that. I am definitely counting on that."

HER PALMS were sweating as the nondescript sedan rocked to a halt on the sandy shoulder of the narrow road. She looked around at the rocky, barren landscape, the brown grass, the skeletal trees. A goat trotted down a distant slope and out of sight. Finally, Beth looked at the tiny, weathered house with its peeling paint and drunkenly canted porch behind the chicken wire fence and felt hideously out of place, even wearing stiff, discount-store jeans a size too large and a too-small yellow T-shirt beneath a blue hooded nylon jacket. At least the blue-and-white tennis shoes and plain white socks fit comfortably. She'd zipped up the jacket to hide the fact that she wasn't wearing a bra beneath the snug T-shirt. She lifted the hood to hide the tangle of her hair, wishing that she'd thought to ask Paul for a hair-brush.

She slid a look his way and found him apparently buck-ing up his courage, his pale hands flexing on the steering wheel before he reached down to let himself out of the car. He was halfway around the front end when the door of the little house opened and Ty stepped onto the porch wearing nothing more than socks, jeans and an undershirt. Before he could ask what Paul was doing there, Beth opened her door and got out.

"Hello, Ty."

The look he flashed at Paul was hot enough to sear flesh. Paul stood where he was and leaned a hand against the hood of the car.

"When did you get out of the hospital?" Ty asked tone-lessly.

She closed the car door and moved close to the lopsided plank-and-wire gate in the fence. "About an hour ago."

He made a face that perfectly expressed what he thought of her actions. "You should be at home then."

"It's more important that I talk to you."

"Your mother wouldn't think so."

"My mother forgets that I'm no longer a child."

"I can't think this would make her remember."

"She's not the one I'm trying to get through to just now. Then again, she wouldn't keep me standing out in the cold."

He made a face and yanked his head at the door behind him. "Let's get it over with, then." As invitations went, it lacked a great deal, but she lifted the wire loop that held the gate in position and went inside.

Paul shook his head and walked backward along the same path he'd traveled earlier. "I have to get going," he said. "Nan's expecting me."

Beth hid her surprise, immediately tumbling to the plan. Ty would have to take her to Austin himself. "Thank you, Paul," she called, even as Ty demanded that he stay, then began sputtering hells and damns. Paul ducked into the car and started the engine, executing a neat U-turn. Beth walked up the path beaten into the dirt and climbed two cockeyed steps to the warped boards of the porch. Frowning, Ty shoved open the door and motioned her inside with an angry sweep of his hand.

The little house was warm and redolent with the smell of beans and corn bread. A small television on a rickety table played a game show softly. A squarish, solidly made couch covered in reddish brown fabric stood against one wall beneath a startling painting of a campfire surrounded by Native American dancers in bright costumes. Beth recognized it immediately as one of Ty's. The rest of the furnishings included a rocking chair, rag rug and a tarnished brass floor lamp with a brittle yellow paper shade. A spindly coffee table piled with magazines had been shoved against the wall beneath a window hung with drab green curtains. A darkened hallway opened diagonally from the door to a kitchen that showed graying linoleum and a square table wedged between wall, ancient refrigerator and another door, presumably to the outside. Beth glimpsed just the tiniest corner of a mottled green countertop edged with aluminum stripping before turning to face Ty.

This was a different Ty from any she'd seen so far, defensive, disheveled, distant. His hair hung lank against his face. The undershirt was old and frayed, the jeans soft and faded with age. He frowned, not happy at all to see her. And he still looked good enough to eat, blast the man.

"You put yourself on leave," she accused without preamble.

He looked at her for a long moment, then he turned his face away, squinting into the distance. "I'll get dressed and take you home," he said flatly.

She sat in the center of the couch and folded her arms. "No."

He closed his eyes for a moment. "Damn it, Beth, I'm in no mood for this!"

"Too bad," she said, crossing her legs and bouncing a foot nervously. Frantically she searched her mind for some way to reach him, then out of the corner of her eye, she caught the hungry sweep of his gaze, and suddenly she knew. Turning her head, she asked innocently, "Where's your mother? I'd like to meet her."

"She's not here," he answered tersely.

"When will she be back?"

"Not for a while." He made it sound as if she would not be back for a long while, and Beth decided that was very much to her advantage, if she were audacious enough to do what she was thinking. And why not? She'd already risked everything for this man. What was left to lose? She smiled to find that she was even bolder than she'd realized.

"Good," she said, unzipping the nylon jacket and peeling it off while quickly rising. Ty gulped, watching the sway of her breasts beneath the snug T-shirt, and triumph surged through her. "Where are you sleeping?" she asked pointedly, and his startled gaze flipped to her face. She drew it back where she wanted it by tugging up the hem of her shirt and pulling it over her head. He gasped and backed away.

"What are you doing?"

Shirt gone, she toed off her shoes and stalked him in her

stocking feet, twisting her fingers in the belt loops of her jeans to keep them from sagging. "Trying to talk to you."

His mouth twitched into a grin even as he circled away from her, his eyes glued to her body. "Is *that* what you call it?"

Ducking her head slightly, she gave him her most seductive look. Slowly, sinuously, she moved toward him. "There's nothing to stop us now, Ty."

He put his hands up as she came near, then slipped sideways. "Isn't there?" He couldn't seem to keep his gaze above her chest, and her nipples hardened in response.

She removed her hands from the belt loops and let the jeans sag low. "Nothing but you, Ty," she said breathlessly. He pushed a hand through his hair, licked his lips.

"Th-they could come home at any time."

"Then we'd better hurry," she said, taking two quick steps that brought them chest to chest. His hands came up and skimmed over her back even as he jerked away. She pushed forward, pressing her breasts to his chest and clasping his buttocks. She smiled, feeling the hard length behind the fly of his jeans. "Do you *want* me to be caught naked in your mother's living room?"

He growled, desire and anger flaring in his eyes. "This won't change anything."

Moving against him, she smiled again. "You're right. We're already mad for each other, and this certainly won't change a thing."

He seized her by the wrist and yanked her into the hallway, almost immediately shoving her through a door into a small room with a twin bed, dresser and broken side chair. His shoes stood on the floor beside the foot of the bed. Hot desire throbbed in the pit of her belly as she crawled onto the worn patchwork coverlet. This was Ty's past, the key to the man he was now. She caressed it reverently with her fingers as he ripped off the undershirt and threw it to the floor before wrenching open his jeans as if to show her that he meant business. She matched him and went one better, hanging her legs off the side of the bed and shoving her jeans down until she could curl her legs free. Leaning back, she propped the weight of her upper body onto her elbows. A smile slowly grew across his face. Then abruptly he spun and disappeared. Trusting that he would return, she peeled off her socks and scrambled beneath the covers.

An instant later he reappeared, her shirt and jacket in one hand, shoes in the other. She shoved the covers to her thighs in invitation. Quickly, he dumped her things, closed the door and dragged the chair in front of it. Desire seemed to mingle with amusement and fading anger as he stripped his remaining clothing and came to the bed. She kicked the covers away and lifted her arms to him. He made a sound of surrender in the back of his throat as he sank into them, stretching out atop her. His fingertips brushed the mottled bruise encircling her throat, then he bowed his head to kiss her.

Scant minutes later she screamed hoarsely as climax swirled her away in an explosion of color. Her vision was just beginning to clear when he threw back his head, teeth clenched, and joined her.

THEY LAY chest to chest on the narrow bed, legs tangled damply beneath the covers, hands clasped. He couldn't believe he'd just made wild, heaving love to her in his mother's little house on his boyhood bed. It was beyond foolish. The other members of his family had made a trek to the grocery store at the crossroads a few miles away, leaving him alone with his sullen misery. They could return at any time. He wondered what Beth would make of them, his family, what they would make of her. She had looked around with obvious interest but no discernible disdain at the small, shabby house that his proud mother would not allow him to refurbish. Still, she was good at covering, his Beth, good at so many things.

His Beth. Was it really possible? he wondered.

Such a little while ago he had thought the matter settled. A little while ago, he'd intended to thrash Paul Jester the moment he laid eyes on him. Now he knew he wouldn't, and that nothing was really settled. The problem was, he didn't know what he would do about anything. He sighed in fleeting contentment, wishing that he could sleep with Beth snuggled naked against him. The temptation was so strong that he closed his eyes, but his ears remained alert, and an instant later caught the sound of a car moving toward them.

Reluctantly he sat up and flipped back the covers. "They're coming. Get dressed."

Beth pushed off the bed and looked at him lazily. "You said that before—they. I thought it was just your mother."

He shook his head and put his feet into his jeans, standing as he pulled them up. "My whole family. Sister and husband, my little brother. Quickly now." He tossed her clothing and continued pulling on his own.

"Do you have a hairbrush?"

"There's an extra in the bathroom," he told her as she pushed her head through the neck of that absurdly small T-shirt.

She slid from beneath the covers and into her jeans, her hair a wild tangle of froth. He tried to decide whose socks were whose, finally got them sorted and tossed a pair her way. A door creaked open. He shoved the chair aside.

"Come!" He snapped his fingers and held out his hand. She scooped up her shoes and socks and grabbed his outstretched hand. He hauled her into the hallway, where he unceremoniously hustled her into the tiny bathroom and pulled the door closed behind her as Naomi, Dee, Hardy and Cob spilled into the kitchen, talking and plunking down groceries. Swift and silent as a bird, Ty swept into the bedroom and pulled on his socks, then quickly straightened the bed and hurried into the hall to lean in the living-room doorway. His mother looked up and greeted him in the old language.

"Cob is angry," she said, smiling gently. "The cooler is broken, and all the beer is warm."

Ty recognized the clink of bottles being stowed in the refrigerator and shrugged. "Cob is always angry."

Naomi nodded, her smile unwavering, and went back to unpacking her groceries. Ty shifted his weight and fought the urge to clear his throat, a sure sign of nervousness. "We have company," he announced mildly.

Everyone stopped what they were doing. It was his sister, Dee, who turned and moved forward, peering into the living room. "Who? Where?"

"A friend," he answered obliquely. "She's in the bathroom."

Dee's slender, winged brows rose sharply. Before she could ask who this mysterious "she" was, the bathroom door opened and Beth stepped beside him, a smile on her face. She had brushed her hair until it crackled and stood out around her shoulders like a dark nimbus. He grasped her hand and pulled her into the living room.

"Mother, this is Beth Maitland." He glanced at Beth, adding, "My mother, Naomi."

Beth inclined her head, almost bowing. "I'm so glad to meet you," she said warmly.

Naomi pushed past Dee into the living area, her wide eyes studying Beth Maitland carefully before she offered her hand. "Welcome to our home, Beth Maitland."

"Thank you."

He indicated the other faces in the kitchen doorway. "My sister, Dee, her husband, Hardy, my brother, Cob."

Beth nodded to each in turn, curiosity lighting her eyes. It was to Dee that she spoke. "You teach at the university on the tribal lands in Montana."

Dee glanced at Ty. "Yes, history and computer technology."

"Well, that's covering both ends of the spectrum!" Beth exclaimed.

"So it is," Dee agreed, laughing. "I hadn't thought of it that way, the old and the new."

"And you teach, as well?" Beth asked Hardy.

"Biology."

Beth winced. "Ow. My worst subject. I had to take it twice to get my degree."

A true academic, Hardy slid as easily into business mode as he did through the door into the living room. "What degree would that be?"

"Child development."

"Ah, a field with strong ties to biology. Human emotional development is grounded in physical development."

"That part I got," Beth said, "but I understand it better now. You can learn so much by just watching a child grow—they're living textbooks. Fascinating."

"You work with children, then?" Dee asked conversationally.

"Yes, I work in the day-care facility at a maternity clinic."

"She's *director* of the day-care facility at *Maitland* Maternity Clinic," Ty corrected wryly. Beth shot him a disappointed glance that took him completely by surprise. In that instant he realized how eager she was to have his family approve of her. She didn't want them to think that she had been given her job out of favoritism, because of who she was rather than what she had to offer. He had stung her pride unjustifiably. All at once, the doubts that had plagued him so mercilessly for so long fell away. It was as if the sun had come out from behind the clouds at last. Problems remained, yes. The differences could not be papered over, but they had enough to begin, surely. Ty moved close and slid an arm around Beth's waist. "Any other child-care center in town would fight to have her," he said, "but the Maitlands are big on family loyalty."

Beth relaxed her stance so that her hip slid against his. "Yes, we are," she said, a little catch in her voice.

Cob lounged in the doorway next to Dee, his arms folded. Ty recognized the sneer that flattened his mouth. "Whites know nothing of true loyalty," he said bluntly. Ty bristled, aware of Beth tensing beside him. He barked an order at his brother in Crow, demanding respect for himself and his woman. Cob blanched. "Not a *white* woman!" he accused angrily. "If you were a true Crow—"

"I am Crow!" Ty shouted. "More importantly, I am your brother!" He felt Beth lay her hand gently upon his chest. It was Dee who turned Cob into the kitchen, scolding softly in the old language. Hardy looked embarrassed. Naomi moved to the couch and sat down, waving at Ty to bring Beth to her. He bit his tongue and did so, crouching at her feet when she was seated.

"My son is young," Naomi began apologetically. "He remembers only the injustice done to his father by white men and not the father who bore the injustice. And I fear that he is infected just now with the political talk in the Indian lands."

"We try hard to instill pride in our young people," Hardy volunteered. "Sometimes a person with a grievance takes it too far and succumbs to the very discriminatory views we fight against."

"I understand," Beth said softly. "It's the same everywhere, a weakness in our common humanity, but understandable, I think, when one has suffered shame or loss or injustice."

Approval glinted in Hardy's gaze. Naomi touched a fingertip to the narrow bruise cuffing Beth's throat, then took her hand. "Why are you here, Beth Maitland?" she asked softly.

"I'm here," Beth said simply, "because your son saved my life."

Ty bowed his head, laying it against her knee, love overwhelming him in that moment. He heard the back door bang shut and was aware of his sister coming into the room without Cob, of Beth's gentle voice as she told her version of the nightmare that had seemed to eat him alive these last days. He let it go, the fear for her, the anger at everyone involved, until only the love and relief remained. He wanted to weep with fragile joy, but he thought of his brother, and disappointment speared through him. Yes, problems remained, big ones.

She had turned his life upside down and inside out, this woman. Hell, she'd destroyed his life. The life he'd made for himself before he knew her was gone forever, all but the foundation, and only with her could he build upon that again.

His Beth. Yes, she was his. She was his mate, his heart, his family, his tribe. Cob wouldn't understand that. He couldn't possibly. Ty wasn't even sure that Beth truly understood it yet. He had come to the knowledge so recently that it felt unique, his alone, his own creation, his reality. He held it tight, unwilling even to share it.

Nothing to stop us now. Nothing to stop us now.

CHAPTER THIRTEEN

BETH TOLD the whole story with as little emotion and as
much honesty as she could manage, beginning with the
engagement and ending with the rescue. She made it very
plain that Ty had done his job and done it well, investigating her for the murder and uncovering the truth in the
process. When it came to the undercover operation, she
noted Ty's objections to the risk involved and also admitted
that he had been right to be so concerned. In answer to
Hardy's questions, she explained the operation in detail.

Dee's queries were more insightful and much more personal. Beth found it difficult to skirt some answers, evasion
being as uncomfortable as an outright lie in the face of the
other woman's discerning gaze. Nevertheless, Beth strove
to keep private matters just that, ever mindful of the fact
that she was speaking to Ty's family. How successful she
was, she couldn't know, but she suspected the relationship
was no secret.

Naomi said nothing, merely listened with a still watchfulness that seemed to see and hear and feel more than she
indicated. Beth found her presence oddly peaceful and un-
settling at the same time, and she saw much of Naomi in
Ty.

It was Dee who truly intrigued Beth, though. She had
never seen a more beautiful woman. Cob was a handsome
devil, too, with his long black hair and dark, flashing eyes,
his face a younger, slightly softer version of Ty's. As yet,
he lacked Ty's utter manliness but seemingly none of his

strength of personality. It pained Beth that he didn't like her. She realized Ty had feared something like this, and she wanted to believe Cob would relent once he came to know her. In contrast, the others were friendly and amiable, Hardy especially, his laid-back attitude a perfect foil for his wife's intensity. He was somewhat beefier than Ty and his brother but also shorter. All displayed a fierce intelligence, especially Naomi, who was small and birdlike, unlike her tall, strong children. Beth speculated that their father must have been a very large, imposing man and regretted that she would never meet him.

Ty was clearly uncomfortable with the talk about the police operation and the rescue, especially his part in it, but Beth made sure they all understood how truly wonderful he was. No one had been prepared for that locked office door and the absence of the secretary. If Ty had not insisted on being in that stairwell and listening to every word being said in that office, if he had not been armed and quickly used his gun to shoot off the door handle, she would not be there. She had no doubt of it.

"He even saw to it that my brother Jake was on-site as an extra measure of caution," she said proudly.

"It was actually Jake who got to Dumont first," Ty clarified. "He pulled him off you."

"And then held your gun on him while you tended to me," Beth added pointedly. "You did everything right, Ty. Face it, you're a hero." She turned to his family. "By the time the EMTs got upstairs, I was breathing, conscious and sitting up, thanks to Ty's knowledge of first aid and CPR." She clutched his hand and smiled. "He's my very own personal hero."

A snort from the doorway alerted everyone to Cob's return. He stood leaning against the doorjamb, his arms folded against his chest, the sleeves of his blue plaid flannel shirt rolled back to display the corded muscles of his forearms. His long, straight hair hung about his face from a center part like a black silk curtain flanking an open window. "The white woman's hero," he said with a sneer. "How much good you do for our people by rescuing rich white women from their own folly."

A protective anger shot through Beth. He might disapprove of her as he wished, but how dare he mock his brother's bravery? Before she knew what she was going to do, before she could even think, she was on her feet, glaring at Ty's younger brother. Intellectually she knew that she ought to let the remark go, but that didn't put the brakes on her tongue, and once she started, she couldn't seem to stop. She was like a runaway train on an embankment, going faster and faster every moment.

"For your information, Ty does a great deal of good," she told Cob loudly. "He's the most respected investigator on the force. He's the most decent, insightful, hardworking, caring man I've ever known, and that's saying something in *my* family, mister! The Maitlands are wealthy, yes, and great wealth means great responsibility. We were taught from childhood to do good for others, and we found out quick that we had to behave better than anyone else. And no matter how hard we work, everyone always thinks everything is handed to us on silver platters! *Your* poor manners won't show up on the evening news, but mine very well could because of who I am, never mind *what* I am!"

"Whatever you think of me, though, you should have nothing but respect for your brother! Ty's the best. He's more than just a good cop, more than a Native American doing what you seem to think is a white job. He's a *man* doing a *man's* job—and doing it better than anyone else out there."

When she finally ran out of steam, she found that she wasn't the only one on her feet, and that Ty's arm was wrapped firmly around her shoulders. For a long, sharp moment, no one said anything. Cob's belligerence had faded, and Beth was suddenly struck by how very young he was, barely more than a teenager. For an instant, confusion clouded his face, but then his anger asserted itself.

"You don't know anything about being Native American!" he said scathingly.

"No, I don't," she replied smoothly, "but I know at least as much about being a human being as you do. Maybe more."

That last remark seemed to hit home with the force of a bullet. He was knocked back, but the next instant he shoved away from the door and stomped out, weaving and twisting through the crowded living room with angry movements. Ty sighed heavily and dropped his arm from her shoulders.

"I'm sorry," he muttered.

"No, it's all right," Beth said, already regretting her outburst.

"I'd better go talk to him," Ty insisted.

She nodded, feeling abandoned and conspicuous. He left her with his mother and sister and brother-in-law. "I'm so sorry. I shouldn't have said anything," she began, but Naomi shook her head.

"Ty will tend to him," she said. "Let us put aside unpleasantness. We should be celebrating my one son, not worrying about the other." She took the entire situation in hand then, directing it with simple nods and gestures. "Dee, our guest should have something to drink. Hardy, there are sandwiches already made in the refrigerator. Miss Maitland is going to tell me about her work now, and then I would like to hear about her family."

Naomi's was the kind of firm, gentle authority one dared not question. Much like a child presenting in school, Beth reported on her job, her family and, ultimately, the clinic, but the mood had been spoiled, and Beth felt a deepening well of doubt inside. Family meant so much to Ty. He loved his brother. How could she live with herself if she caused a split between them? Perhaps this was what Ty had been trying to tell her all this time, that he would have to choose between her and his family and that he couldn't do it.

She thought of her brothers and sisters, of her mother. If one or all of them disapproved of an individual as obviously as Cob disapproved of her, she would have to do some serious thinking. Could she win Cob over? Should she try? At that moment she didn't know. She believed that Ty loved her; she knew that he loved his brother. And loving him as she did, she could never ask him to choose.

TY WAS MORTIFIED. All this time he'd wanted to believe the prejudice and false superiority lay on the Maitland side of the tracks. Oh, he'd known that Cob would not be thrilled by the idea of his big brother being involved with Beth Maitland, but then Cob was not much thrilled with anything Ty did. Ty was not Crow enough for Cob these days, not Indian enough.

Ty made allowances for him, of course. Cob had gotten the shortest end of the stick in their family. He barely remembered their proud, gentle father. He knew nothing of the dignity and patience with which that man had borne the injustices heaped upon him. He knew only the poverty that came from having the breadwinner removed from the family circle, the loneliness of growing up without a father. Ty had tried to be as much father as older brother to him. The ten years between them should have facilitated that, but Ty had been away for long periods of time getting an education and, he realized, much too consumed by his quest to see justice served for his father.

By the time he'd taken notice of his brother's needs, Cob had been a rebellious teenager with a chip on his shoulder, a couple years behind his peers. Ty had tried to bridge the gap with varying degrees of success, but they'd never managed to overcome their basic difference, which was primarily one of personality. Cob's natural instinct was to rush into every battle proudly screaming his defiance. Ty took a quieter, more careful approach, preferring to fight with cunning and intelligence rather than physical and emotional strength.

Ty understood all this, but he had never expected that the boy's anger toward the single white man who had framed their father for a crime he'd never committed would translate itself into intolerance for a whole race, especially not for the woman he, Ty, loved. Still, Ty could not believe that his brother would nurse his prejudices indefinitely. One day, maturity would claim him, and with it would come wisdom. But until that time, Ty couldn't sit by and let Cob insult Beth. No man could allow that. Besides, what sort of future did they have if Cob could not accept her? Ty didn't want to lose his brother, but losing Beth was no longer thinkable.

After making his way around the house and yard, he finally spied his lanky brother sitting on the trunk of Naomi's old sedan, a dim silhouette in the deepening gloom of twilight. He looked very alone, and Ty couldn't help thinking it must be an image that perversely pleased his difficult brother. Casually, he strolled over and leaned a hip against the spiked fender.

"You're not the lone warrior fighting a losing battle, you know."

Cob's square jaw firmed; Ty could hear the boy grinding his teeth. "In this family, I am."

Ty sighed and folded his arms. "That's not true, and you know it. Dee and Hardy could teach at any university in the country, but they choose to serve the tribal needs. If they're not as militant as you would like, that's your problem, and maybe, just maybe, it has something to do with their maturity."

"You and Mother," Cob began angrily, but Ty cut him off.

"Mother and I have done the best we could, Cob, given our circumstances, and you have no right to judge either of us, but especially not Mother. Yes, she could have gone back to the reservation after Father died, but for what, Cob? Her life was never there. This is her land, and she's fought her own personal battles for it. She's happy here. Why can't that be enough for you? She deserves whatever happiness she can find after losing her husband and raising three children on her own. Can't you see that all she wants now is some peace? Doesn't she deserve that?''

Cob bowed his head, and Ty could feel his roiling confusion, the battle between need and understanding. He waited for the confusion to recede, for Cob to formulate his next argument. He didn't have to wait long. Cob slid off the trunk of the car and rounded on him, hands slashing in the faint light.

''Why have you decided to be a white man?''

A dry laugh escaped before Ty could rein it in. ''Cob, we've been over this before. I couldn't be a white man if I wanted to. I am Absaroka, Crow. I am Tonkawa and Caddo. I am the same as you, Cob, except that I learned early on that all whites are not my enemies. I'll admit at first it was a matter of beating them at their own games. A white man robbed me of my father. I meant to bring him to justice using their methods. But a white man helped me do it, and along the way I realized that it was not their methods I used, but ours, as well. I laid claim to justice, and I won't relinquish it just because you can't see the sense in it. And I won't give up Beth, either. I love her, and I won't let your prejudice rob me of her.''

Agitation showed in every line of Cob's body, in the way he fisted his hands and shifted his weight restlessly. ''Why couldn't you love an Indian girl?'' Cob wanted to know, and he asked it in the same voice that he had once used to demand a new toy or treat.

Ty shook his head. ''Because life is not that neat or simple, Cob. How easy it would be to wall ourselves up inside our reservations, see only our own and blame all our woes on the outside world. You don't need a tribe or a reservation to do that. You can accomplish the same thing by walking into the house, bolting the doors and refusing to come out. I choose to live life to the fullest, to take everything from it that I can, and that includes Beth.''

"But why her?" Cob demanded.

He shrugged. "Just lucky, I guess. Or it could be Isakawuate, the Trickster. I can't think of any other reason she'd keep reaching for me like I was some sort of brass ring. All I know for sure, Cob, is that I'm going to catch that brass ring with her and hold on as if my life depends on it, because I think it does.''

"I think you're making a mistake," Cob argued sullenly.

"Not too long ago I'd have agreed with you. See, I tried to get out of the way at first because I thought she and her family would ultimately reject me. Then I began to see through that lie, so I told myself that I didn't have anything to offer her. Now I'm ashamed to say that it was my own cowardice that was the problem. I was afraid to love a white woman, Cob. Hell, I was afraid to love any woman. I almost lost her. And now I can no more walk away from her, Cob, than I can walk away from myself. Or you.''

Cob shook his head. "If she leaves you, you'll wind up like Mama, pining for the rest of your life.''

"Yes, I suppose I will, and that's exactly what I've been so afraid of. But you know what, Cob, the idea of never having her at all is even worse.''

Cob's agitation had gradually eased. He slumped, regarding Ty from beneath the handsome jut of his brow. "What are you going to do?''

Ty renegotiated his position, shifting more of his weight against the car. "I'm going to marry her," he said flatly. "And I'm going to kick your butt if you ever again speak to her the way you did just now. You're my brother, Cob, and I love you, but Beth is my heart. Reject her, and you reject me. That's your decision, frankly, but before you write us off as too white for your taste, you should know two things. One, I'll always love you no matter what. Two, I won't ever again tolerate the type of behavior you displayed in there earlier. It's time you learned to walk in the world into which you were born, instead of simply longing for a world of ideals.'' With that he lounged back and waited.

For the longest time, Cob stood with shoulders hunched, hands shoved into his jeans pockets. Then he turned and walked away, feet scuffing against the hard, packed dirt. Ty bowed his head, disappointment lancing deep.

He'd said it all wrong, obviously. As so often happened, he hadn't managed to reach his bright but troubled brother. Sadness filled him, but he knew he wouldn't back down. He couldn't. All that he'd told Cob was true. He was only sorry he hadn't realized it earlier. Perhaps if Beth hadn't come to him today, if he'd never seen her again after that last moment in the hospital when she'd smiled so bravely through the pain as they'd wheeled her away, he might have been able to convince himself that it was for the best. But not now. She had battered down the last of his defenses with her frankness, her blatant sexuality and her beauty. The courage she'd displayed in so many ways—calmly convincing him of her innocence, interfering in his investigation, making wild love with him without the least promise from him, walking into Dumont's office with only that wire to protect her, coming here today uninvited to challenge him with only the weapon of her love—humbled and overwhelmed him. He would not dishonor that with his cowardice. She had won, and he was glad, whatever the cost, but the battle had undeniably wearied him.

After a while, Ty became aware of the deep chill invading his skin. Reluctantly, he shoved himself away from the car and trudged toward the house. He pushed through the door, automatically glancing at the clock on the wall. The hour was growing late, and the rasp of Beth's fading voice

warned him that her strength was waning. He ignored the
questioning looks of his sister and mother and paid attention instead to the way Beth's hand rested protectively on
her throat. Concern for her outweighed everything else.

"We'd best head back," he said, intending to brook no
argument.

"You haven't had supper," Dee commented. Naomi rose
and said, "I'll pack you some sandwiches."

"Oh, I've had plenty, thank you," Beth said awkwardly,
indicating the half-eaten sandwich on the plate beside her.
Ty nodded at his mother and moved purposefully through
the room behind her.

"I'll just grab my things and be right back." He glanced
at his brother-in-law. "Hardy, you could warm up the car,
if you wouldn't mind. Keys are on the peg beside the back
door."

Hardy was already on his feet.

"Do you have to rush?" Dee demanded. "We've barely
gotten to know one another."

"She just got out of the hospital, Dee," Ty replied. "I'm
taking her home."

"Yes, of course," his sister said, subsiding immediately.

Ty moved quickly to the bedroom, pulled on a sweater,
then gathered his things and tossed them into his bag. He
hadn't brought much, never did. Within seconds he was
zipping the small duffel. As he reached for the light switch
next to the door, he looked one more time at the small bed
shoved against the wall beneath the window, and a smile
curled his mouth. Never in his wildest dreams had he imagined anything like what had happened there today. But then
he'd never imagined anyone like Beth Maitland. He didn't
know how they were going to do it, fully blend their lives,
make their home, but that didn't matter now. Perhaps it
never had. They would find a way.

Beth and Dee had joined his mother in the kitchen by
the time he'd grabbed his black leather jacket from the tiny

hall cupboard. He stood in the doorway, watching the three of them bag sandwiches and a thermos of steaming apple cider that Naomi had heated in the microwave, and let the richness of the moment fill him. It seemed right to him, that the three women he loved best in this world should all be in the same place at the same time. He sensed the underlying awkwardness and sensed, too, that it would soon fade. The next time they met, these three, they would be old friends and soon, he hoped, family.

He walked into the room and draped his jacket around Beth's shoulders. He ought to shake her for coming out without a proper coat, but if he did, he'd just wind up kissing her, and he knew well where that would lead. Much safer to kiss his mother and sister.

"Thank you, Mama," he whispered to Naomi. She said nothing, but he read her loving acceptance in her embrace.

"I'm glad you came," he told Dee warmly. At first he'd scolded her for making the long trip when she'd heard he'd taken a leave. He was no longer irritated that their mother had called her. In fact, he was no longer any of the things he'd been when he'd tossed his bag into his truck and headed out of Austin.

"So am I," she replied, looking meaningfully at Beth. "Take care."

"Absolutely."

He moved to open the back door and ushered Beth onto the small covered porch. His SUV waited, exhaust pluming white in the cold night air. Hardy got out and left the door standing open. Ty ushered Beth down the steps. She looked over her shoulder.

"It was so nice to have met you all."

"We will meet again," Naomi said. "Come any time."

"Thank you, especially after... I do apologize."

"Never mind Cob," Naomi said. "Just take care of yourself."

"She will," Ty promised.

Hardy slapped him on the back. "Have a safe trip."

"You, too. And take care of Cob."

"We'll try," Hardy promised.

Ty nodded understandingly before opening the door for Beth and handing her into her seat. He saw that she fastened her safety belt, then locked and closed the door, aware that he was being a tad overprotective and happy to be so. He hurried around and got in behind the steering wheel. His family was already retreating by the time he turned on the headlights, but he waved and received waves in return before putting the transmission into gear, backing around his mother's old car and heading down the drive.

"How are you feeling?" he asked as he turned the truck out onto the narrow road.

"I'm fine." She sounded oddly subdued.

"What about your throat?" he asked, concerned.

"It's a little sore."

"There's a million things I'd like to do to you for pulling this stunt," he said, softening his words with a smile, "but we both know how we'd wind up if I did."

She didn't misunderstand him. The glow in her eyes proved it, but then she dropped her gaze. "Do you want to wind up there, Ty?"

Did he want to make love to her? That was like asking if he wanted to breathe. But he put other considerations first for a change. "I want to get you home before you seriously damage your health," he said firmly. She turned up the collar of his coat and slumped into the corner. He reached for the control knob of the heater fan and cranked it up a notch as he spotted Cob walking along the side of the road.

Cob stopped and waved both hands, making a crossing motion. The vehicle was well past him by the time Ty brought it to a stop. Hope burgeoning, he slammed the transmission into park and yanked open the door, ordering Beth to stay put. He slammed the door behind him, sealing in the heat as he turned to face his brother. Cob seemed uncertain now that Ty had stopped, but Ty didn't give him a chance to change his mind. He moved forward swiftly, and to his relief, Cob came to meet him.

"I'm sorry, Ty. I never meant to hurt you."

Ty threw both arms around him and hauled him close. "It's okay. Doesn't matter now. Everything's okay."

"If you really love her, you should be with her," Cob conceded.

Ty held his brother by the shoulders and looked him squarely in the eye. "I do, Cob, as much as I love you and Mom and Dee, but in a different way. I can't explain it to you. You won't understand until you stumble into it yourself. But it's real, Cob, as real as anything else in my life."

He heard a faint sound like the noise of a car window being rolled down, but he dismissed it automatically as far less important than what was taking place.

"You're my brother, Ty," Cob stated firmly, "and brothers are forever."

"Brothers are forever," Ty affirmed, backing off to give his brother's hand a slap and a firm shake.

They left it that way. It was enough, more than enough. Any more and Ty would have found himself reduced to tears. He walked to the vehicle and got inside, his euphoria waning at the sight of Beth's pale face.

"You okay?" He noticed that her window was rolled part way down and adjusted the heater.

She nodded mutely, reclined her seat and settled back. He was still a little too choked up to speak easily, and was concerned that she'd overused her voice, so he let the silence be enough. Before long, Beth drifted into an exhausted slumber.

During the remainder of the drive, he debated taking her home with him, but she had nothing with her other than the ill-fitting clothes she was wearing, and he suspected that her mother would have the entire Austin police force out looking for her if he didn't get her home soon. Besides, he had loose ends to tie up.

He had to get his job back, for one thing. Oh, he hadn't quit outright, but he'd been on the verge, and the captain had known it. That was another thing. He could face his own mistakes, but he saw no reason to saddle himself with anyone else's. It hadn't seemed important before, but it did now. He knew he'd have a battle on his hands. The captain had been only too happy to let Ty take the blame for the harm done Beth. He wasn't going to like it now that the scapegoat had decided to fight back, but so be it. Ty's world was coming right again, more right than it had ever been. Besides, no permanent harm had been done. Beth was going to be fine in a few days. Dumont was behind bars where he belonged, probably for the rest of his life. Ty was not going to let his career go down the drain for nothing. That decided, he knew that it would be better to take Beth home to her mother's house where she would have the care she needed until she was completely well again.

When they pulled up into the drive, the guard stopped them, and Beth awoke. "What's wrong?" she demanded groggily.

"Reporters have been all over the place since this morning, Miss Maitland," the guard warned her. "We've had to call in extra security and be very vigilant. Frankly, we all thought you'd be in the hospital more than one night."

Beth sighed. "Let's just say I was motivated to get on with my life."

"Your mother said you were cleared, miss. We're all real glad."

"Thank you."

"Good thing you disappeared from the hospital when you did. I understand that some of the press managed to get into your room."

Beth glanced at Ty, who shrugged wryly. "A good thing,

indeed. Keep your eyes open, though. I doubt it's over yet.''

"Yes, ma'am." He saluted and backed away from the car window.

Ty shook his head as he drove the car forward. "I don't know how you bear the press scrutiny."

She sighed and shoved at her hair, sitting up straighter. "It gets tiring, but mostly I just ignore it. Now that I'm cleared, their interest will wane."

"I suppose, unless…" He'd been about to suggest that marrying the detective who'd investigated her for murder might reignite the whole media circus, but the front door of the mansion opened and people began spilling down the front steps, obviously alerted by the guard at the gate. He decided that the time wasn't right to declare himself.

"I've got some explaining to do," Beth groaned.

"I can see that," he replied dryly, bringing the vehicle to a halt.

Surprisingly, she seemed overcome by timidity. She turned to him. "You'll take yourself off leave, won't you, Ty? You'll go back to work where you belong?"

He smiled and nodded, wanting to put her at ease. "Yes. First thing tomorrow."

"I'm glad. I'm really glad."

Megan was at the door, yanking at the handle and demanding to know what Beth thought she was doing, gallivanting around who knew where. Beth tossed him a troubled glance. "I'm sorry, Ty, for everything that happened today. I overstepped."

"Don't worry about it," he said dismissively, irritated and distracted by the obvious fact that they weren't going to get a moment alone to make a proper goodbye. Well, there was tomorrow, all their tomorrows. "You'd better go in now. They're worried about you."

She nodded and reached for the door handle. At the last moment, she hesitated, and he came very close to saying to hell with everyone and everything else and dragging her off someplace private. But then she opened the door and slid into her mother's arms. A moment later he was sitting in the idling vehicle alone, watching his Beth being ushered off by concerned, well-meaning relatives. He hadn't even managed a good-night kiss, but he consoled himself with the thought that they would soon be together permanently. He wondered briefly what Megan Maitland was going to do with herself once she was all alone in that big old mausoleum. As for himself, he'd take a pup tent if Beth was with him. And he had the crazy notion that she'd go for it even if that was all he had to offer her.

Joke's on you this time, Isakawuate, he thought gaily. As insane as it seemed, the woman truly loved him. He didn't doubt it. But he'd soon learn not to tweak Old Man Coyote's tail quite so thoughtlessly.

CHAPTER FOURTEEN

BETH SIGHED and pushed away the photocopied article on childhood aggression she'd been trying to read for the past half-hour. Her mind would not cooperate. She could think of nothing but Ty and her determination to end the relationship before she caused a split in his family. She had to wonder if Ty would allow it to come to that. No doubt he would end the relationship himself, as he'd tried to do from the beginning. She should stop refusing his calls and keeping herself away from him and get it over with. It was so very difficult, though. Every moment she ached for him. Only by forcefully reminding herself that she did this from love could she maintain her resolve.

It was ironic that when Ty had alluded to the differences in their backgrounds, she had assumed he feared rejection by the Maitlands when it was really the other way around. He'd obviously known from the beginning that she could not overcome Cob's disapproval. Perhaps it even went beyond Cob. Perhaps none of them approved of her. Nevertheless, she was glad she had gone to him that day from the hospital. She understood, finally, what it was that stood between them.

At least he had returned to work. She hoped the telephone calls her mother had made on his behalf had helped. Once she and Jake had made Megan understand that Ty was not responsible for the covert operation, that his caution had, indeed, saved Beth's life, Megan had been adamant that he receive the recognition and reward he deserved.

Beth wished, however, that her mother would stop questioning her about "the gentleman's intentions," as if her honor were at stake. She was running out of excuses for why they were not seeing each another, and she knew better than to tell Megan Maitland that anyone deemed one of her children unworthy. Besides, the resulting storm would accomplish nothing. She couldn't change who or what she was.

She had thought returning to work would help her get over him. Work had always taken a very important place in her life. Caring for the children of clinic staff and patients brought her fulfillment. She still welcomed their little faces every morning and experienced the satisfaction of caring for them to the best of her ability, but somehow the work did not lessen the longing that she felt for what—or rather, whom—she could not have. Sighing, she reached for the paper again.

Her hand froze, hovering over the stapled sheets, when a tap at her office door heralded a visitor, the latest of many since her return. She pasted on a smile, expecting one of her siblings or assistants, anyone but the tall, elegant woman who stood there swathed in cashmere.

"Darcy?"

The gorgeous supermodel grinned. "What some people won't do to get into the papers."

Laughing in shock, Beth got to her feet. "Darcy Taylor! I can't believe it!"

"My goodness, just look at you," Darcy said, gushing. "Ellie must be every bit as grown-up and beautiful."

Beth laughed. "Oh, my gosh! How long has it been?"

Darcy made a face. "Let's not go there, please. Too long."

"What are you doing here?"

"Checking on my girl. How are you, Beth?"

"In shock."

Beth hurried around the desk and ushered her old baby-sitter toward a chair. Darcy moved with languid grace, sinking into the hard chair as if it were a down-filled pillow.

"You look marvelous!" Beth exclaimed, astonished, as ever, by the other woman's patrician beauty. She'd always marveled at Darcy's cool radiance, the long, dark hair, the tall, lean body, the huge, expressive eyes, the very perfection of her—and the obvious lack of conceit. If anything, Darcy was a little shy, slow to trust and rather aloof until she decided to do so. Beth remembered all the wonderful times they'd shared. Nine years their senior, Darcy had been the best of baby-sitters for Beth and Ellie on the nanny's day off, never scolding, full of fun ideas and able to tell the twins apart even though they'd tried their best to fool her on occasion.

Darcy blushed at the compliment. "Thank you. You're looking lovely yourself. But are you sure you should be here so soon after everything that's happened? If half of what I hear and read is true, you must be emotionally, if not physically, traumatized."

"You should know better than to believe everything the press puts out," Beth said, waving a hand dismissively.

"Tell me about it," Darcy muttered wryly. Then she leaned forward and clasped Beth's hands in hers. "I mean that. I want to hear all about it."

Beth tamped down her reluctance, took a deep breath and began. "I stupidly tried to convince myself that I was in love with a man named Brandon Dumont. He's a stockbroker, a handsome devil—and I do mean devil—and possesses a certain oily charm."

"Sounds like a dozen men I know," Darcy commented sourly.

"I guess I was tired of waiting for Mr. Right," she went on, "but it didn't take me long to realize I'd made a mistake with Brandon. I was trying to find a way to diplomatically break it off when I heard that he was having an affair with a woman he worked with. He couldn't deny it, and while I was hurt, my overwhelming emotion was sheer relief. I broke it off, of course, but Brandon begged me to tell everyone that he had jilted me and not the other way around. His social standing was very important to him, and he didn't want to be known as the guy who got dumped by a Maitland. I was so glad to be rid of him that I didn't think twice about doing as he asked.''

"You Maitlands always have been cavalier about the family name and influence," Darcy said dryly. "Most people in your position would take every opportunity to lord it over the rest of us mere humans."

"Oh, right." Beth rolled her eyes. "Like your fans wouldn't knock me down and run over me to get an autograph from Darcy Taylor."

"You know what I mean," Darcy argued. "I've never met anyone so conscious of the privilege accorded them or so willing to forgo it. The man cheated on you, and yet you were willing to set aside your own pride in order to bolster his. I couldn't have done that, Beth."

"I wish I hadn't!" Beth exclaimed. "It was all part of his plan, you see. He married Brianne because she claimed to be carrying his child. When he realized the pregnancy was a lie, she threatened to reveal some of his shady dealings. He'd been cheating his clients, you see, and Brianne, who was an accountant, had proof. So he murdered her and left her body here in my office. He orchestrated the whole thing to make it look as though I had killed her out of jealousy. It was his way of paying us both back for upsetting his carefully laid plans to climb the social ladder."

"By marrying a Maitland."

"Exactly."

Darcy shook her head. "You poor thing. It's bad enough, what he did to you, but to have it splattered all over the press. And with so much speculation!"

"I don't suppose you would know anything about that," Beth quipped.

To her surprise, she did not get the teasing retort she'd expected. Instead, Darcy slumped—as much as that perfect posture would allow—and frowned sadly. "It's awful, the things they'll print." She smiled wanly. "I've had enough, frankly. I'm thinking seriously of retiring."

Belatedly Beth became aware that her mouth had dropped open. "But I thought you loved modeling!"

"No," Darcy admitted. "It was never *my* dream. I never wanted to leave Austin. In fact, I've bought a house not far from here. I've come home, Beth. I've finally come home."

"Does Mitchell know?" Beth asked automatically. It was a natural question. He and Darcy were the same age. They'd attended school together and once had seemed close.

"Not yet," Darcy said offhandedly. "But he will. For the moment though, I'd like to keep my presence—and my plans—a secret. How is Mitch, by the way?"

"He's fine."

Darcy nodded as if she expected to hear nothing else. It was a commonplace question and response. Yet Beth remembered how shocked and confused her big brother had been when Darcy had abandoned Austin during their senior year in high school for a life of glamour in New York City. She had kept in touch in the beginning, sending postcards from exotic locales and even making a phone call or two. A few letters had been exchanged between the twins and Darcy early on, but Beth had gotten distracted, and she suspected that Ellie had, too.

"How's Ellie?" Darcy asked, as if reading Beth's mind.

"Ellie is wonderful. She's married now. Did you know?"

Darcy nodded. "I heard something about it."

"She and Sloan have two beautiful daughters, twins, just like us," Beth told her, beaming.

"So Ellie's a mother," Darcy said with sigh. "I envy her that."

"Actually she's a stepmom," Beth said, "but that won't make any difference as far as Ellie's concerned. She loves those girls like her very own."

"I'm sure she does," Darcy murmured wistfully.

"She's also the clinic administrator."

"Why am I not surprised?" Darcy exclaimed. "She was the serious one."

"So true," Beth admitted. "Everyone was shocked when she and Sloan got together, but I've never seen Ellie happier."

"And what about you?" Darcy asked.

"Well, as you must know, I'm director of the day-care center here."

"You always did love babies," Darcy commented knowingly.

"So did you," Beth replied.

"How are you managing the press scrutiny?" Darcy asked, changing the subject.

Beth shrugged, willing to discuss anything Darcy wanted. "I do my best to ignore it. How do you handle it?"

Leaning forward, the famous model confessed conspiratorially, "I do my best to ignore it."

They both smiled. "For all the good it does!" Beth added, and Darcy concurred with a definite nod.

"What's this about a covert operation and rescue?" she asked lightly.

"I wore a wire into Brandon's office and got him to admit that he'd murdered Brianne and framed me," Beth said dispassionately.

"Good grief." Darcy shook her head disbelievingly. "Weren't you frightened?"

"Not really, but I should have been." She instinctively lifted a hand to the collar of her slinky navy blue turtleneck.

"Brandon tried to strangle me just as he had Brianne. Ty and Jake barely got to me in time."

"Thank God for that!" Darcy lifted a hand to her chest and shuddered delicately. "There was no permanent damage?" she asked.

"None, thankfully."

"Jake, that would be your brother, right?"

"Yes."

"And Ty would be?"

Beth looked away. "Oh, um, one of the detectives on the case."

If Darcy suspected that Ty might be more than that, she said nothing, merely shook her head wonderingly. "You've been through so much. I can't tell you how glad I am to know it's all over. It's amazing, isn't it, how so far out of control our lives can become?"

"Everything does seem to get complicated," Beth agreed, thinking how complex her relationship with Ty was, how much it hurt to let it go. "Sometimes love just isn't enough," she murmured more to herself than to Darcy. The dismal truth rushed back, and she gulped down the lump in her throat, the same lump that had been there since Cob Redstone had so bluntly declared what Ty had been trying to tell her all along. Unbidden, she heard Ty's declaration again, just as if she was sitting on that lonely road, waiting for him to come back to the car.

Brothers are forever.

She couldn't argue with the sentiment, and she could never love someone who expected her to choose between him and her siblings, especially her twin, Ellie, so how could she expect it of Ty?

"Beth?"

Startled, she battled tears. How had she forgotten Darcy's presence?

"Honey, are you sure you should be working today? You look a little wan."

Beth managed a weak smile. "You may be right, Darcy. But I'm so glad I was here when you stopped by."

"I'd like to visit longer," Darcy said, rising to her feet and glancing at her diamond-studded wristwatch, "but I have an appointment."

Beth, too, rose, took both of Darcy's hands in hers and led her to the door. "I'm so glad you came. It was very thoughtful of you."

"I had to check up on my girls," Darcy said again. "When things settle down, we'll make a lunch date and catch up. All right?"

"I'd love that," Beth said, squeezing her hands. "We'll find a quiet, private place."

"With no press," Darcy added.

"With no press," Beth echoed, and they both laughed. Impulsively Beth hugged the other woman. "Welcome home, Darcy."

Darcy hugged her back. "Dear Beth. Thank you. Take care of yourself."

"You, too."

They parted with a shared smile. Beth closed the door and leaned against it. It was so good to see Darcy again. She wondered if Mitchell would be equally glad to see her. Beth hoped he would. His wife's death just a year after their wedding had scarred Mitch and left him very much alone. Beth wished something or someone would penetrate that shell of solitariness with which he seemed to shield himself. With a sigh, she pushed away from the door, moved to her desk and once more picked up the article she'd been trying to read all morning.

"So CALL HER AGAIN."

Ty glared at Paul and snapped in frustration, "I've been calling her for days, and I've tried to see her at the mansion twice, for all the good it's done. She's not talking to me."

"She's just busy," Paul said offhandedly. "Call her again."

"She's avoiding me, Paul. Why can't you see that?"

Paul closed the file he'd been reading and sat back in his desk chair. "The kid's crazy about you, Redstone, though I can't for the life of me imagine why. Trust me. I heard it all the way out to your mother's place. 'Ty saved my life. Ty's a true hero. Ty's the best detective in the whole department.' She's wild about you."

"I thought so," Ty muttered, dropping into his chair. He braced his elbows on the desk and pushed a hand through his hair, lifting and tucking the long front strands behind his ears in one easy movement. "Now I don't know what to think."

Paul's hands spread wide in bewilderment. "Something must have gone lame, then, because I'm telling you the woman is nuts about you."

In a gesture of impatience, Ty shoved the telephone across the desk toward his partner. "If you know so much about it, maybe *you* should call her."

"And tell her what? Stop avoiding my boy Redstone?"

"I thought we'd be celebrating by now, with the case successfully concluded and Dumont in jail," Ty said mournfully.

"And you back on the force and in everyone's good graces," Paul added.

"No small thanks to the Maitlands," Ty concluded. "Her mother even called the mayor, for pity's sake."

With one hand Paul stroked his pale chin. "Something's not right, pal. Something's way out of kilter. You sure you didn't say anything to scramble the deal when she showed up at your mom's? You were pretty bent out of shape with both of us."

"I swear it was nothing like that," Ty insisted. "Cob made a fool of himself, but we settled that between us before we left."

Paul sighed. "Don't know what to tell you then." He snagged a pencil from the tray on his desktop and began bouncing the eraser end against the blotter, a sign that he was in deep thought. Suddenly the pencil flipped end over end. "Hey, now. That's the ticket." He reached for the telephone.

"What are you talking about?" Ty demanded.

"You said it yourself, partner mine," Paul told him mysteriously, busily flipping through his card file. He found the number he wanted and began punching it into the telephone he shared with Ty.

"Paul?" Ty demanded, wanting to know what was going on, but his partner held up a stalling hand before speaking into the telephone receiver.

"Yes, hello. Beth Maitland, please.... My name? Paul Jester."

A moment later, Paul sat in his desk chair and grinned. "Beth! How are you? Huh? No, nothing wrong. As a matter of fact, in case you don't know, Brandon Dumont was indicted yesterday and took a plea bargain. Forty-four years before a first chance at parole. The accounts we found hidden in Brianne Dumont's desk were the final nail in his coffin. It's well and truly over. Time for a *celebration*, wouldn't you say?" Paul lifted an eyebrow at Ty, smug as hell.

All Ty could do was shake his head.

"Funny you should say that," Paul went on doggedly. "Ty said the same thing, actually. No reason to celebrate, just doing his job, yada, yada. But really, I'd like to get something besides an ass-chewing out of this deal, pardon my French. So I thought if Ty won't join in, maybe we could convince you to help us celebrate. How about dinner with me and my wife? She's dying to meet you, what with you being our most famous ex-suspect and all. What do you say?"

Ty rolled his eyes. Beth Maitland was too damned smart

to fall for anything so obvious. "Just ask her why..." he began, but Paul instantly covered the mouthpiece with his fingers and sent Ty a stern glare. With Paul's baby face, it was a little bit like being taken to task by Cupid, but Ty reluctantly settled for mouthing the command. "Ask her why she won't talk to me!"

Paul obliged by swiveling in his chair, his back to Ty. Angry, Ty slammed a desk drawer just to make it difficult for Paul to hide the fact that he was not alone, not that Paul took any notice. He was too busy wheedling.

"Aw, come on, Beth. Nan's really counting on this. I promised her she'd get to meet you. You pick the restaurant. How's that? Or, if you'd rather, you can come over to our place. I know you won't mind the kids even if they do get a little loud sometimes. But then I'll just have to take the wife out on my own. You wouldn't know how she is when she doesn't get what she wants. What's that?" He turned to Ty with a triumphant grin that transformed his plump cheeks into twin apples. "The Agnes Room will be just fine. Nan will be thrilled. Honestly. Say about seven-thirty on Friday evening? No, no, I'll make the reservations. And thanks a million. Nan's going to love meeting you."

He spoke a few seconds longer, then rang off, grinning at Ty in such a manner that Ty wanted to smack him—except for one thing. He'd given Ty an opportunity to speak with Beth and find out what was going on.

"I'm going to pay big time for this one, aren't I?" Ty groaned, feigning dismay.

Paul leaned back in his chair, puffing his chest with indecent pride. "Let's just say we're even now, native boy, and let it go at that."

"No score to even, Paul," Ty said seriously. "Everything worked out fine."

Paul shook his head. "The wire was too dangerous," he admitted. "You were right about that."

"And you were right that it was the only way to break

the case," Ty countered. "I'd say that put us at even from the start."

"She was hurt," Paul reminded him.

"Not seriously."

"You warned me how it would be if I let that happen."

"I overreacted."

For a moment, Paul seemed to give that serious thought, forefinger tapping on his desk blotter. Then he grinned unrepentantly. "Yeah, you did. Besides, I hauled the woman all the way out to your mom's. Maybe you do owe me."

Ty laughed and shook his head. But then he frowned, realizing that his worst suspicions had just been confirmed. Beth really was avoiding him, and he couldn't for the life of him think why. Unless it was Cob. Surely she understood that Cob's attitudes were not his own. Cob was a mixed-up kid trying hard to grow up in a world where he felt he had never belonged. Surely Ty could make her see that, given the chance. If not, the cold, hard knot in the pit of his belly told him all too well what the future was going to hold for him.

BETH WORRIED all that Friday that she had made an inappropriate choice. True, Paul had said that he wanted to celebrate and from the way he was talking, his wife liked to splurge once in a while, but the Agnes Room was one of Austin's finer restaurants and could well be outside a detective's means. Perhaps she should offer to pick up the tab. He had cleared her of murder, after all. Well, he and Ty had cleared her.

The thought of Ty brought a pang of deep misery. He hadn't called in two days, and she couldn't help thinking, perversely, that he'd given up awfully easily after everything that had gone on between them. Still, she supposed she couldn't blame him. He probably only wanted to tell her about Brandon anyway. Or to break their relationship off once and for all. Well, he needn't bother. She could

never force him to choose between her and his brother. She
had been right to avoid his calls. She only wished that she
could stop thinking about him. Perhaps with time, she'd
forget Ty Redstone had ever existed. Sure she would. On
her deathbed most likely, and perhaps not even then.

At any rate, while she was grateful to Paul Jester, she'd
rather have eaten glass than see him again. He reminded
her too much of Ty and what might have been. Paul had
been adamant, however. She could only surmise that his
wife was pushing him for the meeting, and it wouldn't hurt
Beth to be gracious for an hour or two. She reflected wryly
that Darcy had been right, after all. What privilege the
Maitlands enjoyed must never be taken lightly. If Detective
Jester's wife wanted to dine with Beth Maitland, Detective
Jester's wife was going to dine with Beth Maitland. If the
evening became too difficult, she could always plead a
headache and leave.

Seven o'clock came all too soon. The previous four days
had dragged by at a snail's pace, but now that the hour she
dreaded was at hand, time flew. She had barely managed
to pull on an appropriate outfit, a sable-brown stretch-velvet
dress and matching shrug, when the clock on the landing
chimed the hour. In a panic, Beth attacked her hair with a
brush, twisted it into a sloppy knot, secured it with an enormous tortoiseshell clip and rushed out of the room.

After telling Harold where she was going and when she
expected to return, should her mother inquire, she hurried
to the garage and her car. She gunned past the group of
reporters milling at the mansion gate, and by the time she
pulled up in front of the restaurant, her watch hand was
sitting exactly on the half-hour. After tossing her keys to
the attendant for valet parking, she hurried inside. The Jesters had already taken their seats and Beth followed the
jacketed waiter through the sumptuous dining room, skirting heavy chrome chairs upholstered in dark red leather and
tables topped in crisp white linen. She spotted the back of

Paul's blond head at some distance and took note of the attractive brunette at his right, but then an all-too-familiar figure rose to his feet, and her heart plummeted.

Ty.

He looked spectacular. His hair was shorter than she'd ever seen it, testament to the fact that he'd recently visited his barber, and blue-black in the candlelight. His collarless shirt was the same blue-black, silk, with pin tucks top-stitched in white, and the dark brown moleskin suit he wore was of a very modish cut. He seemed very tall and imposing, his dark gaze penetrating even in the dim light. For an instant, she considered bolting, but then Paul turned, smiled and climbed to his feet, holding out a hand to welcome her. Beth gulped and proceeded forward reluctantly.

"Beth! You look marvelous," Paul exclaimed, catching her hand and drawing her forward to meet his wife. "This is Nan. Sweetheart, the one, the only Beth Maitland."

"Oh, I've heard so much about you!" Nan Jester fairly gushed. She turned a glance at Ty, "Beth's a very beautiful lady. And so brave, too. Paul's told me all about it." She gasped as if grasping the intensity of the danger for the first time, and turned to Beth. "Going in after a murderer all by yourself! Except Ty was there, wasn't he? Dear Ty."

"Dear Ty" stared at Beth as if he was unaware anyone else was in the room. The waiter had pulled out her chair and gestured toward it with a slight tilt of his head. Recalling herself, Beth slid around the table and into the chair. Paul immediately reclaimed his seat, but Ty hesitated until Beth was well and truly settled. Only then did he sit, resting his forearms on the table and folding his hands. She made an attempt to smile, knew it was abysmal and remarked blithely, "I didn't expect to see you here."

"I know. I've been trying to talk to you for days. This seemed the only way to manage it. Nan's right, by the way. You look stunning tonight. But then you always do."

Beth felt her heart speed up slightly. She fidgeted in her chair. "Th-thank you."

"I went to the mansion," Ty said. "The guard kept telling me that you weren't in. I called on the telephone and was told the same thing. You're avoiding me, Beth. Why?"

Dismayed, she glanced at Paul and Nan, who were watching and listening avidly. Beth felt her face flame. She couldn't discuss this here. "I, uh, I've been terribly busy. I was away from work so long, and..." The excuse sounded horribly lame even to her own ears. What a coward she was. Why hadn't she simply set him free? She swallowed forcefully and tried to find the words, keeping her gaze trained on the rim of the silver charger before her. "You must understand, Ty," she said softly, and he bent his head close to hear her. "I don't expect anything of you. We made no promises. All along you said—"

A harsh flash of light went off directly in her face, almost blinding her. Caught unawares, she blinked and lifted a hand to shield her gaze. Suddenly everything was confusion. Orders were barked. Uniformed waiters crowded around them, trying to push the intruders away. A microphone was shoved in front of her face and she looked into the grinning visage of Chelsea Markum.

"You're having dinner with the detectives who broke your case, I see. Care to tell us what's going on? Is this business, reward or something more? The public wants to know. And what are your comments on Brandon Dumont's guilty plea? Were you surprised? Have you recovered from his attack?"

Beth shoved back her chair, only to find Ty already on his feet, his hand on her elbow. Her usual aplomb had deserted her and she felt perilously close to tears. She'd been dodging the press for days now. Her mother and Ellie had tried to tell her that she would be wise to hold a press conference and tell them all they wanted to know in hopes of getting them permanently out of her hair, but she hadn't felt able to face them. She very much feared that she was going to embarrass and humiliate herself totally. Why hadn't she realized that the reporters would follow her? Naturally they didn't bother following her to the office because of the heavy security there, but in public she was fair game. Fool. What an utter fool!

"Get out of the way!" Ty ordered loudly. The waiters and other restaurant personnel kept trying unsuccessfully to shove the growing horde of reporters aside.

"Freedom of the press, Detective Redstone!" Chelsea Markum shouted, even as she was jostled away by Paul.

Spying a narrow pathway of escape, Beth took it, all but running through the tables of murmuring diners. Ty was right with her. They rushed into the foyer. He shoved open the heavy mahogany door and she plunged through it—straight into someone's arms. Gasping, she looked up, startled to see the familiar face of her handsome brother.

"Beth?"

"Mitch!" Belatedly she recognized the warm, strong body. Without warning, she burst into sobs.

"Get her out of here!" Ty ordered. Mitch looked past her at the advancing reporters and didn't hesitate. A comforting arm about her waist, he started to turn her away, but Ty's hand grasped her elbow, holding her back.

"Beth," he said, "I'm sorry. I…" Without warning, he ducked his head and kissed her hard on the mouth. A light flashed. Stunned out of her tears, Beth jerked back, gaping at him. "Don't keep me away," he pleaded, even as he shoved her at Mitch once more.

"What have you gotten yourself into now?" Mitchell wanted to know, whisking her out of there. Beth could only gape over her shoulder at Ty. Holding the reporters at bay with outstretched arms, he was ordering them to leave her alone. Inanely, she realized she hadn't said goodbye to the

Jesters. She didn't dare think beyond that, not with Ty's kiss still tingling on her lips and the reporters breathing down her neck. She didn't dare even consider that perhaps she was the one who had given up too easily.

CHAPTER FIFTEEN

"WELL, YOU'VE done it now," Paul said, completely dismissing his part in the previous evening's fiasco. Ty turned over the newspaper that Paul had tossed on his desk. He'd already seen the photos and the headline.

"What would you have had me do?" he demanded. "Let them run her to ground?"

"You didn't have to give them an interview," Paul replied blandly.

"I didn't give them an interview. I answered a couple of questions."

"A couple of questions," Paul mocked. He raised his voice to a soprano. "What's your interest in Ms. Maitland now that the case against her has been closed?" He switched to a booming bass. "Very simply, I love her." Once more adopting his own mien, he concluded, "Very adept, native boy. Maybe you ought to consider diplomacy for your next career."

Ty shook his head. "I kept them away from Beth, and I made my point."

"Okay," Paul conceded wryly. "But can you imagine what the press presence around her will be like now?"

Ty turned over the paper again and stared at the two-column shot of him kissing Beth. Set into the lower left corner, a much smaller photo showed him holding his arms wide, mouth open, scowl in place. The headline above the article read, "'I Love Her,' Says Detective."

"You're right," Ty murmured, "I have to get to her before they do."

"You have other problems," Paul told him warningly. "I don't think the captain's a romantic. I heard him shouting as I passed by his office on my way in, and your name was definitely in the air."

He had expected it, really, Ty thought. What he hadn't expected was how he'd feel about it. Perhaps it should matter more. His career had been a priority in his life for a long time, since he'd vindicated his father, in fact. In some very important ways, it defined him. But nothing mattered more than Beth, and he had to be certain she understood that. He wondered if she'd seen the paper yet, and if so, what she'd thought of it.

The phone rang. Ty snatched it up, hoping that it was her. The captain barked into his ear.

"Yes, sir. Right away."

He hung up the phone, folded the paper and smiled ruefully at Paul, lifting his eyebrows to say he didn't know what was going to happen, but that whatever it was didn't unduly concern him. He took his handgun from his desk drawer, in case the captain asked him to turn it in, and slipped it into the shoulder harness beneath his navy blue suit coat.

"Wish me luck," he said blithely, striding out of the cubicle. He should have known that Paul would do more than that.

AT ABOUT the same time Ty's captain was telling him, at full volume, what a disappointment he was to the department, Beth was bending over her mother's desk, a sniffling and wide-eyed three-year-old on one hip, his fist fastened securely in her hair. There hadn't been time to hand him over to anyone after what Jester had told her on the phone.

"Mother you've got to call again," she said.

Megan shoved back from her desk and glared at her

daughter with obvious exasperation. "Beth, I've already done my bit to save this young man's career. Whatever he's done this time, I don't think I should interfere."

"Whatever he's done this time?" Beth echoed disbelievingly. "He hasn't done anything, ever! You know that."

"Then I don't understand why he needs my intervention again."

Beth closed her eyes, opening them just in time to catch a small, sneakered foot as it swung toward the vase of flowers placed on the corner of her mother's desk. "It's all my fault," she said, tucking the foot where it belonged.

"Don't be silly," Megan began.

"They know," Beth interrupted softly. "They know about the affair we were having during the investigation."

Her mother sighed and shoved down the small, tasteful reading glasses perched on her nose in order to pinch the narrow bridge with thumb and forefinger. "I warned you this would happen. How did they find out?"

Beth gulped. "It's in the newspaper."

"The newspaper!"

"Someone gave them a statement."

"Beth, you've gone too far this time," Megan said angrily. "First you want him, then you don't. Now this."

"I didn't do it!"

"Then who?"

"Mother, please just call. Tell them...tell them something! His career is everything to him, Mother, everything."

"All right," Megan said, reached for the telephone, "but this is the last time I trot out the Maitland influence for Ty Redstone. If the two of you don't get your act together after this, I will personally want to know why!"

Silently Beth nodded. She didn't have the heart to lie to her mother, but she knew that she and Ty could not, in Megan's words, get their act together. Nothing had changed as far as she could see, no matter what he had told the reporters. It was a gallant effort, though, announcing in the papers that he loved her. Silly man. How she loved him! Too much to split him from his family and see him slowly come to resent her. Still, the whole thing had to be settled. She couldn't avoid it any longer. She would make arrangements to see him that very night. Biting her lip, she willed back the tears. It was already over. Tonight she would make it official. Why, then, did that make her feel so much worse?

TY STROLLED into the clinic with more cool than he was feeling. Two dozen roses swaddled in green paper rested in the curve of one arm. It had been a near thing, keeping his badge. The captain had not appreciated having his ears pinned by his superiors after the Dumont operation. Ty had foolishly offered himself as scapegoat, and the captain hadn't been happy to turn him loose again. Someone had to be held accountable when a Maitland was injured during a police operation, after all. Admitting publicly to a personal romantic involvement with said Maitland had not, perhaps, been Ty's finest hour, but he was glad it was out. He loved Beth, and he didn't care any longer who knew it. Now it was time to settle with her.

He still wasn't sure why the chief of police had intervened on his behalf, but he had his suspicions after learning that Paul had informed Beth of what was going down. These Maitlands, they knew how to stand with a guy—or against him, if the need arose. Apparently they had decided to stand with him, and he was properly grateful. Once he had secured Beth's approval, he would tell them exactly that.

After all that had happened in the past twenty-four hours, he expected a welcome, tepid if not warm. Instead, the security guard at the desk made him wait while he called Michael Lord, the head of the clinic's security staff. The first stirrings of unease touched him when Lord sauntered into view wearing a determined expression.

"Redstone."

He didn't offer his hand, so Ty didn't, either. "Lord," he said warily. "I need to see Beth Maitland."

Michael shook his head. "I'm sorry, Ty. No can do."

No. Ty laid aside the roses, appropriating a corner of the guard's desk. "Now, look," he said, his patience at an end, "I need to see Beth, and I'm going to see her, one way or another."

"Sorry. I have my orders," Michael insisted, widening his stance. "Ms. Maitland asked that you be kept away earlier this week, and no one's rescinded that directive."

"I'm rescinding it," Ty declared tightly. Michael stared at him. Ty's temper flared. He shoved back the sides of his coat. "I'm going to see Beth Maitland. Now, we can do this the easy way or the hard way, but I am going to see her here today."

Michael sighed. "Please, Ty. Let's not get tough. It won't do any good, and it might do a lot of harm."

Ty couldn't believe this was happening, but he had no intention of backing down. He was mentally reviewing his options when the elevator doors slid open and Mitchell Maitland got off. A newspaper had been folded into the pocket of his lab coat and he was studying a chart, but he glanced up and paused.

"What's going on?"

"We've been ordered to keep Redstone out, but he doesn't much like it," Michael told him, not even looking in his direction.

"I'm going to see Beth," Ty announced stubbornly, never taking his eyes off Michael Lord.

Mitchell strolled to the security desk and glanced at the roses. "I take it those are for her."

Finally, Ty spared him a glance. It seemed to be answer enough for the doctor, who nodded and extracted the folded newspaper from his pocket before dropping it onto the desk beside the roses. "Let him go through," he said.

Surprised, Michael looked at the doctor. Ty breathed a silent sigh of relief. That was the second of Beth's brothers to whom he owed much.

Immediately Michael relaxed. "Whatever you say. Sorry, Ty. Nothing personal."

"I understand," Ty told him, picking up the roses. He looked at Mitchell Maitland. "Thanks. I appreciate it."

Mitch clutched the clipboard in front of him. "I talked to my brother about you."

"That would be Jake, I presume."

"Yes."

Ty glanced at the folded newspaper on the desk corner. "And I take it that you also read this morning's paper."

Beth's brother nodded, studying him blatantly. Then he crooked an eyebrow. "You take a good picture," he commented wryly.

"That's it?" Ty demanded. "That's all you have to say about it?"

Mitch studied him a moment longer, and Ty did the same in return. They were of a height, though Mitchell was a little beefier. His strong Maitland features bore just a touch of arrogance, and his dark hair was tousled slightly. Finally he shook a finger at Ty.

"Treat her well," he warned.

Surprised by the depth of his relief, Ty vowed, "I will!"

"Beth's something of a wild child," Mitch went on, "but at heart she's the very best of us. You hurt her, you have the rest of us to contend with."

Ty grinned. "You Maitlands are your own tribe. Maybe I'll join up."

"You could do worse."

"But not better, I think," Ty replied.

Mitch nodded and spun on one heel. "I expect you know your way to the day-care center."

"I do," Ty said, falling into step beside the doctor as he moved away from the security station.

Mitch pushed back the cuff of his left sleeve, glancing at his watch. "I'll leave you then. I have an appointment." With that he hurried away, lifting a hand in farewell.

These Maitlands, Ty thought, *are an unpredictable lot.* Including Beth. Suddenly chilled, he wondered what he would do if Beth refused him.

BETH CROUCHED on her little stool, her knees drawn up. She'd dressed western-style in blue jeans, shirt and boots in honor of Cowboy Tom, the hero of the book she was reading during today's storytime. In keeping with the costume, she had braided her hair loosely and tied it with a string. She'd had a three-year-old named Morgan hanging on it most of the day.

Upset at having to return a toy to the child from whom he'd taken it, the boy had needed calming and had eagerly allowed her to hold him. He'd proved so unwilling to be set down a short while later that she'd wound up taking him to her mother's office with her. Afterward, he'd wrapped her braid around his wrist and refused to be dislodged until she'd promised that he could accompany her to the changing table with his infant sister. Beth understood that the new baby had upset Morgan's comfortable world and that his behavior would soon stabilize. He sat as close to her as he could get, leaning against her leg. She showed a brightly colored drawing to the eager little faces ranged about her in a semicircle before turning the page and picking up the thread of the story.

"'Tom lifted the lost baby calf onto his shoulder,'" she read. "'"Moooo," said the calf. "I want my mama."'

"'"Hold on there," said Tom. He knew he had to get the little calf warm before he could look for its mama. It was shivering cold.'"

Tiffany, a little girl with twin blond pigtails perched high on the sides of her head, scooted closer and demanded, "I wanna see!"

Other little voices immediately took up the words. "I wanna see! I wanna see! I wanna see!"

Beth calmly turned the book to show them the picture of Cowboy Tom with the shivering, sad-looking calf lying across his shoulders as he led his trusty horse over rocky ground.

"Can I see, too?" asked a warm, familiar voice at her shoulder. She gaped at Ty's smiling face, and her heart turned over in her chest. A quick glance across the room at the door showed her assistant Lizzie looking on benevolently. Before she could answer him, Ty laid a big bouquet of roses in her lap, crossed his ankles and quickly, gracefully lowered himself to the floor, arms resting on his knees as he craned his neck to look at the picture book. "May I?" he asked, taking the book from her suddenly nerveless fingers.

"Uh, I'm not sure."

"Oh, let me," he pleaded. "I don't often get to do this sort of thing, you know."

She couldn't think how to deny him, so she shut her mouth, accepting this lull before the storm. Too soon, they would have to talk about important matters.

As easily as if he did this sort of thing every day, Ty took up reading the story while deftly fielding such questions as, "Who are you? Can I sit in your lap? Where's your kid?" Before he was done, they were all over him, not just on his lap, but hanging about his neck, curled close to his sides beneath the curves of his arms and sitting on his feet. Somehow, despite the many interruptions, Cowboy Tom reunited the frightened calf and worried mother cow in record time. A stream of questions followed.

"What you bring them flowers for?" asked Jared, the boy standing at his shoulder, little arms wrapped tight about Ty's neck.

"For Miss Beth, of course." He slid her a look so rife with longing that she could barely catch her breath.

"We got flowers in pots," said Melanie from his lap, pointing at the window ledge.

"Yes, I know."

"Are you a teacher?" demanded Tiffany, pressing down with both hands on Ty's feet.

"No, I'm a police detective."

"Show your gun!" one of the boys demanded.

"No gun," Ty said sternly. "Guns are not toys. They're not for children." He softened his tone. "I'll show you my shield, though, my badge."

"Yeah, show your badge!"

Dutifully Ty extracted his badge in its leather case from his jacket pocket, flipping it open for the children to ooh and ah over. They looked at the picture on his identity card.

"Policemans is our friends," one of them said.

Another confessed happily, "A cop stopped my mom for speeding."

A few seconds later, Ty tucked away his badge and gently but firmly put an end to the fun. "Okay." He began setting children on their feet one by one. "What's next on the agenda? Think you guys can play quietly for a few minutes while I talk to Miss Beth?"

Beth lifted a hand, signaling Lizzie to come for the children without looking in her direction. She couldn't keep her eyes off Ty. "Time to wash up for lunch now," she announced, getting to her feet.

Ty did likewise, smoothly unfolding his long legs as he pushed to his full height. He looked so good, so very handsome. There were complaints from the children, but Lizzie had them corralled in short order and headed for the bank of low sinks in the next room. Beth was aware of Ty's intense regard all the while the children were filing from the room, but she dared not speak again until they were gone.

"The flowers are lovely, but you didn't have to," she murmured, her arms folded about them.

"A fellow can't make a marriage proposal without some sort of gift," he said baldly.

Marriage proposal? For an instant, Beth's heart soared.

"I didn't know what sort of ring to buy," he said. "I thought you might like to pick it out."

In the very next beat of her heart, she remembered why this could not be, and her hopes crashed to the ground. Overwhelmed with loss, she burst into tears.

Ty's hands fluttered around her. "Beth? Sweetheart? Darling?" With a strangled sound, he gathered her close, crooning words she did not understand. He crushed the roses between them so tightly that her face was buried in their fragrant blooms, the lush petals catching her tears. "I love you, Beth. Please don't cry. Just tell me what's wrong. I've known something wasn't right, but you wouldn't talk to me."

"I couldn't," she sobbed. Finally, she mastered herself and pushed away, swiping at the tearstains on her cheeks. "I can't marry you," she told him shakily.

Beside her, Ty stiffened. "But...I thought for sure you cared for me."

"I do! I love you with all my heart!"

He pulled her against him, shoving the roses away with impatient hands. *My beautiful roses,* she thought forlornly, following their path to the floor with her gaze. He took her braid in his fist and tugged her head back.

Bringing his nose to hers, he said firmly, "If you love me, you will marry me, because I can't make a life without you anymore. I've forgotten how, and even if I could learn again, I don't want to." He framed her face loosely with of his long, lean hands. "Beth," he added, "we didn't come so far, take such chances to lose each other now."

"But what about Cob?" she wailed. "He's your brother.

I can't make you choose between us. I can't! You'll come
to hate me if I do.''

His handsome face clouded with confusion. "What are
you talking about? Cob is my brother. He will always be
my brother. But you are my heart, that wild thing in my
chest that won't let me sleep unless you're in my bed. I
don't want to go home without you there. I can't get
through the day without seeing you. Nothing has meaning
for me if you're not part of it. Cob has nothing to do with
that.''

"He hates me," Beth reminded him forlornly.

Ty made an impatient sound in the back of his throat.
"Cob doesn't hate anyone. He hates that he is so confused,
that he hasn't yet found his place in this world. And he
loves me. Yes, he is rude and he is brusque and he is rash,
but he knows that I can't be happy without you, and he
accepts that. He told me so that night before we left.''

Brothers are forever.

"Do you mean it's all right with him?" Beth queried
dumbly, hearing those fateful words in a whole new con-
text.

"Nothing's all right with Cob just now," Ty admitted,
"but I expect that before long he'll start to find his way.
We must each make our own peace with who and what we
are, Beth. Can't you give him the time to do that?''

"Yes, of course. If he... You are saying that he accepts
me as part of your life, part of the family?''

"What other choice does he have?" Ty asked. "He is
my brother.''

"I know. But I thought, if you had to choose between
us...''

Something very close to anger clouded Ty's face. "You
think I would choose between you? You or my brother?''

"I didn't want to put you in that position!" she explained.

He shoved his hand through his hair in exasperation. "I

have *always* known we have this one thing in common,"
he said fervently. "Family. How we feel about them. How
they feel about us. Your sister Ellie, the way she glared at
me, lifting her chin at me as if I were to blame for Dumont
framing you and all that followed. Jake and Mitchell,
checking me out, sizing me up, letting me know that if
anything happened to their little sister, I would catch hell.
The others, all answering my questions with their calm
good manners, but with that look in their eyes that said
they'd slice me into ribbons if something happened to their
Beth. And your mother!" He winced. "She's the one who
scares me—Queen Maitland, ready to lop off my head if I
hurt her baby—and with the power to do it, too! But that's
all part of the reason I love you. In this one thing, we are
so alike. Could you choose between me and them? Would
they ever ask it of you?"

"No, and no," she admitted. "I see now that it's the
same with you. I saw the first part, Ty. Truly I did. It was
the second I was unsure of. It was Cob I doubted, not you."

"Ah," he said, sauntering closer. "Then you don't see
the correlation."

She frowned. "What correlation?"

"In my family," he said smoothly, "Cob is the wild
child." He tapped the end of her nose with the tip of his
forefinger.

Her jaw dropped, his implication obvious. But wasn't it
true? Hadn't the rest of the family always told her that she
was the uninhibited one, the unthinking one, the impulsive
one? She thought back to the age of eighteen, nineteen,
how she had been bursting with feeling, with this vast ca-
pacity for life, but she'd had no place to aim it, no clear
direction in which to go. The others, all the others, had
known so early what they wanted to do with their lives,
what they wanted to *be*, while she had streaked from one
great amusement to another, plunging headlong into what-

ever offered itself until, finally, she had stumbled upon the right path.

She wasn't executive material. She wasn't driven to science or business. She had a heart full of gaiety and love, and she adored children. She wanted to play with them, to wipe away tears and offer solace in a hug, to teach them and nurture their independence within the safe confines of structure, as had been done for her.

Oh, Cob was angrier than she had been, but what had she ever had to be angry about? The Maitland money and position had cushioned her uncertainties, kept her safe and at the same time curbed her wishes. She had enjoyed the loving presence of her two parents, of brothers and sisters who had indulged, and perhaps even envied, her. She sighed.

"I'm sorry," she told Ty, wiping away her tears. "I'm sorry. You were the one who saw the stumbling blocks, but in the end, I was the one who stumbled. Forgive me, please."

His smile was hot enough to scorch rock. "Come here," he said, obviously preferring to demonstrate.

Obediently, happily, she stepped closer, pressing herself against him. He clamped a hand around the back of her head and another at her waist. His mouth descended, and the wildness that had always been between them flared with renewed strength. He plunged his tongue into her mouth, and she accepted it gratefully, hungrily, wrapping her arms around him. But simply kissing was never enough for them. The wildness demanded intimacy on the deepest level. She tilted her pelvis against him, feeling the steely length and hardness of his response.

An instant later, both his hands dropped to her bottom, cupping and lifting her. She slid her arms around his neck, knowing instinctively what he wanted, so that when he lifted her bodily, she wrapped both legs around him. She thought insanely of her office, the desk, the chair, the service stairwell, anyplace more private.

Then abruptly Ty tore his mouth from hers. "No, no, no," he murmured, as if reading her thoughts. "Not yet." His hands at her waist, he set her firmly on her feet. "This time we will settle it," he gasped, his chest heaving as hard as hers. "Say it. Say you will marry me. Say yes, damn it!"

"Yes, damn it."

He blinked at her. She beamed at him. Intent flared hot in his eyes, and he swung her into his arms, so engaged that when the applause erupted, he nearly dropped her. He swung her around. They were all there—at least nearly all. Ellie, R.J., Mitch, Abby, Janelle and Anna. And her mother, of course.

Lizzie, her assistant, stepped forward shyly. "I, er, made a couple of phone calls," she admitted sheepishly.

A couple? Beth stared, goggle-eyed, at the audience they'd drawn as Ty slowly set her down.

"Well, it's about time," Megan said flatly, "after all the bother the two of you have put me to. But, Beth, you have to do something about that mob at the back door."

"Mob?" Beth asked weakly.

"Reporters," Megan informed her sharply. She pointed an elegant finger at Ty, adding, "And I hold you personally responsible, Detective." Abruptly her face softened. "Or should I say Ty?" She smiled warmly and opened her arms as she strode toward them. "Welcome to the family, Ty."

At Megan's words, everyone began talking, congratulating Ty, teasing about that kiss and the roses that lay in a heap on the floor. Beth felt tears of joy gathering in her eyes. Ty's arm was firm at her waist as he shook hands with her brothers and embraced her sisters and mother. Anna wanted to know when they could start planning the wedding.

Beth couldn't begin to think about it yet. "What are you doing here?" she asked instead.

"Janelle and I had some details for her wedding to go over with Mother."

If Janelle seemed a little miffed that Beth had inadvertently stolen her thunder, at least she said nothing.

"We'll talk about it and let you know," Beth said to her sister, knowing full well that they wouldn't talk about it for some time. The look in Ty's eyes said it all. The moment they were alone, truly alone, they were going to tear off their clothes and make love. As usual. She laughed, so delightedly happy she couldn't do anything else.

The future shone brightly ahead of her as she listened to the excited babble of family and friends and felt Ty's strong presence at her side, in her heart. Ushered by her other assistant, Cheryl, and one of the staff, the under-twos spilled into the room from lunch, ready for their storytime. Shortly they would be joined by the three-year-olds, who were at lunch, and then everyone would take a nap. The kindergartners would start arriving later on, after school. They didn't take older children at the center except on a temporary, often emergency, basis.

One day, my own children will be among them, Beth thought with savage joy, and in the midst of the chaos, she turned her face into Ty's chest, content, for the first time since she'd known him, to simply be held. She knew then what Cob was looking for, what he would one day find and what Brandon never could. It was the very thing that made this world go around, the root of her family and every family like it, the only true way to belong, the foundation on which this clinic was built, the only power or privilege that counted.

I love you, her heart whispered to his.

I love you, too, his whispered back.

And in the distant shadows of yesterday, today and tomorrow, Old Man Coyote laughed, not with derision or scorn, but with satisfaction. The Native son had found his heart's mate. Two families would be joined, and a third come into being. One tribe, one people, with the common language of love.

MAITLAND MATERNITY

continues with

FORMULA: FATHER

by

Karen Hughes

Fertility specialist Mitchell Maitland couldn't believe his eyes when supermodel Darcy Taylor strolled into his office and announced she'd like his help in conceiving a child. He was thirty-nine years old and had never gotten over his teenage crush on Darcy. One thing he *did* know. He was not about to assist the woman of his dreams have another man's child!

Available next month
Here's a preview!

"FOR THE SAME REASON you didn't. I was shy, gawky, inept. I'd never liked anyone before, and I wasn't sure what you felt about me."

He shook his head. "Thank God we don't have to do that again. Go back, I mean."

"I know," she agreed. "Puberty sucked."

He laughed again. "Yes, indeed."

"Maybe we could go back to high school for a day, hmm? Just a day?"

"What would you do?"

Darcy's gaze grew quite serious. "I'd take you behind the gym by the bleachers. And I'd tell you the whole truth. That I loved you. That I dreamed of you, and thought of you all the time. That I had a whole notebook filled with Mr. and Mrs. Mitchell Maitland written in it, in every conceivable form. And then..."

Mitchell leaned toward her, hardly believing what he was hearing. He'd dreamed of her, too. And she was never far from his thoughts. He hadn't had the notebook, but he'd done the equivalent, which was to keep her picture tucked away inside the pages of a contraband *Playboy* magazine. "And then...?"

"I would have kissed you."

"Brazen."

She nodded. "Brazen and wicked and all the other things I was too timid to explore."

"You're not too timid now, are you?"

She shook her head, but before she stilled, he leaned over and kissed her. It was the purest sensation he'd ever known. As if they were those shy teenagers behind the gym, exploring each other for the first time.

Her hand went back to his neck, and she pulled him tighter against her. His rib hit the yearbook and he broke the kiss long enough to grab it and toss it on the floor. Then he took her in his arms, but not as a boy. He took her as the man he was. With twenty years of passion coursing through his veins.

He stood, lifting her with him, holding tight to her arms, afraid to let go for fear she'd disappear. His mouth touched hers again, and her response was instant and electric. She kissed him boldly, opening her mouth to him, exploring in return.

He felt her against him, her body rubbing him seductively, as if she needed to do anything at all to get him incredibly hot and bothered. No textbooks tonight. No hiding his feelings or his response to her.

He rubbed against her, too, letting her know just what she did to him. What she'd always done.

Her moan told him a great deal. Her hand running down his back told him more.

He eased out of the kiss, capturing her gaze. "Darcy…"

"Yes."

"I want you."

She nodded. "Oh, God, yes."

"Are you sure?"

"It's taken so long to get here," she said. "You're not getting rid of me so easily."

He kissed her again, his last shred of reserve fading with the taste of her on his lips, on his tongue. The woman he'd dreamed about from his earliest awareness of the difference between boys and girls was his. And she wanted him in return. The woman on the magazines had come to life.

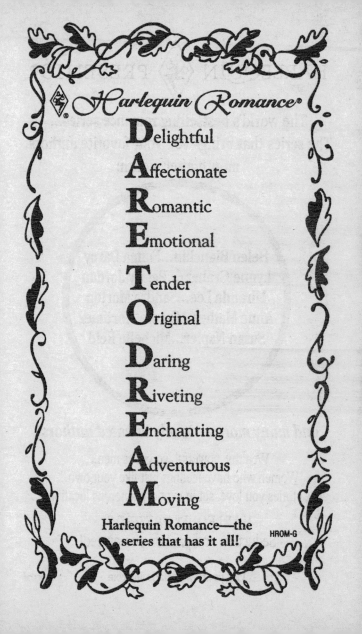

Harlequin Romance®

Delightful

Affectionate

Romantic

Emotional

Tender

Original

Daring

Riveting

Enchanting

Adventurous

Moving

Harlequin Romance—the
series that has it all!

HROM-G

HARLEQUIN PRESENTS®

The world's bestselling romance series...
The series that brings you your favorite authors,
month after month:

Helen Bianchin...Emma Darcy
Lynne Graham...Penny Jordan
Miranda Lee...Sandra Morton
Anne Mather...Carole Mortimer
Susan Napier...Michelle Reid

and many more uniquely talented authors!

Wealthy, powerful, gorgeous men...
Women who have feelings just like your own...
The stories you love, set in exotic, glamorous locations...

HARLEQUIN PRESENTS,
Seduction and passion guaranteed!

Visit us at www.eHarlequin.com   HPGEN00

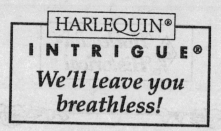

HARLEQUIN®
I N T R I G U E®
We'll leave you breathless!

If you've been looking for thrilling tales of
contemporary passion and sensuous love stories
with taut, edge-of-the-seat suspense—
then you'll *love* Harlequin Intrigue!

Every month, you'll meet four new heroes
who are guaranteed to make your spine tingle
and your pulse pound. With them you'll enter
into the exciting world of Harlequin Intrigue—
where your life is on the line
and so is your heart!

THAT'S INTRIGUE—DYNAMIC ROMANCE AT ITS BEST!

 HARLEQUIN®

I N T R I G U E®

Harlequin® Historical

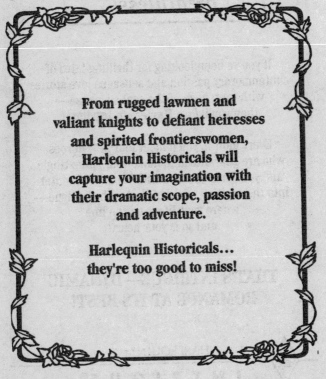

From rugged lawmen and
valiant knights to defiant heiresses
and spirited frontierswomen,
Harlequin Historicals will
capture your imagination with
their dramatic scope, passion
and adventure.

Harlequin Historicals…
they're too good to miss!

Your Romantic Books—find them at

www.eHarlequin.com

Visit the *Author's Alcove*

➤ Find the most complete information anywhere on your favorite author.

➤ Try your hand in the Writing Round Robin—contribute a chapter to an online book in the making.

Enter the *Reading Room*

➤ Experience an interactive novel—help determine the fate of a story being created now by one of your favorite authors.

➤ Join one of our reading groups and discuss your favorite book.

Drop into *Shop eHarlequin*

➤ Find the latest releases—read an excerpt or write a review for this month's Harlequin top sellers.

➤ Try out our amazing search feature—tell us your favorite theme, setting or time period and we'll find a book that's perfect for you.

All this and more available at

www.eHarlequin.com
on Women.com Networks

HEYRB1